RUN FOR YOUR MIDLIFE

GOOD TO THE LAST DEATH, BOOK NINE

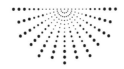

ROBYN PETERMAN

ACKNOWLEDGMENTS

The Good To The Last Death Series is a pleasure to write. Run For Your Midlife took me on a wild ride. Telling stories is my passion and my passion has been fulfilled with this series. Daisy, Gideon and the gang bring me an absurd amount of joy and I hope you feel the same way.

As always, writing may be a solitary sport, but it takes a whole bunch of people to make the magic happen.

Renee — Thank you for my beautiful cover and for being the best badass critique partner in the world. TMB. LOL

Kelli — Your editing makes me look like a better writer. Thank you.

Wanda — You are the freaking bomb. Love you to the moon and back.

Heather, Nancy, Caroline, Susan and Wanda — Thank you for reading early and helping me find the booboos. You all rock.

My Readers — Thank you for loving the stories that come from my warped mind. It thrills me.

Steve, Henry and Audrey — Your love and support makes all of this so much more fun. I love you people endlessly.

DEDICATION

For Kurt the Bastard. I will love you and miss you forever.

MORE IN THE GOOD TO THE LAST DEATH SERIES

ORDER BOOK 10 TODAY!

BOOK DESCRIPTION

RUN FOR YOUR MIDLIFE

Lately, my life has been a big, fat, hairy midlife crisis. I could really go for a boring day or three.

Apparently, there's no rest for the over-forty crowd.

Yes, I have fabulous friends.
Yes, I have a beautiful baby.
Yes, the ghosts are coming back home.
Yes, I'm in love with the Grim Reaper.

However, that sexy Demon has got some major 'splainin' to do...like his possible involvement in the shocking kidnapping of my worst and most deadly enemy.

With a drag queen and an ice queen as my back up, we're going to sashay away into the Darkness to find the truth and turn a wrong into a right.

Although, I'm learning fast that black and white are often clouded with of shades of gray.

Whatever. I'm putting on my rose colored glasses and going for it. I plan to live midlife in peace… not pieces.

Good luck to me.

CHAPTER ONE

I turned and looked. In the midst of being frightened out of my mind, I laughed. Yes, my worst and most dangerous enemy was here in ghostly form and decomposing in my front yard, but on the porch stood the Four Horsemen of the Apocalypse in all their drag queen glory. They were clad in skimpy bathing suits. Their eyes were deep black pools, and their horns were out. Of course, their makeup was perfect and their stilettos matched their suits.

They were terrifyingly gorgeous, and I was happy they were on my team.

Candy Vargo aka Karma stood to their left with the beloved ghost of my gram hovering next to her. Tory—the wild card, who I liked even though she didn't seem to want my friendship—stood by Gram to make sure she didn't flicker away.

"Is that a ghost?" Zadkiel bellowed with rage. What was left of his decaying body trembled with fury. "No ghosts are allowed here."

Before I could answer, the monster flew like a bullet out of a gun toward Gram. Candy Vargo blasted him with an explosion that should have turned him to ash. It didn't. However, the house didn't survive.

The four queens and Tory surrounded Gram to protect her, but it wasn't looking good.

I moved without a thought.

I moved at the speed of light.

I moved to stop the monster from harming another person who I loved. He'd already hurt me enough. It was shocking that even dead he could wreak such destruction.

Tackling Zadkiel to the ground and holding him tight, I felt myself fall. Gideon, the love of my Immortal life, tried to stop the natural progression of what was happening. His roar sounded far away, but his voice was a touchstone to reality that was quickly disappearing.

I'd already set the action in motion, and there was no way to stop it. Actions always had consequences. Reality would have to wait for me.

I'd just accidentally mind dived into my despicable archenemy.

THE COLD. THE COLD WENT ALL THE WAY TO MY BONES AND TORE through my body like sharp, frozen daggers made of ice. Trying to catch my breath, I gasped for air and screamed.

The only sound that left my lips came from so far away I could barely hear it.

My head pounded violently, and every single cell in my body screamed for oxygen. I knew exactly what was happening, and it wasn't good.

I'd entered Zadkiel's mind. Never in a million years would I have wanted to be where I was. Remembering Gram saying that sometimes weird things happened for a reason, I tried with all my might to figure out what was reasonable about the situation.

I was at a loss.

We were floating on air in the vast nothingness. There were no walls or floor to speak of. It was a familiar place to me, but this time I didn't want to stay.

"Well, well, well," Zadkiel said with a raised brow and the barest hint of alarm on his face. "Isn't this fun?"

He didn't like it any more than I did. Using that to my advantage was the new game plan. The question was, how?

Zadkiel was whole. He was no longer a ghost. That's what happened when I went into the minds of the dead. The man's outer beauty belied his putrid insides. I stared at him. He stared back. A sadness overwhelmed me. How had someone who had once been good turned out this way?

Was it simply the inevitability of living forever? Was every Immortal destined to crack? Like Clarissa had? Like Zadkiel had?

I shook my head. No. Gideon wasn't this way. My father had not been this way. Charlie, Heather, Tim and Candy were not this way.

I would never be this way.

However, Gram had been correct. Sometimes weird things did happen for a reason. I had the ability to see the past when I was in the minds of the dead. If I had to make a call about Zadkiel's afterlife —the right call, I could find out the facts emotionlessly.

Granted, I needed the ghosts to come back to stop the destruction of mankind, and Zadkiel held the key. But one moment at a time. It was the only move that made sense.

"Take my hand," I told him, extending mine.

He was wary. He had no clue what was going on. We were in my territory now.

"I think not," he snapped, backing away.

I shrugged. "Fine. Touching you isn't appealing. I just figured you'd like to get out of here."

He was torn. I'd lied by omission. Yes, he needed to touch me to leave. But that was secondary to what I was about to do.

"I'm leaving," I said coldly. "I'm happy to leave you here for the rest of time. It's rather fitting."

"You need me to get your precious dead back," he challenged.

"Do I?" I asked in a casual tone. I twisted the silver streak in my hair so he would notice. "I'm not so sure."

He clearly wasn't either from the crack in his smug expression.

I sent out a silent thank you to the Souls of the Martyrs. I was pulling it out of my ass, but it seemed to be working.

"You do need me," he insisted.

I didn't comment. My hand was extended. I waited. There was strength in stillness and silence.

"You have ten seconds to make up your mind," I told him. "Stay or go. It's up to you."

His eyes flashed with displeasure. He liked to be in charge. He was not. And if I had my way, he never would be again.

His demeanor soured as I slowly began to back away. He didn't think I would leave him. I wasn't sure it was the right thing to do, but if he was going to call my bluff, I'd go through with it and try to find a way back to the dead without him. He was truly a hideous man.

At the eight-second mark, he strode across the nothingness and grasped my hand in his. I held it tighter than I'd ever held anything. I wasn't letting go until I had my answers.

"Take me back," he snarled.

"All in good time, Zadkiel. All in good time."

Pictures raced across my vision so quickly I couldn't make them out. It was like an old static-filled black-and-white TV screen was inside my head. In the past, I'd waited for whatever the dead wanted *me to see to appear. Today was different. I was going to call to the stories I needed to see. If others popped in, so be it.*

"Gabe and Tory," I called out into the vast nothingness.

Zadkiel hissed and tried to break the grip. He failed.

The racing images slowed. The faces of Gabe and Tory came into focus. My breath caught in my throat. Their love was unmistakable.

"I can take some of the pain," Tory whispered to Gabe. "Please let me."

Gabe kissed her and held her close. "No, my love. This is mine to bear alone."

"Do you love me?" she asked, smiling. Her beauty was magical.

"With everything I am," he replied.

"Would you take my pain?" she pressed, playing with his blond hair.

"I would."

"Then love me enough to let me do the same for you," she insisted. "Let me love you."

Zadkiel was nowhere in this picture, but he had to have witnessed the exchange. My stomach started to hurt.

Images of Gabe being physically beaten until he was unconscious filled the screen. Pictures of Tory being whipped like an animal made tears pour from my eyes.

"She told me," Zadkiel roared to Gabe. "She told me what a weak, pathetic Angel you are—unable to take the pain you were created for."

"No," Gabe said, bleeding profusely from the mouth. "She wouldn't do that."

Zadkiel laughed. "She did. And you will pay... No. Actually, she came up with a better punishment. Your brother and sisters will pay for your weakness. Tory wants it that way. I agreed because I'm nice. What say you, Gabe?"

Gabe eyed the man with raw hatred. "I will take the punishment. My brother and sisters had nothing to do with this."

"What a lovely brother you are," Zadkiel sneered. "A thousand years of the most excruciating pain for you. Enjoy."

The picture went fuzzy. It jumped for a while and then grew clear.

Tory lay in a pool of blood as Zadkiel stood over her with a whip in his hand.

"I could have given you the world and you chose him," he roared. "Such a stupid, stupid slave you are. He turned you in."

"No," she choked out.

"Ahhh, but he did," Zadkiel lied. "And now you shall pay. I banish you from the light. Your name was given with reason. I knew I should never have trusted you."

"I don't understand," she said as bloody tears ran down her cheeks.

"From this day forward, you will be known as Purgatory—a vast gray land of nothingness; a slow, ugly death where souls go to wait for Judgement Day—a punishment worse than actual death. Be gone."

Tory screamed as robed and hooded men beat her and tossed her out of the light.

I bit down on my tongue. So many questions had just been answered. But there were more.

"Show me the good," I commanded.

I already knew so much of the devastatingly awful. I'd experienced it. In order to be fair, I needed to know if Zadkiel had indeed been a good man. With a life as long as he'd lived, it would make some sense. He'd once been the Angel of Mercy. However, I was the Angel of Mercy now.

The good was as exquisite as the bad was heinous. It was easy to momentarily love the monster when I saw how much beauty he'd created, but did it outweigh the evil? Tory had asked me if I had a God complex. I didn't. Or did I? I was searching for evidence to judge. All of this sucked hard. It was so much easier to be a forty-year-old human widow in a dead-end job waiting for menopause to hit. It was also sad and empty. I knew I wouldn't change anything. My life now was full and beautiful.

I kept searching Zadkiel's mind. My heart felt pulled in so many directions, I wondered if this was an exercise in futility.

No. I could help Gabe and Tory. It might be far too late for them but they deserved the truth.

"The dead," I called out as Zadkiel fought to release himself from my grip.

"Let me go," he roared.

"Not on your afterlife," I shot back with a smile.

The pictures came in slowly. I shook my head and squeezed Zadkiel's hand so hard I heard the bones crack. He was a son of a bitch.

It was simple. I wasn't sure how long it would have taken me to figure it out. Honestly, I might have never figured it out until it was too late. But thankfully, I didn't have to.

I watched what he'd done. It was difficult to see since it involved my daughter, but it was straightforward in its dastardly brilliance. He'd somehow figured out how to bypass me as the Death Counselor and send the dead to my child—the next Death Counselor, who was an infant and couldn't help them.

I wasn't aware because she wasn't with me. He would have known I would send her to safety. So simple. So evil.

"Tell me how to undo it or I'll leave you here," I said to him as calmly as if I'd asked him about the weather.

"Not part of the deal," he growled.

"There is no deal, Zadkiel," I said sharply. "All you have left is your integrity and it's verging on zero. When Armageddon comes

long before it's due, do you believe no one will know that you are the ultimate cause?"

"YOU are the ultimate cause," he bellowed as spittle gathered on his lips.

"No," I disagreed. "You. Not me. I might have neglected my duties due to the fact I despise you, but when given a second chance, I rose to the occasion. What will you do with your second chance?"

Zadkiel laughed. It was from his gut. "I can't believe this."

I didn't speak.

"I chose you to be the next Angel of Mercy because I knew you would fail."

I refused to take the bait.

"You think you've bested me?" he screamed, trying in vain to release himself.

I didn't let go.

"I'm getting bored," I said. "Time runs differently here. I really need to get home and pump."

"What?" he demanded, completely confused.

I winked at him. He wasn't sure what to do with that. "Not important. You have five seconds to tell me how to reverse what you did. If you can't bring yourself to share, I'll leave and you'll stay. If you tell me, we both go. The choice is yours."

"And if I lie?" he inquired with a smirk.

I laughed. "For being so old, you're seriously stupid. I can see into your mind. Go ahead, lie. See what happens. I dare you."

My smile and my words unsettled him. The game was ending. He was losing. Although, there was still a chance that everyone would lose.

"One. Two. Three..."

"Bring her home," he snapped. "As soon as the dead see there's a Counselor who can aid them, they will leave her. I just increased her light and dimmed yours."

"When?" I ground out. "When did you do this?"

"When you refused me," he snapped. "You didn't think that would come without consequences, did you?"

"She left recently," I said, eyeing him with distrust. "I saw no dead around my child."

"Nothing happens immediately," he said with an eye roll. "They might not have found her yet, but they definitely can't find you."

"That's all?" I asked, searching his past briefly.

It all added up. However, I still had no clue where the man should be sent. Thankfully, I didn't make that decision alone.

"Yes," he said tightly. "I want to leave."

"What's the magic word?" I inquired.

His eyes narrowed. "Fuck you."

I shrugged and laughed. "I prefer please, but whatever floats your boat, asshole."

I closed my eyes and we left.

Sometimes weird things did happen for a reason.

Today would go down in history as one of those days.

CHAPTER TWO

I woke up on the cold, hard ground with my arms wrapped around the ghost of a man who would have happily seen me dead. There was a pile of warm blankets on top of me and Gideon's worried face was inches from mine.

The second I opened my eyes, he dragged me off of Zadkiel so quickly it created a blast of wind.

"How long?" I asked as he helped me to my feet. "How long was I out?"

"Twenty-four hours," he replied, looking like he'd suffered a thousand little deaths.

I nodded and glanced over at the horrid ghost who hovered warily in the air. It still amazed me how time ran differently on the different planes. I would have sworn I'd only been gone an hour.

"I know how to bring the dead back," I said.

"Course you do, motherfucker," Candy Vargo said, handing me a toothpick. "You're a badass. Expected nothin' less."

Putting the toothpick in my mouth, I looked around. I hadn't realized anyone else was even with us. Although, I should have known. We worked as a team. Candy Vargo, Tim, Gabe, Tory and the Four Horsemen of the Apocalypse—Carl, Dirk, Fred and Wally—were only feet away. The queens were in faux fur parkas, but their horns were still on full display.

"The dead are with Alana Catherine. As soon as we bring her home, they'll come back to me." I glanced around. Gram was nowhere to be seen. "Where's Gram?"

"Safe," Candy assured me, staring icily at Zadkiel.

I blew out a long, slow breath of relief. Part three was done. That left part four. Figuring out where Zadkiel was to go had to be the last part of the game. It didn't sit right in my gut, but it was the only available option.

I was pretty sure I knew the person who should make the call. Up until now, it had been a duo who decided where a soul in question was to reside in the afterlife. But that had been when I'd thought there were only two options.

There were three.

The duo must now become a trio—a trinity, so to speak. I had no clue if Tory would go for it.

"He lied to both of you," I told Tory and Gabe.

Gabe's swift and furious intake of breath was expected. Tory's blank response was not. Maybe it was just too late.

"Neither of you turned on the other. I'm so sorry."

"What's done is done," Tory said flatly. "There's no going back. The Grim Reaper was correct. I'm a slow, gray death."

Gabe's expression was filled with raw, agonized pain. He glanced over at Tory. She refused to meet his gaze.

Zadkiel had won. His smug smile was disgusting. If he spoke a word, I would tear him apart and not glue him back together.

My warning glare was abundantly clear.

"A decision needs to be made," Gideon announced. "I don't believe I can send the abomination into the light."

"And I don't think I can send him into the darkness," I said, to the shock of everyone.

Gideon stared at the ground. He wasn't happy. I wasn't either, but if we were working without our personal hatred for the man, we had to speak from the heart.

"How do we solve this?" he asked in a clipped tone. "The longer he's here, the more harm he causes."

"I agree," I said. "There's a third place he can go."

Zadkiel hissed and began to float away. Candy Vargo was having none of it and dropped a raging fire cage around the ghost.

"Try to get out of that, ugly motherfucker," she told him. "It's enchanted with shit that will mess you up for longer than you've been alive."

"Stellar," Wally said, clapping his hands.

"LOVE IT," Carl added.

I looked over at Tory. She was staring at me with a confused expression.

"Purgatory," I whispered, walking over to her and taking her hands in mine.

"He told you?" she asked shakily.

"I saw," I replied.

Tory pulled away from me. She walked over to the fire cage that Candy Vargo had created and observed Zadkiel as if he was an animal in the zoo. After a few minutes, she smiled. It was kind of scary. Zadkiel wasn't pleased.

Tory's voice was clear. She glimmered from head to toe like diamonds. "I accept. It's fitting that the abhorrent man who sent the Souls of the Martyrs into limbo join them in their unending, torturous pain."

17

Gideon appeared shocked. "How did I not know this?" he asked aloud, not expecting an answer. "Purgatory is a state of mind, like Heaven and Hell—not a destination."

I was so glad it wasn't just me. My lack of Bible knowledge kept biting me in the ass, but not this time.

"It's real," Tory announced in a hollow tone. "Not everything is light or dark. There are many shades of gray in between."

"I must learn more," Tim said, rapidly taking notes. "While there is rumor of Limbo also known as Purgatory, I've never heard hard evidence until now. Quite fascinating."

"Has everyone lost their damned minds?" Gabe shouted, pulling a tree out of the ground and throwing it.

Thankfully, not at us.

"I will *not* accept that Tory will have to watch over that bastard until the end of time," he ground out. "He goes to the darkness where he belongs."

"I agree," Gideon said in a cool tone.

"Now, now, darlings," Dirk chimed in, strutting around like it was Paris Fashion Week. "I do believe that you boys might be a little too close to the subject to make the call. The gals seem to have a better grip than the guys. Normally, I prefer the grip of a big sexy man, but not today."

"Girlfriend, I hear you," Fred said, joining the grass and dirt catwalk that Dirk was sashaying around. "A nice strong grip of a man is a lovely thing until you realize that the wise, gentle and creative grip of a woman is magical. As a drag queen, I feel I encompass both."

"Amen, sister," Wally joined in. "Decisions based on high emotion never end well. That's how I ended up with a tattoo on my left testicle."

"Yes, yes," Carl said, patting Wally on the back. "Doing

things of permanence in the heat of passion or anger or even joy isn't prudent. Trust us, we've been around that block many times."

"And we have the silicone butt injections and tattoos to show for it," Wally added.

The particulars around the lessons were bizarre, but the wisdom was undeniable. Even Gideon seemed to pause.

"Keeper of Fate," Tory said, bowing to Candy. "Please remove the cage. We will be leaving shortly."

"Tory, Sugar Pie," Wally said, approaching her with caution. "You must say goodbye to your new friends."

Tory didn't spare the queen a glance. "I have no friends. I work alone."

Purgatory clapped her hands and the Souls of the Martyrs appeared in an Arctic blast of wind. They salivated as they swarmed the fire cage with Zadkiel in it.

"Judgement shall be theirs," Tory whispered.

Candy Vargo eliminated the cage with a wave of her hand. The wraiths dove at a screaming Zadkiel and snatched him from this plane. The wind and the wailing were an eerie farewell to a man who had done as much irreparable damage as he had done good.

Tory nodded her head at the group without making eye contact with anyone. She disappeared in a blinding blast of silver crystals.

It was strangely anticlimactic. But mostly it was a relief. Very soon, I would hold my baby in my arms. The thought made me feel whole again.

Gabe was crushed. He walked away from us and into the fields. Gideon followed. That was unusual, but nice. It made me happy to see the man I loved go to comfort my brother who I adored.

"Crap," I muttered as the two men disappeared from sight. "I don't know where Alana Catherine is. I want her home."

"I got this," Candy Vargo said. "I'll bring them all back fuckin' pronto."

She saluted us and vanished in a flash of orange and purple light. Candy Vargo could be a handful, but I would have her back until the end of time.

"What about you queens?" I asked. "Would you like to stay for a while? My home…"

I blanched. I didn't actually have one of those at the moment.

"Do you need a hand, friend?" Tim inquired with a giggle. "I'm as good at healing property as I am at healing Immortals. Being friends with Candy has taught me many skills. She's quite the destructive gal."

I grinned. Tim to the rescue again. "I would be forever grateful, friend."

In the blink of an eye, my home was back. I had no clue if the insides were the same, but I didn't care. All I needed was a roof over my head, my baby, Gideon and a coffee pot. The rest could be dealt with later.

"Voila!" Tim said, taking a bow as the queens cheered wildly.

"So, as I was saying," I told them. "My home is your home."

"So lovely of you, Sugar Pants," Wally said, giving me a hug. "But we have exciting news!"

"Do tell," I said with a smile.

"We've been called in for a live audition for *RuPaul's Drag Race* next week," Carl screamed. "We're going out early to stalk and harass our competitors."

"THRILLING!" Fred squealed.

I winced. "Gram wouldn't want you harassing the other contestants."

"What about a little stalking, darling?" Dirk inquired.

"Nope."

"We can make that work, girlfriend," Fred promised. "We don't need to cheat. After Drag Queen Boot Camp, I feel ready to win!"

"I'm going to miss you guys," I told them, hugging each crazy queen.

"Ohhh, we'll be back, darling," Dirk said. "You do fabu karaoke parties."

"LOVE IT!" Carl shouted. "And Tim, you're a prince. Keep up the good work. And if you decide to shift careers, I'd totally be willing to invest in a restaurant if you're the head chef!"

Tim blushed bright red. "Much appreciated."

I squinted at the queens. "You guys have money?"

They giggled like naughty kids. "No!" Wally announced with a sly grin. "But you do."

I sighed and laughed. "Right you are. Can I ask a question before you go?"

"Absolutely, Sugar Pants," Wally said.

I walked up to the house and sat down on the porch swing. Tim and the queens followed. "I feel like the game isn't over. I can't shake the feeling."

The queens exchanged glances.

"We had a brief kiki and we're concerned, as well," Dirk admitted ruefully. "Truly, only three parts played out, but we could have been wrong about it being a four-part game."

I nodded. "I kind of thought that figuring out where Zadkiel went in the end was part four, but I'm not as sure now."

"Don't worry your gorgeous head, girlfriend," Fred told me.

"The bottom line is that you succeeded in averting Armageddon. The ghosts will be coming home soon and Zadkiel is gone for good. Win. Win. Win."

"We, not I," I corrected him. "It was a team effort."

"The very best way," Carl sang.

"OH SHIT!" Dirk screeched as Tory came tumbling out of the sky and landed with a sickening thud on the front lawn.

Tim, the queens and I ran like there was a ten-alarm fire on our butts. Tory was shaking from head to toe. She could barely get her words out.

"Calm down," I said, grabbing her shoulders and giving her a gentle shake. "Just breathe."

"Gone," she gasped out.

My stomach dropped. "Who's gone?"

"Zadkiel," she choked out. "Ripped a hole in Purgatory. All the wraiths are escaping. It's bad."

"Zadkiel escaped?" I shouted, beginning to freak out for real.

"No." She shook her head. "Kidnapped."

"Wait. What?" That didn't sound even a little bit right. "Who kidnapped him?"

Tory took a deep breath and looked me in the eye. "The Archangel Gabriel and the Grim Reaper."

"Bullshit," I hissed. She was lying. "No one even knew that Purgatory existed until today. How did they find it?"

"Blood," she said, looking away.

I was ready to blow. I glanced over at Tim, who was eyeing Tory distrustfully. "I need a sec," I ground out. "Tim, if I level the house, can you fix it again?"

"Not a problem," he assured me.

"Thank you," I said, remembering my manners even in a time of crisis.

Without a backward glance, I strode toward the house. Raising my arms over my head, I slashed them through the air, and a scream left my lips that came from the bottom of my soul. It was incredibly good that we lived in the middle of nowhere. The explosion was loud and fiery.

Taking a deep, cleansing breath, I walked back over to the open-mouthed group.

"Serve, girlfriend. You know how to bring it every time," Fred said. "Remind me never to get on your bad side."

"Explain," I demanded in a tight voice to Tory. "Leave nothing out."

She nodded and backed away a bit. Everyone did.

"Over a thousand years ago, Gabriel and I exchanged blood. It was a way to always be able to find each other. I've never used it since the day he betrayed me and, as far as I know, he's never used it… until today."

It was still so hard to believe. "You *saw* them? You *saw* Gabe and Gideon?"

She looked down at the ground. "I did," she whispered.

I closed my eyes and tried to calm my racing heart. Part four of the game had just revealed itself. I couldn't think of any explanation that would excuse what Gideon and Gabe had done.

However, I was going to find out if I had to tear down the light and the darkness and everything in between to find them and the reason.

I opened my eyes and turned to the Horsemen. "Queens, how badly would you feel if you didn't get to audition this time around for *RuPaul's Drag Race?*"

"Not a problem, Sugar Pants," Wally said as the others nodded their agreement. "What do you have in mind?"

I looked at my lovely, crazy friends. Carl was Conquest.

That didn't quite fit. Fred was Famine. That didn't fit at all. Wally was War. That was closer, but not perfect. Dirk was Death.

Death for the win.

"Dirk, I need to dive into your mind to get to the darkness. Does that work for you?"

He looked thrilled. "Oh, darling! I say YES! Just stay away from my memories from when I was a stripper in Vegas. Really messy stuff."

"I won't touch your memories," I promised.

I turned and looked at Tory, who was still standing a healthy distance away from me after my house demolition stunt. "Do you want to come? I could use an extra hand."

"I work alone," she reminded me.

"Not anymore."

After a stare down that felt like it lasted an hour, she finally nodded.

"Tim, Carl, Fred and Wally, will you be in charge here and let everyone know what's going on when Candy brings them home?"

"Yes," they said in unison.

"Also, Tim, put word out to Abaddon that I might need him, please."

"Are you sure?" Tim asked with displeasure punctuating each word.

I knew there was no love lost between Abaddon and Tim, but I still didn't know why. Honestly, I didn't care. Abaddon was a Demon who had Gideon's trust. If I needed him, I would ask. His price was high, but the stakes were higher.

"Positive," I said, not wanting to lose another minute. "I'm going to hug Dirk. Tory, you'll put your arms around me. Don't let go. The initial descent is painful then it's all good."

"Pain means nothing to me," she replied.

Her words made me sad. If I'd had time, I would have consoled her.

I didn't have time.

"Ready?"

Dirk and Tory nodded.

Gideon had better have an excellent explanation. I might be the Angel of Mercy, but I was having a hard time thinking about showing any mercy right now.

It was turning out to be one hell of a hard-knock midlife.

CHAPTER THREE

"WAIT! WE MUST WAIT," TIM SAID, HOLDING UP HIS HAND AS I prepared to hug Dirk and enter his mind. "Information is power. We don't have all of it."

"We don't have any of it," I said, frustrated. Running my hands through my hair, I tried to stay calm. In a crazy world where little made sense, the new wrinkle of Zadkiel's apparent kidnapping took the cake for senselessness.

My fur babies, Donna and Karen, zoomed around the yard without a care in the world. I envied them. It was cold and gray outside and I felt the chill all the way to my bones. I wasn't sure if it was the weather or the situation, but my shivers were real.

"Tim is correct, Sugar Pants," Wally said, snapping his fingers and conjuring up a warm puffer coat for me. "We mustn't light ourselves on fire to stay warm."

I took it gratefully and gave him a stressed smile. I felt the insane need to go for a run to clear my mind, but that wasn't a good idea. I needed to run towards the problem, not away.

Carl pulled a bright pink beanie from his pocket and put it

on my head. The queens had excellent mothering instincts. It made me miss Alana Catherine desperately. She was safe, and on her way home soon. That was all that mattered.

Carl adjusted the hat then spoke. "Let us not forget that a fact is information without emotion. An opinion is information plus experience. Ignorance is an opinion lacking information. Stupidity is an opinion that does away with fact. And, flats before noon are totally acceptable."

The flats line almost made me smile, but my lips refused to curl up. I paced the yard. The need to blow something up gnawed at me. None of what was happening added up.

"And I vote that we don't go with the stupidity option," Fred announced, conjuring up a coat for Tory and putting it on her, much to her annoyance. "Very unattractive."

Tim nodded and pulled a notebook out of the pocket of his uniform. "A chaotic mind will reap chaotic results, Daisy."

I stopped dead in my tracks. I might be a grown-ass forty-year-old woman, but my friends had centuries on me. At the rate I was going, I was going to inadvertently choose the stupid option. However, getting my body on board with my brain seemed impossible. Nothing was impossible as long as I believed. I just had no clue what to believe right now.

"Help me," I said. "Please."

Tim smiled. "But of course. Wally, we need some comfortable seating, please."

"On it," Wally squealed, snapping his fingers. A garish lime-green velvet sectional appeared in my front yard. It was so bright, I had to squint. Tory's eyes grew huge and she winced. I agreed with her reaction but didn't say a word.

Fred clapped his hands and provided space heaters. Dirk wiggled his fingers and added a lacquered red and pink coffee table with an array of warm drinks and snacks. And Carl, not wanting to be left out, waved his hand and finished off the hideous outdoor arrangement with a karaoke machine and boas.

It made me laugh. I couldn't believe in the midst of what was going on I could even smile, but the boys were something else in the best way.

"I have a question," I said, as Wally led me over to the outdoor den.

"What's the question, girlfriend?" Fred inquired, pulling a reluctant Tory towards the eyesore of a seating area.

"Tory said the wraiths escaped as well. What does that mean to the world? What does that mean for the wraiths?"

Tory's lips compressed to a flat line and the grayness that surrounded her grew darker. Her hands balled into fists at her sides. "Most will go back. They can't harm humans, only Immortals," she said flatly. "The ones who don't return to Purgatory will ultimately die."

Tim looked confused. "They're already dead."

Tory nodded. "My mistake. The Souls of the Martyrs who don't return to Purgatory will disintegrate to ash and nothingness."

My stomach dropped, and I was glad I had a place to sit, even if it was ugly. "That's not fair."

Tory's laugh was brittle. "Fair doesn't figure into our world. There's very little that's in accordance with humane rules or standards."

I didn't completely disagree, but if we accepted what had always been, there was no going forward. Getting into a fight with Tory wasn't going to end well. I needed her. Plus, I was very aware that I would sound like an idiot. Her long life had been anything but fair. It had been tragic.

The afterlives of the Souls of the Martyrs had been tragic as well. Although, the word tragic didn't come close to describing what Tory or the wraiths had gone through.

"Can you help them?" I asked her.

She stared at me for a long moment. "I thought you needed me here. I'm simply following orders."

Did I need her? My gut said yes, but not at the expense of the wraiths. Time was of the essence, but if Gideon and Gabe had taken Zadkiel to the darkness, time ran very differently there. Staring at my feet, I tried to make a call that was right. As the Angel of Mercy and the Death Counselor, the thought of the wraiths fading away to nothing after the heartbreaking penance they'd paid because of Zadkiel's jealousy didn't work for me.

The fact that Zadkiel was connected to everything bad that was happening didn't escape me. It infuriated me, but fury wasn't going to get me anywhere fast.

"How long would you need to get them to safety?" I asked.

Tory shrugged. "An hour. Maybe two."

The queens and Tim watched the exchange silently. It would have been awesome if they'd chimed in with some sage wisdom, but no such luck. It was all me. Guilt consumed me. Tory had said I had a God complex. She was wrong. I wasn't going to choose who lived and who died. That wasn't my job. My job was aiding the dead as the Death Counselor and being the Angel of Mercy. I might have plenty of bad qualities, but lack of compassion and mercy were not among them. Protecting the wraiths was her job and it wasn't my call to keep her from it.

"Guilt is worthwhile if it can point you towards something that can change," Tim said softly. "Shame is not worthwhile."

I squinted at the man. Did he read my mind?

Tim smiled kindly. "You have a very expressive face, Daisy."

"Go," I instructed Tory. "I'll wait for you and pull my shit together in the meantime. Unless you need my help."

The woman's face was expressionless. She stared at me for a long beat. The air around her swirled a glittery silver and her pale skin sparkled.

For a hot sec, I thought she was going to say something kind.

"I work alone. I need no one. Moreover, I don't need you."

So much for being kind.

In a blast of shimmering mist, Tory disappeared.

My mind still felt chaotic, but sending Tory away felt right. The fact that she believed she worked alone and didn't need me was wrong. I'd make her see the light somehow.

Dirk sat down next to me on the lime green sectional and kissed the top of my head. "According to the lovely Dalai Lama, 'Compassion is the wish to see others free from suffering.'"

"Correct!" Wally said, waltzing over and seating his huge self practically on my lap. "The wise and lovely man also said, 'If you want others to be happy, practice compassion. If you want to be happy, practice compassion.'"

I glanced around and noted the irony. The Four Horsemen of the Apocalypse were some of the best people I knew. It didn't necessarily add up with the stories from the Bible—which I still hadn't read, much to everyone's horror—but the queens had told me that many of the stories hadn't gotten it right. They were clearly a shining example.

"Oh yes, girlfriends!" Fred said with a giggle. "And the wonderful dame Helen Keller had some very wise words to say. 'Life is an exciting business, and most exciting when it is lived for others.'"

Tim handed me a steaming cup of hot chocolate and sat on the edge of the coffee table. "The wounds are there, my friend.

They're always there. However, compassion is the only known cure to heal the scars that haunt us."

A strange sense of peace consumed me. I'd made the compassionate call. My world was still imploding around me, but I'd handle each explosion as it came and try not to cause any unnecessary damage. It was either that or screw everything up. One problem hopefully solved, so many more to go…

"Okay." I took a sip of the yummy drink and felt the warm, sweet heat travel from my mouth to my stomach. "Do you have more wisdom for me while we wait for Tory to return?"

"But of course, darling!" Dirk announced. "Get ready for your mind to be blown!"

I tilted my head. My expression was one of concern. Dirk aka Death aka Rhoda Dendron just giggled.

"Not literally," he assured me.

I sighed with relief. Immortals were exacting beings. Making sure I wasn't going to be left without my head was common sense.

My life was insane.

"Alrighty then, queens." Tim pulled a thick notebook from his mailbag. "Let's begin."

I was wary. Tim's notebooks were filled with disgusting facts that he and our buddy Jennifer liked to pull out at parties. I'd been hoping for some sensible knowledge.

Too bad, so sad.

"I shall start," Tim announced with a wide smile. "Lobsters communicate with pee. They urinate on each other with the bladders on each side of their head!"

All five men stared at me in anticipation. Was I supposed to say something? This wasn't how the game usually worked. However, times were not usual.

"Umm… okay," I said, still not quite sure if my comments

were wanted. "That makes me very happy that I'm a vegetarian."

"Excellent!" Tim congratulated me.

"My turn!" Wally squealed. "Did you know that Dolly Parton once lost a look-alike contest?"

"Seriously?" Now I was confused. How was that even possible?

"Ohhhh, yes!" Fred chimed in. "Our beloved Dolly entered a celebrity look-alike contest as herself and lost."

"To a DRAG QUEEN!" Carl shouted with glee. "Granted, our Goddess of the Universe, Dolly, had exaggerated her gorgeous features with makeup just a tad. She got the least amount of applause of anyone there! Shocking!"

I was wildly unsure how any of this was supposed to help me.

"Peanuts are used in dynamite," Tim shared.

"Love peanuts, darling," Dirk gushed. "How about this nugget of absurd? A gentleman once hired someone to slap him to avoid checking the Book of Faces!"

"Not real," I said with a laugh.

"Very real, Snookie Bottom," Dirk insisted. "He paid a dedicated gal to slap him in the face each time he went online and checked the Book of Faces! Paid her eight dollars an hour."

"Ingenious!" Tim said, impressed. "German chocolate cake is named after a guy."

"Wait, what?" I asked. "It's not German?"

"No, friend," Tim assured me with a giggle. "Contrary to the name, German chocolate cake is named after the brilliant gentleman who created the delicacy—Sam German!"

"Fascinating," Fred said, shoving cookies into his mouth. "Animals who lay eggs do not have belly buttons."

"Lizards communicate by doing pushups," Carl informed

us. "And boanthropy is the disorder in which a person believes they're a cow."

"How adorable," Dirk said with a giggle.

I didn't agree, but I had to admit my mind was so filled with bizarre facts, I didn't feel as out of control anymore.

"Coats off!" Wally commanded with a delightfully naughty grin. "Roll your sleeves up and get ready to be amazed."

"By what?" I asked, following the directions. There were so many space heaters blowing at full blast, it felt like summer around the lime green sectional couch tragedy.

"Hush now, darling," Dirk said with a giggle. "We don't want to spoil the surprise!"

Wally extended his arm and cleared his throat. "Did you know that you can pinch a weenus as hard as you want and feel no pain?"

I was gobsmacked and horrified. Was I about to witness five of my closest male buddies squeeze their junk?

"Is this true?" Tim asked, shocked.

"Definitely, darling," Dirk told Tim. "All of that wonderfully wrinkled skin has no pain receptors."

"Oh my God," I muttered. This game had taken a turn to a place I didn't want to go.

"And," Wally announced grandly. "I will place a thousand-dollar bet that my weenus is larger than all of yours!"

I winced as my mouth moved before my brain was able to stop it. "You don't have any money," I reminded him.

"Don't need it," he replied with a grin. "My weenus will not let me down!"

I really needed to put an end to this conversation. It reminded me of the pebble in the vagina exercise that Jennifer had taught the queens, Candy and Tim to strengthen vaginal walls. Tim and the queens didn't even have vaginas. While I adored my friends, I didn't want to see their *weenuses*. "How about we move on?" I suggested.

"Are you afraid your weenus won't stack up?" Fred asked.

I sucked some air in between my teeth. I was positive they were aware that I was a female and didn't have a weenus... My horrified expression as I covertly glanced down to make sure I hadn't somehow grown male genitalia gave me away and made the queens laugh. Hard. Even Tim giggled. What the hell was happening?

Carl pulled himself together first and tossed the long locks of his wig over his shoulder. "Daisy, sweetikins, what exactly do you think a weenus is?"

I narrowed my eyes at him. "Is that a trick question?"

"Not at all," Carl promised with a naughty grin.

Pretty sure I was about to be the butt of a joke, I just went for it. "A weenus is a penis."

I was definitely the butt of a joke that I didn't get. The laughter was uproarious and went on for entirely too long. My face heated up and I was tempted to electrocute all of them. That would be mean. I wasn't mean. However, I was embarrassed.

"What is a weenus?" I shouted over the bellows of laughter.

Dirk swallowed back his giggles and swiped the tears from his eyes. He was obviously wearing waterproof mascara since none of it was running down his face. "The weenus is the extra skin on your elbow," he explained. "Scientifically known as the olecranal skin, but we like to refer to it colloquially as the weenus!"

"Not to be confused with the flagina," Fred chimed in.

I closed my eyes. I didn't want to ask for the definition, but far be it from me not to satisfy my morbid curiosity. "Which is?"

Fred squealed with delight, which was terrifying.

"The flagina is that awkward piece of skin between the thumb and the pointer finger."

"Scientifically referred to as the thenar web space," Wally added.

"Got it," I said, relieved that it wasn't something located in the vagina.

"Are we ready?" Dirk bellowed.

"For?" I asked warily.

"To pinch our weenuses!"

I gave up. If they were going to squeeze their weenuses, I was in. I was also dying to know if they were correct.

"On the count of three," Tim announced gleefully. "One. Two. THREE!"

I pinched my weenus. Shocked that I felt nothing, I squeezed harder. Still nothing. It was kind of addicting. Tim was literally twisting his weenus. Dirk was squashing his weenus so hard it looked like his fingers were touching each other. Wally shrieked with joy as he gripped and flattened his weenus. Carl had his arms crossed over each other and was doing a double weenus yank. And Fred had mashed his weenus in a full hand grip.

I was laughing so hard my stomach hurt. The absurdity of the activity was hilarious.

"And our work here is done," Wally announced with a wide grin.

I glanced at him in confusion.

He patted my head. "Are you as stressed, Sugar Pants?"

"No," I said, realizing what they'd done for me. "I'm not."

"Is your mind clearer, girlfriend?" Fred inquired sweetly.

Shockingly it was. "Yes."

Tim nodded his head. "Often to clear the mind, it's prudent to give it something to occupy and relax it."

"And nonsense is what the doctor ordered, sweetie!" Carl said. "Tell me that squeezing your weenus didn't make you happy!"

"Happy is kind of pushing it," I admitted, realizing I was still pinching my weenus. I groaned. "Okay, yes. Squeezing my weenus made me happy. Not sure what that says about me though."

"Says you're open to new and exciting things," Tim replied. "It also says that you're smart enough to let your friends help you. No man or woman is an island, friend."

I sat quietly and took in what he said. I didn't think of myself as an island. I was confident in my power, but smart enough to ask for help. You can't receive unless you ask. I'd asked and my friends had given.

I wasn't sure what the next move was, but we had to start somewhere. "I'd suggest we search the field where we believe Gideon and Gabe disappeared. There might be a message of sorts left behind. I'm still having a hard time believing they kidnapped Zadkiel."

"Wonderful plan," Wally said, wrapping his faux fur coat tightly around him. "There will be traces of their magical footprints. It might tell us nothing, but then again, who knows?"

Immortals left magical trails, so to speak. I wasn't sure what that would tell us other than where they'd stood before they'd committed a crime that could lead to God only knew what, but I worked better with a team. I wasn't about to go rogue.

Inhaling deeply, I willed myself to stay calm. I didn't want to undo the bizarre weenus magic. But, wrapping my head around being betrayed by the person I loved beyond reason was almost debilitating. The evidence was bad, but going directly to blaming Gideon was worse. Too many times, I'd jumped to the wrong conclusion. I wasn't going there again no matter how bad the evidence looked.

Tim was correct. There was more to the story and diving in without the facts could end in disaster.

"Let's go," I said, quickly walking in the direction I'd seen Gideon and Gabe walk earlier.

As I led the brigade of Immortals, a human issue popped up. An inconvenient and alarming human issue. There was a siren in the distance that sounded like it was headed our way.

"Do you hear that?" I asked as my stress went from one to ten.

"I do," Tim said, looking confused. "Sounds like a police siren."

"Odd," Carl said. "If the house explosion was detected, I'd think the fire department would be involved."

"Shit," I muttered. "Tim, fix the house, please."

"Right away," he said, waving his hands and setting the rubble that was my home back to a house.

The siren grew louder. My stomach tightened. Why were the police on their way?

"Queens, please get rid of the outdoor den," I instructed. "That might look odd to a human."

"On it," Fred said, clapping his hands. The lime green sectional and all the other extras disappeared.

Magic still astounded me. It shouldn't, considering what I could do, but it did.

"Boys," Dirk said. "Go boring."

"Do we have to?" Wally complained.

Dirk raised his brow. "If RuPaul can wear man clothes, we can wear man clothes."

"Pants strangle my balls," Fred bitched.

"Then don't choose skinny jeans," Dirk snapped.

"Fine," Fred huffed.

Before my eyes, the Four Horsemen of the Apocalypse went from their gorgeous queeny glory into bland-looking guys. They wore jeans and flannels with work boots. It was somehow sad to me.

"I don't think you have to go that far," I told the guys as the siren grew closer.

"You're accepting of everyone, Daisy," Carl said in a very serious tone. "Not everyone is so open to those who are different."

It was terrible that his words were true.

Wally patted my back. "Don't worry your pretty little head, Sugar Pants. In order to cleanse our palates, we shall wear glittering ball gowns after the po-po departs."

As the cruiser pulled into the driveway, I had a terrible sense of foreboding. "I'll do the talking."

"Roger that," Tim said. "We're with you all the way."

"And if they've come to arrest you, we shall kill them, girlfriend," Fred added.

"Nope. No killing," I said firmly.

"As you wish," Fred said.

CHAPTER FOUR

THE SENSE OF FOREBODING IN MY GUT DISAPPEARED AS SOON AS I saw who was behind the wheel of the police car. I was still wary and a tiny bit annoyed. With all the stuff I had going on, dealing with an idiot wasn't on the schedule.

Officer Micky Muggles hopped out of the cruiser, waving spastically. He plopped a big box down on the hood of the vehicle and grinned like a fool. He had shown up alone. That was a good sign. If I was in trouble with the law—which I couldn't for the life of me figure out why I would be—more cops would have arrived with him.

Micky was a strange little guy I'd gone to high school with many years ago. He'd become a police officer much to the surprise of everyone, since he'd been the dude who'd gotten busted for hot-wiring cars back in the day. While the man might have changed his illegal ways, he hadn't changed his hairstyle. His mullet was a sight to behold—business in the front and party in the back. Of course, it was scarier since he'd lost most of the hair on the top of his head and had combed over the few strands that were left. It was a seriously bad look.

"Howdy, y'all," he yelled, pointing at the box on his car as if I should know what it was.

I was clueless.

"Is there a problem?" I asked in the most pleasant voice I could muster up. I was Southern. I had manners. Also, it wasn't good form to piss off a cop no matter how dumb he was.

"Nope-arooni!" Micky announced, putting one hand on his hip and the other on his gun holster.

A gun couldn't kill any of us if that was the crazy little dude's intention. I didn't think so, but at this point nothing would surprise me.

Tim muttered under his breath from behind me. "This is kind of like when your house is on fire and you have to decide whether to mow the lawn or weed the garden first."

It took all I had not to laugh.

"Bet you're wonderin' why I came out here with the sirens blasting," he said, puffing out his scrawny chest.

"That question did cross my mind," I replied.

Micky Muggles gave me a sly grin that made my skin crawl. "Well, now, you did say you were interested…"

The queens quietly growled. I was worried their horns were about to pop out. I needed to handle this before my friends decided to help me with the situation.

Holding back a gag was difficult. "I don't recall ever saying that in this lifetime. I'm with someone and have a child."

The mullet-sporting dumbass threw his head back and guffawed. He got so red in the face I was concerned he was about to have a heart attack. Having a cop die on my property wasn't a good look. I didn't need EMTs and the rest of the department here today. I had huge problems already. A dead Micky Muggles didn't figure into the plans.

Plus, dealing with his ghost wasn't on the top of my list.

Imagining what he needed to fix before he moved on was gross, to put it kindly.

"Shoooowheee! I ain't hittin' on ya, Daisy!" he shouted, still choking on laughter. "That's just dang hilarious!"

"Is he braindead?" Carl whispered in my ear.

"Close," I muttered then turned my attention back to Micky. "Apparently, I misunderstood. My apologies."

"I should say so," he told me. "I'm seeing that busty gal, Rhoda Lee, who works at the Piggly Wiggly."

I winced. Her name was Rhoda Lou, but I wasn't about to correct him. "Congrats."

"Thanks," he said. "Also seeing Sally Ann."

"Sally Ann?" I asked, before I could stop myself. My need to work on my curiosity filter was getting imperative.

"You know Sally Ann," Micky said. "She's the well-endowed waitress from the Beef Barn."

My eye roll was as small as I could possibly make it. Her name was Sally Sue and I was pretty sure she was married. Instead of commenting, I simply gave the breast-obsessed loser a weak thumbs up. Hearing anymore about his collection of gal pals was unappetizing. We needed to get to the point of his uninvited visit and get him out of here. There was a fine chance that either Tory or Candy and the rest of the gang would materialize on my lawn in a blast of magic. As bizarre as Micky Muggles was, I was pretty sure the heart attack I didn't want to happen would occur if something that unexplainable happened

"What's in the box?" I asked, getting right to the point.

"Wrapping paper," he said with a groan. "You said you'd buy some of this shit. It's one of them damned fundraisers for my kid's school. Ex-wife dumped the whole dang box on me since I'm behind on my child support. Can you believe that?"

I made a mental note to talk to Jennifer's boyfriend, Sheriff Dip Doody, about Micky Muggles and his lack of monetary support for his kid. I was pretty sure child support could be garnished from wages. It was bullshit not to pay for his child. Heather could help too. My sister was a badass lawyer with a vengeance for justice who happened to be the Arbitrator between the Darkness and the Light. Of course, there was no way I was telling Candy Vargo. The Keeper of Fate, as profane and obnoxious as she was, had a very soft spot for kids. Imagining what she would do to Micky Muggles was nightmare-inducing.

"Could we do this another time?" I asked politely. What I wanted to do was rake his sorry ass over the coals, but he wasn't my problem and I wasn't going to let him become one. I had enough of those.

"Nosiree," he said, grabbing the box and ambling over. "Gotta get this crap sold by today. You did tell me to come on over and you'd buy some."

He was correct. I had. Shit.

"I'd like some wrapping paper," Tim said, examining the contents of the big box that Micky had dropped at our feet.

"Well, now," he said, scratching the top of his sparsely haired head and staring at the queens in confusion. "I know Tim, but I can't say I've had the pleasure of meetin' the other fellas here. I thought I knew everyone in these here parts."

All of a sudden, I was wildly relieved that the queens had conjured up boring man clothes. The last time I'd seen Micky was at the scene of a crime committed by the queens. Granted, he hadn't actually seen them since they'd already left the scene, but he did tell me that he'd heard *four big-assed women* had stolen horses from Old Man Jenkins' riding barn. In the queens' defense, they didn't realize they were supposed to rent the horses. It was a weak defense, but the Four Horsemen of the Apocalypse weren't on the Earthly plane all that much.

If the boys had looked like *big-assed women* right now, Micky's pea-brain might have gotten suspicious.

I was a shitty liar, but a whopper left my mouth without any brain support. "They're my cousins, Bo, Bob, Bubba and Bill."

Dirk almost choked on his spit. Carl had a small but noticeable coughing fit. Wally just giggled and Fred gasped out a horrified huff. Yes, the names were bad, but I didn't think giving their real names was a great idea.

"Nice to meet ya! I'm Micky Muggles, Daisy's high school boyfriend," he told my *cousins*. "Nickname, the Draaagoon."

"Huh," I said with a half-laugh, half-grown. I wasn't sure when he'd picked up the ridiculous nickname, but I'd *never* dated the goon. "Not accurate, but neither here nor there at this point."

"Lordy have mercy," Gram shouted as she popped up from out of nowhere. "What on earth is goin' on with that boy's hair? He looks like ten miles of bad road. If I had a dog that looked like that, I'd shave his butt and make him walk backwards."

I almost screamed. While I was thrilled Gram was fine, sneaking up on me wasn't helpful. What she'd just said was accurate and I was relieved that Micky Muggles couldn't see or hear her. However, the queens and Tim could and just about lost it.

Since talking back to Gram's ghost would make me look like I'd lost my marbles, I waved my hand in the air to let her know to zip the lip. It got confusing dealing with the dead when humans were present. Messing up and answering someone who wasn't there would be unwise. Buying wrapping paper and sending Micky on his way was smart.

Smart was my MO right now.

"Ohhhhh, I love the paper with the ponies!" Dirk said, holding it up.

"Really, *Bubba*?" Carl asked with a grin. "I'm partial to the ones with the little pink polka dots."

"Well, *Bo*," Dirk huffed, clearly put out that he was Bubba. "There's no accounting for taste."

This was going south fast. If a smackdown started over the crappy names I'd given them, they could end up in the back of Micky Muggles' cruiser.

"How much is the paper?" I asked quickly.

"Five bucks a package," he said, rolling his eyes. "Pricey for a bunch of paper, but I don't make the rules, I just follow them."

That was debatable. He not only didn't follow the rules, he was breaking the law for skipping out on child support. I didn't like the man at all.

"How many packages are in the box?" I asked.

Micky grinned. If he thought he'd just hit the jackpot, he was correct. I'd buy all of it to get his sorry ass off my front lawn.

"Fifty," he said.

"I don't do math," I muttered to Tim.

Tim smiled and pulled a checkbook out of one of his many pockets. "My treat, friend," he said.

"Tim, you've gone and lost your dang mind," Gram chastised him, pointing her bony ghostly finger in his face. "That paper fell out of an ugly tree and hit every branch on the way down. Ain't worth no two-hundred and fifty dollars!"

Crap. I made a mental note to pay Tim back. I didn't carry a checkbook around with me and didn't want to leave Micky Muggles alone with my *cousins* to go inside and get it.

Tim just smiled and wrote the check.

"You can make that check out to me," Micky said quickly.

Tim raised a brow and stared at the greedy man until he blushed a deep red and began rocking back and forth on his little feet.

"The package clearly states to make the check out to the school," Tim said in a cool tone that made mullet-man squirm.

"My bad," he said, nervously pulling a comb from his back pocket and combing the four hairs on the top of his head.

"I should say so," Tim replied flatly, handing over the check.

"Lemme get your change," he said, puffing out his chest and holding one of his hands in the air.

Tim was confused. I wasn't. Micky was an idiot. His hobby in high school was pulling quarters out from behind his strangely large ears.

He wiggled his fingers, hopped up and down then reached behind his ear and produced a quarter. The mullet-loving fool shouted "tada" and took a bow. No one knew what to do. Carl, being the polite queen that he was, clapped for the trick. Micky preened and handed Tim his change.

"Well, I better get goin'," Micky said, saluting us and shoving the check into his pocket with the greasy comb. "Gotta go pick up Molly May from the feed store for a little afternoon delight! If you know what I mean."

I did know what he meant and the bile rose in my throat. First off, her name was Maggie May. Secondly, she was about half his age.

Again, my mouth led with zero approval from my brain and common sense. "You certainly have a collection of lady friends."

The icky little dude winked. "I'm a collector," he said. "Beer cans, rabbits' feet and beautiful chest-blessed women, among other things. Can't call me stupid even though my ex-wife does."

I plastered a huge and fake smile on my face. "That's open to a controversial debate," I said as I walked Micky Muggles back to his cruiser.

His look of confusion told me he wasn't sure if I'd insulted him or congratulated him. However, my smile led the imbecile to believe I'd been complimentary. Wiggling my fingers in the pocket of my coat, I conjured up a box of condoms, size small.

"Here you go, Micky," I said, tossing the box to him. "You don't want any more kids you have to support."

"Good thinking!" he said. "You always were smart back in high school. Dang shame we never went out. Would have just buttered my biscuit if you'd been in my collection. You just never know, some day you might be!"

I was so close to up-chucking I could taste it. "My guess is that you couldn't find your posterior with both appendages in your backside material compartments."

"You got that right!" he said, looking so perplexed I almost laughed.

Big words spewed at tiny minds were awesome.

Officer Micky Muggles got into his police car, turned on the siren and sped away.

Gram was the first to comment. "That man's as worthless as gum on a boot heel."

I shook my head and blew out a long, audible breath. "I'd go so far as to say he's lower than a snake's belly in a wagon rut."

Dirk laughed. "Did you get a good look at his pants?"

"Oh my," Carl said with a snort. "Normally, I do like a man

in tight trousers, but his pants were so tight if he farts, it'll blow his boots off."

I laughed. I glanced back at the house, hoping to see my baby and the rest of my friends and family. No one was there. It seemed like it was taking a long time for them to come home, but maybe Alana Catherine was napping. Or eating.

"They'll be here soon," Tim assured me.

It seemed suspicious that my dear buddy was able to read my mind, but his words were comforting.

"Shall we examine the field?" Fred inquired. "I'm quite sure *Bubba* wants to do that."

Dirk punched him in the head. Fred laughed and electrocuted him. Carl chastised both of them and Wally just giggled at the violent antics.

"I'm sorry," I yelled at them before the fighting left them without body parts. "The names just came out."

"Apology accepted, Sugar Pants," Wally said with a chuckle. He waved his hands and the queens went from non-descript boring guys to resplendent drag queens in stunning ball gowns.

"So much better!" Carl squealed, turning in circles and admiring his frock.

It *was* better. They were gorgeous. Having to hide who they were due to prejudice sucked. In a perfect world, that wouldn't be the case.

The world wasn't perfect—far from it.

Now it was time to figure out how to make my little world better—not perfect, but better. It certainly couldn't get much worse.

"Field. Now," I instructed.

"As you wish," Tim said, taking my hand in his and leading the way.

CHAPTER FIVE

THE CRUNCHY GRASS SNAPPED AND CRACKLED BENEATH MY FEET as I walked the area where Gideon and Gabe had gone. At first, I saw nothing—just dead brown grass and leafless trees. Letting my head fall back on my shoulders, I groaned up at the watery winter sun trying its damnedest to push through the murky clouds.

"I feel you," I whispered to the sun.

A light touch on my shoulder pulled me back into the moment. "Sometimes looking with your eyes makes you blind," Tim said softly. "It's never prudent to look directly at the sun."

His cryptic advice always made sense eventually. I wasn't sure how closing my eyes would help.

"How old is the sun?" I asked.

"Four-point-five billion years old," Tim replied. "Why?"

I shook my head. "Not sure," I told him. "But I kind of feel like I'm the sun trying to force my way out of the clouds and shed some light. If the sun is older than dirt and can't do it, not sure I can either."

I wasn't a defeatist. I was an optimist. However, if Gideon

had done what I thought he'd done, I wasn't sure how we could go forward. The thought was devastating and depressing. Pushing away the sick feeling in my stomach was difficult. If the roles were reversed, he would get to the bottom of the problem rather than condemn me.

I owed him as much.

"Did you know that in ancient civilizations, many believed the sun was a God?" Fred asked.

"I can see why." Reaching up into the air, I wiggled my fingers and tried to pierce a hole in the clouds for the sun. It didn't work. No surprise there. It was a metaphor of sorts. A crappy one, but I called them like I saw them.

"The sun has a crown, darling," Dirk explained in a hushed tone. "It's quite thin and faint, but it's there. All true beauty wears a crown—even if you can't see it."

"Sugar Pants," Wally said, putting his arm around my shoulders. "If you want to see the full glory of the sun, you must weather the storm first."

I looked up at the huge, beautiful and wise man. "What if the storm's a tsunami? What if I drown and can't get back to the surface?"

The ball-gown-clad queen hugged me close. "To win, you must create your own sunshine."

I knew the words were prophetic. That was how it worked with Immortals. Glancing back up at the sky, I sighed. The sun was now completely covered in dull gray clouds.

"Nothing is impossible. I just have to believe," I whispered.

I wanted to believe in Gideon. I wanted to believe in Gabe. I needed to believe that Gideon and I were a forever thing. The alternative was heart-shredding. We had a daughter and a life.

"Fine," I said, getting over my mentally destructive pity party with effort. "I'm going to make my sun shine bright."

"That's the spirit, girlfriend!" Fred said. "As Rihanna says, shine bright like a diamond."

AFTER THIRTY MINUTES OF EXAMINING THE FIELD, WE WERE NO closer to learning anything new. However, Tim had been correct. Once I stopped staring at the ground to detect Immortal footprints, I could see them as clear as day. Letting my gaze roam lazily over the area was the key.

Problem was there were tons of them in every color of the rainbow. Pretty much all of the Immortals in my life had been all over the property. There was no decerning who'd left the prints. Some had even overlapped and combined to create new colors.

"This is quite the conundrum," Tim muttered, taking notes.

Wally nodded. "Looks like a disco dance floor."

That was one way to put it. And then it got more colorful.

In a blast of what I could only describe as pissed-off orange glitter with a medium-sized explosion, Candy Vargo appeared. The woman was agitated and chewing ten toothpicks.

My body tensed up and I didn't waste any time. "Where's Alana Catherine?" I demanded.

"Safe," she assured me, spitting out the wood and marching around the open field. "Everyone's in the house. Charlie and Heather are on their way out."

My sigh of relief made my knees buckle. Carl steadied me and gave me a quick squeeze. "The storm has arrived. Time to find the sun, my friend."

"What the actual fuck is going on here?" Candy Vargo shouted.

Never a good sign when Candy was losing her shit.

"Gideon and Gabe kidnapped Zadkiel and took him to the darkness," I told her, feeling incredible distaste for the words that left my lips.

"Says who?" she demanded.

"Tory."

The Keeper of Fate's eyes narrowed to slits. It was looking like everyone in her path might end up missing body parts. I didn't have enough glue or time to put everyone back together. I was barely holding myself together.

"I thought Gram had gotten into the sauce," Candy snapped, pulling out another box of toothpicks and going to town. "You're tellin' me she wasn't wasted and making up yarns?"

"One, she's dead and can't drink. Two, she never drank in real life. Three, I'm not sure what she told you, but from your reaction, it sounds like it's generally correct."

Candy blew a crater in the ground that would house a swimming pool. "Motherfucker," she bellowed. "Forget about Armageddon. That ain't the end. This is."

"What are you talking about?" I shouted, adding another crater to the collection. It was that or electrocute Candy Vargo. That seemed like a really bad idea. "After all the crap that Immortals have done, this would cause the end?"

I punctuated the crater with a blast and made it a sinkhole. I was just getting started. "After what Clarissa did? After what Zadkiel has done? You're telling me that the *alleged* ghost-napping of a murderous asshole will bring on the end?"

"*Alleged* might be slightly underplaying the situation," Tim pointed out.

I wanted to peel my skin off. Sadly, I probably could and live to tell. "Fine," I conceded. "But I don't believe this one incident is going to cause the destruction of the world. Period."

In a shimmering blue mist, Charlie and Heather arrived. I wasn't sure if the presence of the Arbitrator between the Darkness and the Light and the Enforcer was a welcome sight. If they believed what Candy Vargo did, I didn't need them. What I needed was for Tory to come back so I could find Gideon and Gabe.

Or did I? Tory didn't want to come. Did I want an unwilling partner? My mind raced too quickly to gather my train of thought. My gut had told me I needed Tory. Following my gut had gone well so far. However, new wrinkles presented different problems.

"Shit," I yelled, squatting low to the ground and trying to make sense of bullshit.

Charlie approached me with a concerned expression on his face. His power was on full display. It was difficult to breathe, but I didn't say a word—just took shallow breaths and prayed I didn't pass out.

Normally, he looked in his sixties, slightly overweight, with a contagious laugh and twinkling blue eyes. Lately, he appeared to be around thirty. Immortals could play with their ages. He played with his to match the age of his beloved June. In a terrifying moment of desperation, I'd put June's soul back into her body after Clarissa had stolen it. It had resulted in our fifty-seven-year-old dear friend looking around twenty-five after the successful and unfathomable magical operation. None of us were sure of her human status anymore. She'd taken it far better than I had when I thought I'd lost my marbles and saw dead people.

Charlie squatted next to me and looked me in the eye. "Talk to me."

"Kinda hard," I choked out.

He smiled and waved his hand. Tamping back the magic, he gently pulled me to my feet. "Better?"

"Much," I said.

Heather joined him. My sister's enchanted tattoos danced and raced over her skin. It was a stunning and macabre sight to behold. She looked like a living piece of art.

"I'm having a hard time wrapping my mind around what I've been told," she said, tucking my wild dark curls behind my ear.

"Join the club," I muttered. "Tory saw it happen."

Charlie inhaled deeply. "Do we trust her?"

I shrugged. "I think so… I don't know."

"Is it a possibility that she's exacting payback from Gabe?" Tim inquired.

"For?" Heather asked, confused.

For several minutes, I went back over the story with everyone. Including the part where Zadkiel had destroyed both Tory and Gabe thousands of years ago. It didn't make sense that she would want to harm Gabe. But sense wasn't the name of the game right now.

Charlie paced and his eyes spit steel blue sparks. Heather's tattoos swirled so fast it was dizzying to look at her. Candy glowed dangerously. Only the queens and Tim were calm. I wasn't sure what I was. It felt a bit like I was floating above my body and looking down at a shitshow.

"I'm walking the conversation back," I finally said. "How is this the end?"

"Interpretation is the key," Charlie said tersely.

"Charlie," I said, trying my best not to snarl at the man.

The Enforcer was the sweetest man I knew… along with being one hell of a scary badass. Being polite was in my DNA, but my limits were being tested.

"Yes?"

"Cryptic isn't gonna work for me today."

He sighed and his brow wrinkled in thought. "The short answer is I don't know, and I would surmise Candy Vargo doesn't know either."

Candy simply growled.

Awesome.

"Is there a long answer?" I pressed, knowing it was futile to get blood from a stone.

Heather ran her hands through her sleek pixie cut. "An ending can be a new beginning," she said. "Some would argue that there's no clear beginning therefore, no clear end—more of a cyclical motion. Life is a never-ending circle."

"More confused," I said, annoyed. I adored my sister. I knew she was wise. But this conversation was giving me a migraine.

"Howfuckingever," Candy Vargo jumped into the fray. "If the balance of what we hold to be the truth is fucked with, it signals the end for us. Screw Zadkiel and Clarissa. They lost their minds. What they did wasn't remotely excusable, but when an Immortal breaks, it's never pretty."

"Understatement," Tim said.

"Gideon and Gabe ain't lost it as far as I know," she went on. "If those sons of bitches destroyed the balance with full knowledge of right and wrong, we're all fucked. I mean, if the Grim Reaper and the Archangel have gone rogue, it's not long before the higher power calls it a day and does away with all of us."

And the silence was loud. The higher power was a concept I didn't quite understand. It wasn't as simple as God or goodness. Nothing in the Immortal world was black and white.

Pressing the bridge of my nose, I decided to only deal with

what I could handle. I'd find Gideon and Gabe and get the bastard Zadkiel back to Purgatory. Period.

All the ifs made me itchy and unsettled.

"House," Candy Vargo commanded. "I'm fuckin' cold and Alana Catherine needs some boob."

She didn't have to ask twice. I sprinted so fast, I left everyone in my dust. I needed light in my world. My baby shone more than the sun in all its fiery glory.

CHAPTER SIX

THE GANG WAS ALL HERE. MY HOUSE FELT LIKE A HOME WITH people I loved in it. Gideon and Gabe were missing, but that was beyond my control. However, seeing my people centered me and made my purpose beyond clear. I refused to believe any kind of end was in sight. Even if Gideon and Gabe had committed the crime, there was a thing called forgiveness and redemption.

I hoped.

Compassion. If I wanted to see the full glory of the sun, I needed to weather the storm first. For Alana Catherine, I'd weather the most devastating of storms. Always.

Holding my child in my arms was as close to perfect as it would ever get.

"She's so happy to be with her mamma," June cooed, sitting next to me as I nursed Alana Catherine.

June was a good and kind person—like a mom to all. Her steadiness and openness to love were her superpowers. I counted myself wildly lucky to be her friend and would do anything for her. She would do the same for me. It made every kind of sense that the Enforcer had chosen a human mate with such simple and beautiful gifts.

June also made the best cookies in the Universe, but that paled in comparison to all of her other qualities. Although, one of June's peanut butter cookies sounded incredible right now.

Alana Catherine's slurping noises and sweet milk-drunk expression glued me together. My eyes feasted on the small bundle. Her life amazed me and I wouldn't let it be in vain. Glancing around for ghosts, I didn't spot any except for Gram. My guess was that they'd come back soon now that Alana Catherine was home.

Rafe, Prue and Abby sat silently steaming after learning what Zadkiel had done to Gabe and Tory. Their lives had been lived under the vicious and evil fist of Zadkiel. However, Gabe's and Tory's existences had been far worse. It was hard to imagine. Abby's face was twisted in fury and Prue had sworn more than I'd ever heard Candy Vargo go at it. Gram didn't chastise her. None of us did. Today, she got a pass.

There was a tiny part of me that didn't blame Gideon and Gabe, but that didn't mean I agreed.

Our human friends were slightly confused, but that was to be expected. Amelia sat next to Rafe and held his hand. Missy, my BFF and Heather's partner, understood more than Amelia since she was the Soul Keeper, but the full magnitude was lost on them.

Heck, it was kind of lost on me...

"Plans?" Candy Vargo demanded, building a tower on the coffee table with chewed-up toothpicks.

The tension in the room was high. Working with little to no information was dicey. Didn't matter. It was what it was. Complaining wasn't going to change it.

"When Tory gets back, I'm going into the darkness through Dirk. I'll find them," I said flatly.

"And?" Candy pressed harshly, not looking at me.

"And what?" I asked, frustrated. I was a pull-it-out-of-my-rear-end kind of gal lately. Planning it out then sticking to it never seemed to go right in this farked-up world.

"You gonna kick some ass?" Candy Vargo demanded.

Alana Catherine had fallen asleep in my arms. Handing her off to June felt like I ripped out part of my heart. I did it anyway. I was getting antsy and didn't need to put that on my baby. "If necessary, yes."

"Are you sure they went into the darkness?" Charlie inquired.

I paused. It was a question I hadn't considered. It was the logical guess since neither of them had wanted Zadkiel to go to Purgatory. "No," I admitted hesitantly. "Where would they have gone if not there?"

Charlie didn't answer me.

"Karma's a bitch," Candy mumbled right before she began to glow an eerie bluish color.

"Oh shit," Heather said, jumping to her feet. "Everyone back up. Now."

The power filled the room quickly and made everything blurry. With a wave of my hand, I transported June, Amelia and Missy upstairs with Alana Catherine. It was safer there.

The Keeper of Fate's messy hair blew around her head and she began to chant a haunting tune. When her eyes rolled back in her head and she hit the floor with a thud, my body tightened all over.

I'd seen this before.

"Is she about to get a message through her ass?" I whispered.

"Not her ass, so to speak," Tim said without cracking a smile. Shit was serious. "Her left butt cheek tingles when an Immortal needs assistance—a magical SOS, if you will."

"Right ass cheek," Heather corrected Tim.

"Of course," Tim replied. "My mistake."

Candy's voice was low and ominous. It sent shivers skittering up my spine. The wind in my house picked up. Pillows, lamps and knickknacks fell to the floor. The queens ran around and tried to save a few objects, but gave up when funnels of purple glitter began to burst all over the place. Candy Vargo's body convulsed then stilled. She looked like a lifeless doll.

"With the collection of knowledge, treading cautiously is the best plan of action," she sang in a monotone. "The collection is deeply personal. Do not wake the monster."

Orange crystals rained down from above and covered every surface of the living room. Candy Vargo passed out. Tim and the queens gently picked her up and placed her on the couch. Flicking the shimmering pieces off my eyelashes, I looked around to see if anyone knew what she'd meant.

"What was she talking about?" I asked.

Charlie pressed the bridge of his nose and began to pace the room. "I wish I knew."

Not what I was looking for. He was the oldest and the wisest of us and he was clueless.

"Do we know who sent the message?" I asked, searching for at least something in the words.

No one answered. The ass message was as muddy as every other clue we had, or rather, didn't have...

"Doesn't matter," I announced, feeling light-headed but ready for action. Doing nothing was not the way to go. My gut told me to get moving. "With or without Tory, I have to leave."

"And do what exactly?" Prue asked coolly.

I didn't reply. I didn't know the answer. Bottom line was to find Gideon and Gabe... and Zadkiel. From there, I was winging it.

"Howdyho," Jennifer shouted coming through the front door with my dogs, Donna and Karen, on her heels. "I got some hot gossip!"

The gust of cold wind that followed her in blew the crystals of magic all over. The entire room looked like an explosion of orange and purple glitter on crack.

"Darling," Dirk said, leading Jennifer into the house and giving her a hug. "No time for gossip. The world might be coming to an end."

"Well, that sucks," Jennifer said, glancing around at the sparkling living room. "Oh my gosh! Is Candy Vargo dead?"

"No, no," Tim assured his good buddy. "She ass-messaged us and is recuperating. She'll come to shortly."

Jennifer scratched her head and pulled a bottle of wine from her bag. "That's a new one for me. Didn't realize asses could talk."

"You'd be surprised what asses can do," Heather muttered.

I stood up and centered myself. I'd give Tory five more minutes. After that, I was out. "Jennifer, tell me some gossip. I need something in my brain that isn't life-threatening, please."

"Can do," she announced, sitting down next to Candy on the couch and checking her ass. Once she was satisfied that Candy's ass wasn't in danger, she continued. "First off, the mayor fell asleep at the town council meeting and farted in his sleep so loud, they had to clear the chamber."

Wally gasped and clasped his hands over his heart. "On no, girlfriend! Is this a normal occurrence?"

Jennifer offered the wine to Wally, who took it. "Yep. Man's gassy. Rumor has it he ate beans for lunch. Did you know the average speed of a fart is six-point-eight miles an hour?"

"I did know that," Tim replied.

Heather rolled her eyes. "Of course, you did."

Tim smiled with pride. He took his gross facts very seriously. "And while most call a very quiet and odiferous fart a silent-but-deadly aka SBD, the technical term is foist."

I winced. The visuals weren't good, but it was definitely a relief to hear about problems that didn't concern me—even stinky ones. "You got more?" I asked.

Heather groaned. "Are you serious?"

"Totally," I replied, grabbing my weenus and squeezing. I needed the magic of the mind-calming weenus.

"Daisy, may I ask what you're doing?" Charlie questioned, looking at me like I'd gone and lost it.

He wouldn't be wrong, but he was about to get a lesson in the joys of pinching elbow skin. It took all of one minute and twenty seconds to have everyone in the room pinching their weenuses.

"I rest my case," I said to the room of weenus-squeezers.

"Thrilling!" Carl announced. "It's the simple things in life that help in a crisis."

"You know what isn't exactly thrilling or simple, but dang funny?" Jennifer asked, doing thorough elbow skin workout.

"Do tell," Wally insisted, grabbing a broom and making a valiant attempt to clean up the room.

It wasn't working.

"Old Man Jenkins streaked at the high school basketball game last night," she said with a hoot of laughter.

"He did not," Dirk gasped with a giggle.

"He sure did," Jennifer told him. "Right in the middle of Prudie Lane's crapola rendition of the national anthem." She whipped out her phone and passed it around. "Went viral on the internet. Best part was when the Ladies Garden Club tackled his naked ass to the floor. Ref called a foul."

Jennifer slapped her thighs and laughed like a loon. Our small town wasn't boring.

"How do you know all this garbage?" Heather asked, shaking her head while looking over Tim's shoulder at Old Man Jenkins' wrinkled junk.

"Dip's police radio," Jennifer admitted with no shame whatsoever. "It's where all the action is!"

I squinted at her. "Are you supposed to be listening to official business?"

"Hell to the no," she said with a naughty grin. "But Dip made me a deal. If I don't get any more Botox, I can listen for thirty minutes a day."

She'd recently gotten a double dose of Botox. Her face was just beginning to show expression. My adorable buddy didn't need all that crap. She was a terrific-looking sixty-five-year-old gal who'd been divorced five times. She'd gotten into a horrible habit of using her divorce settlements for *self-improvements*. Her new man, Sheriff Dip Doody, didn't think she should mess with that junk. He was correct. If bribery worked, who was I to judge?

Heather groaned. "I shouldn't know this," she said with a chuckle. "I'm an attorney."

"And I work for you, you lucky gal!" Jennifer reminded her with a wide grin.

Heather laughed. "Correct."

"One more," Jennifer said, nodding to Fred who had brought out wine glasses. "This one's a doozy."

"Spit it out." I checked my watch. Tory had one more minute before Dirk and I were leaving... Not physically, since when I mind dived, my body went nowhere, but mentally we would be taking a trip.

"Micky Muggles got fired about an hour ago," she shared.

"Oh my God." I scrunched my nose. The only thing that was too bad about that piece of news was that I couldn't have Sheriff Dip garnish his wages. Whatever. I'd have Heather go after the loser. "Why?"

"Got busted for cruising in the cruiser, if you know what I mean," she said. "Rumor has it he also pilfered the collection of Civil War coins from the art gallery—worth a couple hundred thousand."

"Whoopsiedoodle!" Dirk sang. "If you're going to fuck around on the city's dime, you're gonna find out!"

"Sure 'nuff. Never did like that greasy little guy," Jennifer agreed. "Where are June and the baby?"

"Upstairs," I told her.

My buddy rubbed her small hands together and hopped to her feet. "I need to kiss some chunky baby cheeks!"

"Go," I told her. Mind diving was serious business. I didn't want to listen to gross facts about mullet-sporting idiots when I was leaving this plane on a mission of potential life and death. Walking over to Dirk, I extended my hand. "You ready?"

"Yes, darling," he assured me with a smile. "Am I overdressed?"

I eyed his ball gown and smiled. "You're gorgeous."

"Aren't I just?" he replied with a giggle as he took my hand.

"I'm going to hug you," I explained, leading him over to the couch. "It'll be a little painful during the initial descent, but just stay calm."

"As a cucumber, darling," Dirk promised. "This is wildly exciting!"

Candy Vargo was still passed out. Prue, Rafe and Gabby

were still fuming. Heather was pensive and wore a worried expression. Charlie continued to pace. Carl, Fred and Wally sipped wine and kept the comments to a minimum. Only Tim seemed to be in good spirits.

"Nothing is impossible," he reminded me. "You just have to believe, friend."

It was our mantra. It was time to test it out… again.

The blast of silver mist came in the nick of time. Tory had returned.

"Fabulous entrance!" Wally announced, clapping enthusiastically.

It was. Tory's beauty was almost off-putting. The moment I thought I was used to it I was reminded I was not. The Immortal stood only about five feet tall but owned all the space she occupied. Her eyes were a piercing blue and her skin was alabaster. Her hair was the kicker—the most unusual silver hue I'd ever seen. The woman was stunning.

I'd secretly named her the Ice Queen the first time I'd seen her. The truth was far more complicated.

"The wraiths?" I asked, as she glanced around and took in the occupants of the room.

"Are safe," she said tonelessly.

Something was off. My Spidey senses tingled. It didn't help that Candy Vargo woke up and let a burp rip that made me gag.

"Jesus," Heather muttered, eyeing Candy. "Manners much?"

"Fuck you," Candy grumbled. "It was better than a fart."

"Not by much," Abby added with a wince.

Candy Vargo grunted and sat up. She looked at me like I was contagious. "What the fuck are you waiting for? Did you hear what my ass said?"

"Ease up," I told her, feeling my stress skyrocket. I considered pinching my weenus, but even that wouldn't help right now. "Do you know what you meant?"

The Keeper of Fate rolled her eyes so hard they should have gotten stuck in the back of her rude head. "Not how it works, dumbass. All I know is, with the collection of knowledge, treading cautiously is the best plan of action. The collection is deeply personal. Do not wake the monster."

"Right," I said flatly. "You have anything else?"

"I'm just the messenger," she shot back as frustrated as me. "It's up to you to interpret the shit."

Biting back all of the useless and profane words that were on the tip of my tongue was hard. Gram had been very quiet, which was odd. I didn't need her ripping me a new one for using the F-bomb as a verb, noun and adverb. I might be losing it, but the illusion of holding my shit together seemed to be the way to roll. If I could pretend it, I could be it.

I motioned for Tory to join me and Dirk. She didn't look pleased, but didn't fight me. This wasn't the best situation. However, I couldn't for the life of me figure out another way.

One move at a time. Be flexible. Handle each disaster as it unfolds.

"Don't fight the pain," I advised.

"No pain, no gain," Tory replied.

"From your mouth…" I whispered.

It was time to find the sun.

CHAPTER SEVEN

THE COLD. THE COLD WENT ALL THE WAY TO MY BONES AND TORE through my body like sharp, frozen daggers made of ice. Trying to catch my breath, I gasped for air.

The only sound that left my lips came from so far away I could barely hear it.

My head pounded violently and every single cell in my body screamed for oxygen. I knew it was momentary, but it still sucked.

My mind went numb, and my limbs felt as if they'd turned to stone.

Tory tried to pull away from me and Dirk but we were locked together in an enchanted embrace. I held her tight and refused to let go. We were in my territory now, not hers. I'd never lost anyone in the darkness and I wasn't going to break my record today.

When the pain subsided, we stood in a small circle and stared at each other. The surreal feeling was almost funny. Almost. This wasn't fiction. It was real and there was very little fun about it.

Closing my eyes, I pictured Gideon's face. Tragically, he was the reason I was here. The Grim Reaper was the ridiculous kind of beautiful—gray-blue eyes, messy blond hair and muscular body. His outer shell was breathtaking, but it was what was inside that was even more stunning. His eyes lit up when he laughed. He went from plain gorgeous to otherworldly beautiful. I craved the sound of his laugh. It filled me with a happiness that was hard to explain.

His darker side was as glorious as his lighter side in a different way. In his beast form, the Grim Reaper was a raven-winged being with blood-red eyes and power that was mind-boggling. The pain of his past was evident, but it hadn't broken him. I refused to believe that Zadkiel's fate would be the catalyst to bring down the man I loved.

My tears were close to the surface. Crying would solve nothing. Finding Gideon and Gabe and getting answers was the plan.

"Oh my!" Dirk said, glancing around in surprise. "Far more boring than I expected."

"What did you expect?" I asked, trying to look at the space with new eyes.

We were floating on air in the vast nothingness. There were no walls or floor to speak of. It was a familiar place to me. Everything had a grayish haze and the emptiness was resounding.

"I don't know," he replied. "Something fiery and evil... not quite so dull. I thought it would be more lively than this eerie silent void. Maybe clanking chains, bloodcurdling screams, howling, grinding, hissing, moaning..."

He had a point. I'd had similar thoughts when I'd first experienced the darkness. But the barren landscape was a picture waiting to be painted. The color came to life when I watched the memories of the dead I'd been charged with helping. This situation was very different. None of us were dead. Dirk and Tory didn't need my help to move on.

What we were doing was uncharted and possibly stupid.

Tory was quiet. That wasn't unusual. Dirk was not. I was unsure how to proceed. That was bad.

"So," Dirk said, clapping his huge and expertly manicured hands. "Do we just wait for the action to start?"

I shook my head. "No, we find it," I told him. "Normally, it's forbidden to walk towards the light or the dark. However, new day, new rules."

Tory huffed out a put-upon sigh. I was over her crap and we'd just begun.

"You want to add to the conversation?" I asked.

"No."

"Awesome," I muttered, pointing at a path that led into the darkness. "Follow me."

I'd found Gideon in the darkness once before. It had been terrifying. I walked toward the corridor I'd followed the last time. It didn't look the same. With each step we took, an ominous echo trailed us. My idea of finding them in the darkness started to seem like a deadly folly.

Dirk halted both of us and leaned forward. The tall queen cupped his hand to his ear and squinted his falsely lashed eyes. "Do you hear that?"

I listened. I heard nothing. "No."

"I do," Tory whispered.

Trying again, I still heard nothing but silence. "What do you hear?"

Dirk looked a bit confused. "Sounds like a party."

"Agreed," Tory said.

I had no clue what they were listening to. Pretty sure there weren't parties in the darkness, I just shrugged and went with it. "Fine. I say we get the party started."

"You go, gurl," Dirk said. "Pink would be proud!"

∾

"*WHAT THE ACTUAL HELL?*" *I MUTTERED UNDER MY BREATH AS WE approached what looked like a bar in the middle of nowhere. The large rectangular building floated on the air like we did. It wasn't anchored, but it didn't move. There was no grass or trees or anything natural, just concrete and sultry red lighting. I would have sworn the building was breathing. A blindingly bright neon sign illuminated the carved black door at the front of the establishment. It read "Ignis Pit".*

"Literal," Tory commented.

"Someone has a sense of humor, darlings," Dirk said, glancing around warily. "The Fire Pit is a fabu name for a bar in Hell."

We'd carefully walked along a rocky and dimly lit path towards the party I couldn't hear for twenty minutes before we arrived at the odd destination. Or, at least, what felt like twenty minutes. Time on other planes ran differently. Five minutes or five days could have passed at home. Didn't matter. There was no way to control it.

"It's a bar?" I asked, shaking my head and wondering what was happening. "Like a business? That serves alcohol?"

"Looks to be," Dirk said. "Is this not the norm?"

My laugh sounded a little unhinged. The word norm and a bar in the darkness didn't equate. "Umm... no. Nothing normal about it."

"Shall we go in?" Dirk inquired.

"I don't even know how to answer that." Was I picking up on Dirk or Tory's past memories? I wasn't touching them. They weren't dead. It was a logical option, but logic didn't apply to magic.

I glanced over at my partners. "Do either of you recognize the place? Have you ever been to it before?"

Tory shook her head.

"No. Not my cup of tea," Dirk said. "I prefer more flamboyant to dark, depressing and deadly, doll face."

Tory rolled her eyes. "Whatever. Rarely does anything happen without reason in our world. If there's a bar, someone's in there who is expecting us. Mark my words."

Of all the bizarre and weird as of late, this one felt off.

"I wonder if we're about to die," I muttered. For the most part, I didn't think we could actually die here. Our physical bodies were on my couch in Georgia even though we felt solid. However, I wouldn't bet on anything right now.

"Only one way to find out," Dirk said, adjusting the bodice of his gown. "Did you bring money, darling?"

Had he lost his marbles? "Umm... nope. Never needed money in the darkness before."

The queen patted my head. "Not to worry. I'm sure we can run a tab if necessary."

"At what price?" Tory snapped.

Dirk raised a brow. "At any price. When the end game draws nigh, the cost is irrelevant."

"Shit." I took a deep breath. If Gideon and Gabe were throwing back beers, I was going to skin both of them alive. "Let's go."

The interior of the bar was seedy yet strangely luxurious. Deep red velvet couches and heavy black wooden tables dotted the area. Tall light towers flanked the ornately carved wooden bar and flashed red and blinding white to the beat of the sultry drum music from hidden speakers. I half expected strippers to appear.

"It's empty," Tory noted.

I touched a table. My hand went right through it. "Is it even real?"

"Define real," Dirk said.

A disembodied voice answered the Horseman of the Apocalypse known as Death before I had the chance to.

"Definition of real," the female voice said in a forbidding tone. "Actual existing as a thing or occurring in fact... not imagined or supposed."

"Who said that?" I demanded, pushing Dirk and Tory behind me.

I wasn't sure how much protection I could provide, but it was instinct.

"I did," the voice answered as the owner appeared in a thick haze of red mist.

I recognized her immediately. It was the Goddess Lilith. Her wild dark curls blew around her head, and her pupils were shaped identically to a goat's. They glowed red. She wore a shimmering scarlet gown that hugged her body. The iridescent fabric danced around her and sparkled in the neon lights. Her expression was neutral, but she didn't seem delighted to have guests.

I wasn't delighted to be here either.

Hell, or the darkness, for a more accurate term, was a matriarchal society. Satan was more of a concept than a being, from what I'd been told. I was pretty sure none of this information was in the Bible... that I hadn't read.

The Goddess Lilith and the Goddess Pandora ran the show. From the stories, there was no love lost between the powerful women. They despised each other. If I had to run into one of them, I'd definitely choose Lilith. Pandora was rumored to be batshit crazy.

Lilith didn't seem sane, but she didn't appear to be off her rocker... yet.

Lilith was also Gideon's sister. Wrapping my mind around all of it was exhausting. I'd met her once. It hadn't been what I would describe as pleasant, but she hadn't tried to kill me. In the Immortal world that was considered a win.

"Lilith," I said, nodding my head in respect.

"Daisy," she replied coolly with a curt and mostly unfriendly nod in reply. "It's not wise to go where one is not invited."

"I agree," I replied.

The woman had no backup that I could detect. She most likely didn't need it. We were on her turf.

"And who are your friends?" she inquired.

Dirk stepped forward and bowed. "I'm the Pale Rider."

Lilith wasn't impressed. She looked annoyed. "Why are you here?" she demanded. "Armageddon is not on the schedule."

"I come bearing no ill will," he replied quickly. "I am simply the conduit to the darkness for the Angel of Mercy. No more. No less."

The Goddess inhaled deeply and her expression relaxed. "Your gown is lovely."

Dirk giggled and winked at her. "And yours is to die for, Goddess Lilith."

"I have no plans to die today," she replied with a hint of a smile. Her laser gaze then rested on Tory. "And you?"

"Tory," she said. "Purgatory."

Lilith's brows shot up so high it was comical. "Do not fuck with me," she hissed. "You're a myth."

"No," I said, stepping in front of Tory and effectively challenging a Goddess. I didn't care. Tory had been through enough. No one was going to harm her on my watch. "She's not a myth. She's also not the enemy."

"Fascinating." Lilith snapped her fingers. The music stopped. The lights went dark and the building around us literally disappeared. "I suppose one learns something new every day."

Introductions were over and we were still breathing. So far, so good.

"I'm looking for Gideon," I said, getting right to the point. If she was going to throw us out of the darkness, I may as well try to do what I came here to do.

"Interesting," she commented.

If she knew anything, she wasn't talking.

"He did something uncharacteristic," I tried again. "I need to find him."

"Not my monkey, not my circus," she said, watching us with unabashed curiosity. "Shall we go for a stroll?"

I was pretty sure it wasn't a request. "Yes."

"Excellent," she replied.

The Goddess waved her hand and the walls that didn't exist felt like they were closing in. I wasn't sure how Tory or Dirk were doing, but my head pounded, and my skin felt as if it was melting off my bones. My eyes were open, but I couldn't see a thing. An arid wind swirled around me, and I reached out to grab onto something.

There was nothing to hold on to.

Coming to the darkness had been a bullshit plan.

"We're here," Lilith said.

Slowly, I looked around. Dirk was next to me on the left and Tory was on my right. All three of us gasped for air. Lilith's idea of a stroll sucked.

A vast mountainous landscape of raging fire was in front of us. It seemed to go on forever. It was terrifying, wicked and sensual all at the same time. Alarmingly, I felt closer to Gideon in this place. My eyes scanned the area as I looked for him.

He wasn't there.

Roaring flames licked up the sides of trees I'd never seen before. Prehistoric-looking birds swooped through the air and attacked each other with a bloody vengeance. A huge red sun hung low in a purple-blue sky. The heat was almost unbearable. I reminded myself that I wasn't really here in body, but now I wasn't as sure.

"What do you see?" Lilith demanded over the screeching sounds of the birds.

The words left my mouth before I had time to sensor them. "Hell. I see Hell."

The Goddess threw her head back and laughed. It was a stunningly scary picture. The fiery landscape trembled at her delight. Her gown blew around her slim body as she raised her hands high. Everything, including time, appeared to lean toward her.

"Interesting," she said, then clapped her hands.

We went from one version of Hell to another. We were back in the vast gray nothingness.

While I didn't want to be rude, considering she could end me with a blink of her eyes, I didn't have time for a tour.

"Was there a reason for that, Lilith?" I asked tightly.

She eyed me for a long beat, then smiled. "There's a reason for everything, Angel of Mercy."

I waited for more. She didn't disappoint.

"Gideon is not here," she said. "I would know if he was. Would you like to be more forthcoming as to why you came to the darkness to find him?"

Honesty could either piss her off or set me free... or both. I wasn't a hundred percent sure Gideon and Gabe had actually kidnapped Zadkiel. Candy Vargo had lost her shit when she found out about the possible crime. I certainly didn't want to witness Lilith's reaction to the possible end of everything. "No. I would not."

The Goddess raised a perfectly plucked brow. "As you wish."

She turned and began to fade away. It felt wrong. Tory had pointed out that very little happened in our world without a reason. There was a reason we'd found Lilith.

"Help me," I said before she completely faded away.

Her eyes narrowed to slits. Even furious, she was gorgeous. "What price are you willing to pay, Angel of Mercy?"

"Whatever price I have to," I shot back evenly.

I didn't turn my head when Dirk squeaked and gasped. I didn't move a muscle when Tory swore viciously under her breath. I kind of wanted to curl into a ball and rock for an hour, but that wasn't a badass move. I had lady-balls, and I was going to honor them.

Lilith's smile was feral. I regretted my rash offer, but it was too late to take it back. I prayed that the price wouldn't break me.

"Illusion," she said. "Illusions are often hidden in plain sight—right under one's nose."

"Like this place?" I asked, referring to the gray nothingness surrounding us.

She shrugged. "If you give, you get, Daisy. There is only so much I can reveal when I'm in the dark."

She was fishing. Sadly, so was I, but I wasn't stupid enough to trust her completely. Gideon only trusted her to a point. While my gut told me not to lay everything out, I was willing to part with some information.

"With the collection of knowledge, treading cautiously is the best plan of action. The collection is deeply personal. Do not wake the monster."

Lilith's body tensed and sprays of blood-red crystals exploded around her. Her expression was pinched and she hissed. "Where did that information come from?"

"The Keeper of Fate," I replied, feeling ill. "Do you know what it means?"

Her lips compressed to a thin line. After what felt like an eternity, she spoke. "That's not the way it works, Angel of Mercy. You know that as well as I do. However, listen closely to the words. They might be as much of an illusion as the answers you seek. While I do not feel that Gideon is in mortal danger... yet... I'd suggest you listen carefully to the warning of the Keeper of Fate."

"Thank you," I said, not much wiser than when I'd arrived. However, the fact that she thought Gideon wasn't in danger yet was comforting. "What is the price?"

She smiled. It didn't reach her beautiful and unusual eyes. "To be determined. I shall collect when the time is right. And remember, chasing your tail will result in dizziness. Oftentimes, you're in a stronger position when evil decides to show its hand. The strength in stillness cannot be denied. The dead don't talk."

"The dead do talk," I corrected her.

Lilith eyed me for a bit. "Yes, but they're dead."

I wasn't sure what her point was, but asking was an exercise in futility.

I knew I was barking up a tree with no branches, but I needed more. My gut said to tell her the truth. To get real information, even if it was cryptic and I had to decipher it later, I had to give something. Prices had to be paid. If I lived to regret what I was about to share, I'd never follow my instincts again. "Gideon and the Archangel Gabriel kidnapped Zadkiel from Purgatory after the decision had been made to send him there to live out his afterlife."

Lilith's brows shot up a second time, but this time she laughed. Hard. "Bullshit. Utter bullshit. The Grim Reaper is many things, but my brother is not stupid. The higher power would not be pleased with such an aggressive dismissal of balance. I refuse to believe that tall tale."

I was starting to like her a whole lot better. But if she was right, I had no freaking clue what was going on. If they hadn't taken Zadkiel, who had? And where were they?

"I saw it," Tory snapped. "I saw them take Zadkiel with my own eyes."

"Did you?" Lilith inquired. "Are you quite sure it wasn't an illusion?"

My stomach began to roil. If it was an illusion like Lilith implied, did that mean that Zadkiel had fooled both Gideon and Gabe somehow? Had he won in the end after all? Could the ghost of the most vile man in existence have set up the end?

"Shit." My chin dropped to my chest.

"Bad words will not solve problems," Lilith said.

"Correct," I agreed. "But they feel nice."

She chuckled. "You," she said, pointing a manicured finger at Tory. "Anger is only healthy when it's productive. The barrier between the worlds may be thin, but not all that lies behind it is savage."

Tory just stared at the Goddess. She didn't flinch or comment.

Lilith was impressed. She approached Tory and touched a strand of her silver hair.

"Use the pain for a purpose," she said, cupping Tory's cheek in her hand. "Otherwise, it will end you."

Tory nodded jerkily.

"Pale Rider," she said, turning to Dirk. "I expect to watch you and your lovely cohorts next season on RuPaul's Drag Race."

"From your lips, girlfriend," Dirk said with a giggle.

"And finally," Lilith said, staring at me. "You are a force like no other. Separate the heart from the head or one of them will break. The words are important. Collect them and when the monster arrives... which it will... be ready to beat it at its game. Come not between the monster and its wrath."

I tilted my head at the Goddess and raised a brow. "I believe you just misquoted King Lear."

"Did I?" she inquired. "By all means, correct me, Angel of Mercy."

"The line from the play is, 'Do not come between the dragon and his wrath.'"

She winked at me. "I'm old. Sue me. I've given you many pieces of the puzzle. Don't waste the collection of words."

In a blast of red mist, the Goddess Lilith disappeared.

"Well, that was something, darlings!" Dirk said.

"Understatement," I replied, committing all that was said to memory. I'd be writing it all down when I got home. It was clear a whole lot more information had been imparted than I'd realized. "Did you follow any of that?"

Dirk fanned himself. "Basically, she doesn't believe that Gideon and Gabe took the bastard, and now we have to wait for the monster to show its hand."

I looked at Tory. She closed her eyes for a moment. "Same. But there are hidden messages in all that she said."

"Do you think she knows where they are?" I asked.

Tory shook her head. "I don't, but I wouldn't put money on it."

I nodded and sighed. The rules were muddy. The game was deadly. I couldn't catch a damn break if it bit me in the ass. My worry was for Gideon and Gabe. Although, if there were two people who could take care of themselves, they were those people.

I hoped. I hoped with everything I had.

"Ready to go back?" I asked, extending my hands to Dirk and Tory.

"Do we click the heels of our ruby slippers three times and say, 'There's no place like home?'"

I smiled at the silly queen. "Sure. On three. One. Two. Three."

There was no place like home, and I couldn't wait to get back. Gideon might not be there, but I would find him. It wasn't home without him.

CHAPTER EIGHT

I OPENED MY EYES, THEN SHUT THEM IMMEDIATELY. THE CHAOS was too much. My thinking was if I couldn't see them, they couldn't see me.

The method didn't work when I was a kid, and it wasn't working now.

Heather sat down beside me on the couch. I knew it was her from the clean citrusy scent of her perfume. My sister was one of my rocks. I knew she would tell me the truth.

"How long was I out?" I asked with my eyes still screwed shut.

"Twenty-four hours," she said.

"Alana Catherine?"

"Is fine and safe," she assured me. "You pumped enough breast milk for a month. She's napping. June, Missy, Jennifer and Amelia are with her."

"Correct me if I'm wrong, but are there about fifty dead people squeezing their weenuses in my living room?"

"More like seventy-five," Heather reported. "A little hard to tell since they kind of float in and out of each other, but best guess is in the seventies."

"I see. And how did they learn about the magic of the weenus?" I inquired.

"Wally, Carl and Fred," she confirmed.

I was pretty sure she was trying not to laugh. It was an odd sight to see a bunch of ghosts in different states of decomposition going to town on their elbow skin.

"Sugar Pants," Wally squealed, sitting down beside me. "The specters were quite panicky upon arrival. We thought it prudent to give them something constructive to do to calm down. I think it's positively darling to see the deceased pinch their weenuses!"

Weird was the word I'd use. I still didn't open my eyes. If I could see it, I had to deal with it. I just needed a few more minutes of forced oblivion.

"How many detached body parts?" I asked.

"Ummm…" Heather said.

"You know what? Don't answer that," I said, opening my eyes and taking in the scene.

As happy as I was that the dead had come back to me, I didn't have time to deal with them right now.

"Well, slap my butt and call me Bertha!" Gram shouted with a wide grin as she zipped over and hovered in front of me. "It's a passed-on party here, Daisy girl!"

"I can see that," I said with a wince as an arm fell off of an older gentleman doing the Hustle by the chandelier. "Not sure I have enough superglue for this shindig."

"Not to worry," Carl said, showing one of the dead the correct way to pinch a weenus. "Fred went to the store and procured a few cases."

"With what?" I asked.

Carl looked perplexed. "With his hands."

"Right," I said, blowing out a long and loud breath. "Did he happen to use money?"

"Why would he do that?" Carl inquired.

"Oh dear," Fred lamented, tossing his long wig-locks over his shoulder in distress. "I wondered why people were lined up at the counter at the front of the store. I'd be delighted to go back and pay. Although, I shall need to borrow money."

"Never mind," I said. The queens were grounded until further notice. They were lovely people but a menace to society.

Tory sat open-mouthed on the couch and watched the melee. She and Dirk appeared to be fine after the mind dive. It was fifty-fifty on that. When I'd first dived, I'd slept for days afterward. Since Tory and Dirk were older than time, they were clearly heartier than me. That was terrific. I needed them. Tory's expression at the ghostly antics was one of shock. Dirk was loving it. Even I had to admit it was a lot. I wanted to have a powwow with the people who still breathed ASAP. There was a heck of a lot of info to be deciphered.

But first things first. I was a good host. It was in my DNA.

"Okay, dead friends," I said in my outdoor voice. "Welcome. I'm Daisy the Death Counselor, and I'm delighted that you're here. However, I need an hour or two to do some business. If you'd be so kind as to pick up your body parts and keep them with you, I'll put you back together shortly."

The things I said nowadays were beyond absurd. Last year, I would have committed myself to a looney bin if seventy-five ghosts were pinching their weenuses in my living room. Today, I rolled with it.

"What if we're not sure which ones belong to us, Puddin'?"

a tiny ghostly gal asked with a naughty grin. She held a male leg with the rear end attached that clearly wasn't hers.

Her smile made *me* smile.

My guess was that she'd died recently since she was in good shape and spoke clearly. She looked to be around sixty and had a dyed-blonde hairdo straight out of the eighties—teased high and her bangs defied gravity. She wore sweatpants, Uggs and an oversized t-shirt. Since I was a comfort dresser, I dug her choice. I liked her immediately.

"I'm going out on a limb—no pun intended... well, kind of —and saying that's definitely not your leg or butt."

She threw her head back and laughed. Not a single hair on her head moved. "You got that right, Puddin'! But it sure is a nice rear end."

She wasn't wrong, but it wasn't hers. "Who's missing a leg and a butt?" I called out.

"Meeeeeah," a fifty-ish-year-old man said, floating over.

He was correct. He was also missing both of his arms. I wasn't sure if they'd dropped off during the impromptu dance party or if he'd died missing his appendages.

"Mmkay," I said, not wanting to embarrass him. "Maybe... umm... what's your name?" I asked the happy gal holding the gentleman's ass and leg.

"Agnes Bubbala!" she said. "At your service."

"Shut the fuck up," Candy Vargo bellowed, shoving her way through the dead. "*The* Agnes Bubbala?"

I had no clue who Agnes Bubbala was but, apparently, Candy did and was impressed.

"The one and only," Agnes told Candy.

"Shit," Candy yelled. "Did you finish *Call Me Daddy Dragon* before you bit it?"

Agnes sighed dramatically. "Sadly, no. I had a pesky heart

attack right in the middle of the epic tome. Strange since I had a doctor's appointment last week and was told I had the heart of a forty-year-old. However, if I had to go, it's nice I was doing something I loved."

That didn't sound right to me. "How do you know it was a heart attack?"

"I heard my handyman talking on the phone after I died. He was crying like a baby," she explained, shaking her head sadly. "He was such a dear little man. Made me breakfast every morning before he fixed stuff around the house! Toast and Tang."

"Tang?" I asked. I wasn't sure if that was food or a euphemism for nookie. Maybe Agnes and her handyman were a *thing*.

"Tang like the astronauts drank. If it's good enough for NASA, it's good enough for me," she said with a laugh. "Also, the Tang hid the taste of my potassium supplement. Sitting all the time for work gave me leg cramps. My handyman was so sad. Broke my heart… no pun intended."

"So… umm… your handyman was with you when you died?" I pressed, still unable to get rid of the feeling she might have been murdered.

"Oh yes, we ate breakfast together every morning," Agnes said with a smile. "Writing is a rather solitary sport. I used to break things around the house just to give him something to do."

"Was he in your will?" Heather asked, following my train of thought.

"Oh no, no, no," Agnes said. "All my money is going to char-ity. I never married or had children, and my parents passed a long time ago. My books were my babies."

Heather and I exchanged glances. I didn't want to accuse

the handyman of murder, but I couldn't shake the thought. Agnes Bubbala might not realize it yet, but her unfinished business might be solving her death.

"Agnes, do you know when you died?" I asked. Normally, I let the dead come to me when they were ready, but my curiosity was piqued.

"What day is it today?" she asked.

"The sixteenth," I replied.

"Yesterday," she confirmed.

I wondered briefly if the handyman had called an ambulance or if her body was still behind her desk. The thought of her alone with her Tang and toast kind of haunted me. My job wasn't to deal with the cadavers of my guests. It was to help them in their ghost form solve their unfinished business so they could move on. If Agnes wasn't concerned about her heart attack, then I shouldn't be either.

"I can't believe you're fuckin' DEAD!" Candy Vargo screamed and proceeded to have a tantrum that would have horrified a two-year-old. It was violent and profane. I was now down a coffee table and a couch. If she kept going, I'd be down a house.

"Okay," I said, not sure what to do here. I was tempted to electrocute Candy, but didn't want to scare my new guests. "That's enough."

"You don't understand," Candy hissed. "It was the last fucking book in the series. Number thirty-three. I have it preordered—e-book, paperback, hardcover and audio. I was gonna go stand in line at a bookstore in New Jersey, of all places that give me gas, and get it fuckin' signed. I'm PISSED! Now I'll never know if Delboth, The Strong Minded banged Pethyntae, Lady of the Skies."

"They banged," Agnes promised Candy Vargo.

Candy paused her tantrum and eyed Agnes Bubbala. "What about Qylzrog, The Skinny One? Did he get the job at the IT firm? And what about Pyvnin, The Scary? Did she tell Ardun, The Dragonlord to fuck off and that she wasn't losing weight for any dumbass motherfucker no matter how fine his pecs are? If I was writin' the dang book, I would have castrated Ardun and fed him his pecker."

"Wow, Cupcake," Agnes said with a giggle. "You seem to be very invested in my characters."

"Fuckin' A I am," Candy groused. "I can't believe you had the audacity to die. Now I'll never know if Grurda, The Tall dealt with his erectile dysfunction. It chaps my ass that Bayrliessys, The Great got away with cheating on her fuckin' taxes. Not to mention she blew Daydho, Protector of the Sky, when he was mated to Bioterth, The Adorable. And now... now I will never know how it all fuckin' ends. My life sucks ASS!"

"Holy shit," Heather said under her breath.

I agreed, but knew what it felt like to be into a book series. Candy Vargo was beginning to glow dangerously. That wasn't good. If she incinerated my house, I was going to kick her ass. My baby was upstairs.

I was tempted to ask Agnes Bubbala what the heck she wrote, but didn't. Setting Candy Vargo off again wasn't smart.

Gram swooped in and saved the day. She got right up in Candy's face and told her how it was. "Little missy, you need to pull your dang panties out of your bunghole. You're makin' my hiney itch and you're asking for a whoopin'! Your behavior ain't becommin' for a lady and if you don't stop all that cryin', I'm gonna give you something to cry about. You hear me, girlie? You best start sayin' you're sorry right now!"

Candy's mouth dropped open. No words came out. She blushed a deep red and her chin dropped to her chest. Candy

Vargo was violent, profane and rude. However, with all those crappy traits, she also loved hard. She adored Gram. Gram had become a de facto mom to the Keeper of Fate. Disappointing Gram was awful for Candy.

"I'm sorry," she whispered.

"You ain't gotta apologize to me," Gram said, smacking Candy in the noggin.

Her ghostly hand went right through Candy's head, but it was the thought that counted.

Candy was confused. "Who the fuck do I have to apologize to?"

"Agnes Bubbala," Gram snapped. "If you love the woman's books, you need to stop goin' round your ass to get to your elbow."

As if on cue, every ghost in the crowded living room began pinching their weenuses. The mention of an elbow was just too tempting. Hell, I was tempted.

"I'm sorry, Agnes Bubbala," Candy mumbled.

"It's fine. No worries at all!" Agnes told her. "I'm used to it. When I wrote Oavirth, The Clean as a hoarder, I got heck from my readers."

"But darling," Dirk said, confused. "I thought all dragons were hoarders."

Agnes Bubbala clasped her hands and giggled. "There's a big difference in having a hoard and being a hoarder, Pumpkin! A dragon's hoard represents the vanity of human wishes as well as the uncertain shifts in time. The treasure-trove holds wealth and power, but it is of no use to the greater good of mankind or dragon-kind because it's hidden away for the enjoyment of one."

"But of course," Dirk agreed.

"What about Ummyraer, The Puny?" Candy demanded.

"What about him?" Agnes asked.

"Did he get betrothed to Rordis, The Bunny Killer?"

Agnes, shook her head. "I don't know, Cupcake. I didn't get that far."

"FUCKING UNFAIR!" Candy bellowed then pulled her shit back together when Gram threatened to wash her mouth out with soap.

Granted, Gram couldn't actually dole out the punishment due to being a ghost, but Candy Vargo—as powerful as she was, feared the wrath of Gram. Too many times to count, Candy had washed her own mouth out with soap under the watchful eye of the woman she considered a mom.

"What's your name?" Agnes asked the ranting lunatic.

Candy looked wildly guilty and refused to answer. Then she lied. "Cindy umm… Bindy," she mumbled.

"I'm sorry, what?" I asked with a laugh. "That's not your name, Candy Vargo."

Candy was so busted.

"Oh my!" Agnes said, horrified. "I know who you are."

"Well now, that don't sound good," Gram said, giving *Cindy Bindy* the stink eye.

"You're the nutjob who wrote me letters… weekly… for the last twenty years," Agnes said with a wince. "Your imagination is quite… umm…"

"Warped?" Heather chimed in.

"One way to put it," Agnes said with a somewhat terrified chuckle. "The sheer amount of castration suggested was rather unappetizing. And the insistence on the ingesting of foes was quite stomach churning. However, Candy Vargo… I did model a character after you."

Candy was ecstatic. The batshit crazy Immortal looked like she was going to cry. "You did? Which one?"

"Sisses, Eater of All," Agnes confirmed.

"Fitting," Tim said.

Happy tears fell from Candy Vargo's eyes and she offered Agnes a box of toothpicks. Agnes passed.

Candy Vargo wiped her nose on the sleeve of her shirt and got down on one knee before Agnes Bubbala. "I'm fuckin' honored. The way Sisses, Eater of All died horrifically violent deaths in every single book then came back from the dead to only be killed again is humbling. To think that you intentionally offed me in every story is my wildest dream come true."

"You're quite welcome, Cupcake," Agnes told her. "Trust me, after reading the letters you sent, it was very satisfying to murder you repeatedly."

"Threatening letters via the mail is a federal offense," Tim pointed out.

"Your face is a federal offense," Candy shot back.

Tim raised a brow and grinned. "Weak."

Candy Vargo shrugged and flipped her buddy off.

While all of this was interesting in a strange way, it wasn't helpful. We needed to get back to business.

"What's your name?" I asked the gentleman missing his leg, ass and arms.

"Eeeeeerrick," he said with a sweet smile.

"It's nice to meet you Erick," I told him. "Agnes, could you hand me Erick's leg and butt, please. I'll put it in a safe place until I can glue it back on."

"Absolutely, Puddin'!" she said, handing them over. "Erick, you have lovely appendages!"

"Thaauanuak yooouah," he said. "Yoooouah tooooah, Agganussssah."

I was pretty sure he winked at her, but since he was in an

<figure>92</figure>

advanced state of decomposition, I couldn't be positive. It was either a wink or an odd tic.

"Well, aren't you just the charmer," Agnes cooed and added a shimmy for good measure.

This was going south quickly. I wasn't running a dead dating service.

"Alrighty then, if all the ghosts could go with Gram for a bit, it would be greatly appreciated," I announced.

"Hot diggity dawg," Gram shouted. "Do you people like *The Price is Right?*"

The cheers were loud and garbled. The sound was actually scary, but I'd gotten used to the cadence of the dead. The queens and Tory were a tad alarmed, but no one else batted an eye. The answer was obviously yes. Gram was a very happy camper.

"We can all take bets on the big showcase," she informed the deceased crew. "Whoever gets the closest to the right price gets their body parts glued on first!"

Again, with the eerie cheers. In a gust of chilly wind, the dead followed Gram to the kitchen, chattering with excitement. The TV was on 24/7 to the game show channel. In my experience, the ghosts hated the news and loved sitcoms, soaps and game shows.

I glanced around the room. My brow wrinkled in confusion. I saw Charlie, Tory, Tim, Candy Vargo, Heather and the four queens. We were missing a few.

"Where are Prue, Rafe and Abby?" I asked.

Charlie sighed. "They're searching for Gabe. There was no stopping them."

I closed my eyes and groaned. That was not good. After meeting with Lilith, I was ninety-nine percent sure Gideon and Gabe had not kidnapped Zadkiel. I had no clue what had gone down or what Tory had actually seen. Now, my siblings had put themselves in danger. Of what? I didn't know.

"No one else goes rogue," I said in a tight voice as my fingers began to spark. "Until we understand what's happening, we stay together as one."

"Agreed," Heather said. "What happened in the darkness?"

"Ohhhh," Dirk said, fluttering his hands in the air. "We met up with Lilith in a bar! Shocking and thrilling, darlings!"

Charlie's eyes turned icy blue and began to spit sparks. "Unheard of. Debrief us now, please."

I did. In the process, I lost a beautiful area rug, three lamps and my favorite overstuffed armchair. Candy Vargo was on a destructive tear.

"We're in trouble," Heather finally said after I'd electrocuted Candy for her out-of-control behavior.

"Would you like to be more specific?" I asked, pressing the bridge of my nose.

"I'd love to," Heather admitted. "But I can't."

I rolled my eyes. Yep, I loved my sister, but the cryptic shit was going to make me start blowing up my belongings. "You mean you won't."

Heather shook her head. "No. I can't because I don't know."

This was turning out to be a day with more questions than answers. It wasn't working for me. Anything is possible if I believed.

I still had no clue what to believe.

CHAPTER NINE

After a thirty-minute break, during which Candy repaired all she'd destroyed and I'd nursed and cuddled with Alana Catherine, we'd convened back in the living room.

Tim had been busy in the kitchen whipping up a stinky concoction consisting of cheese puffs, chili, hotdogs, catsup, croutons and spam. I was gobsmacked that I'd had those ingredients in my house. Tim quickly let me know that he'd brought them over to share. Agnes Bubbala had instructed him. While the dish looked somewhat more appetizing than usual, the stench was not good. I was thrilled to be a vegetarian.

The queens, on the other hand, gushed over the vomitous-looking dish much to Tim's pure joy. Candy had congratulated him on another culinary masterpiece. That didn't surprise me. I was pretty sure she would eat garbage.

Candy Vargo had also been busy. After she'd cleaned up the living room, she'd whipped herself up a matching outfit with Agnes. Even Candy's hair matched her idol's. On a normal day, the Keeper of Fate was a hot mess. Today, she was a hot mess with 1980s flair. I noticed Heather snapping blackmail pics. I'd need a few of those.

My panic started to rise again. Squeezing my weenus didn't help. Taking a deep breath didn't calm me. Basically, Lilith had said that there was strength in stillness and that I'd be in a stronger position when the evil decided to show its hand. Did that mean I waited until the monster came to me?

Waiting wasn't my forte. Not to mention, I didn't know who the monster was...

She'd also said the dead didn't talk and she'd misquoted Shakespeare. The Goddess wasn't correct about everything. How did I trust anything she'd said?

Lilith had given me pieces to a large and confusing puzzle.

"I'd like to make an announcement," Candy Vargo said, practically sitting on top of poor Agnes Bubbala.

We all stared at her and waited. Candy's crap was a welcome distraction.

"I'm gonna ghostwrite *Call Me Daddy Dragon!* No fucking pun intended, motherfuckers. I'm gonna castrate and dismember all of the bastards who I don't like. AND Sisses, Eater of All, is gonna get a boyfriend named Frisyrryg, The Loud. He'll have the honor of violently murdering her in the final installment."

Agnes looked like she'd swallowed a lemon—a large one. She'd very obviously not agreed to the plan.

"Nope. Not happening," I said immediately. "If you're going to ghostwrite—pun totally intended—you're simply going to write down what Agnes tells you to. Period."

Agnes mouthed the words "thank you" while Candy pouted.

The idiot crossed her arms over her chest and glared at me. "I don't see how that's fair."

"Fair doesn't come into the equation," I said in a brook-no-bullshit tone. "How are you going to make that happen? Agnes is dead. Sorry, Agnes." I gave her an apologetic smile.

"No worries, Puddin'," she said. "The truth is the truth."

"Got it all figured out," Candy replied. "I'm goin' up to Agnes' house and gonna steal her laptop. My hero can then dictate the rest of the story and I'll type it."

"You can type?" Tim asked, dishing up plates for those brave enough to eat his creation.

"Well, shit." Candy smacked herself in the forehead. "No, I can't type. You're gonna type it, mail boy."

I scrunched my nose. "Agnes, are you okay with this?"

The adorable ghost giggled. "Not seeing I have much of a choice," she admitted. "But it might be fun to finish it off."

"How will you get it published?" Charlie asked.

He'd been quiet since I'd told the story of the mind dive. I knew his brain was racing. His eyes were glittering. It was kind of scary and I was glad Charlie was on my team. June sat close to her husband and held his hand.

Amelia had insisted on watching over Alana Catherine while she slept. I knew Amelia was worried about Rafe. I was too. I couldn't believe Rafe, Abby and Prue had gone out on their own to search.

"I'll just beat the shit out of the publisher if they give me any crap," Candy told him, sticking a toothpick into her mouth while she ate from the plate Tim had served her.

If I watched her eat, I'd puke. "Again, I'm going to veto that plan. If you finish the book, we'll deal with what comes next."

I had no idea how to get a deceased author's work published, but I'd figure it out if I had to.

"I'd like to make a suggestion," Heather said, declining the plate Tim offered her as politely as she could without hurting his feelings.

I was impressed she didn't gag.

"Spit it out," Candy said with a mouthful of ick.

"I hate to say it, but I think we should send Alana Catherine away again," Heather stated.

"I second that suggestion," Tory said flatly.

She'd seated herself away from everyone and just watched until now. The grayness around her was pronounced and it was clear she didn't want to be here.

Too bad. So sad. Until we knew what was happening, my gut told me I needed her.

My stomach tightened and my eyes filled at the thought of sending my baby away from me again. But Heather and Tory were correct. If we were unable to tell what was real and what was illusion, it wasn't safe to have my baby in the mix.

"Where?" I asked.

"Back to where she was—Gideon's place," Heather said.

Gideon had safe houses all around the world. Alana Catherine would be protected there. I was glad she was a baby and wouldn't remember any of this. As much as it pained me to send her away again, losing her wasn't on the table. If she was going, she needed to eat. I might not be able to protect her from illusions, but I could most definitely make sure she had food. I stood up and grabbed my breast pump. "Will this bother anyone?" I asked before I pulled my boob out.

"Of course not, dear," June said with a smile. "A woman's body is a glorious thing. You go right ahead."

Charlie nodded and gave me a kind smile. "It's as beautifully natural as it gets."

"June and Charlie are right," Jennifer said, toasting me with a glass of wine. "Ain't nothing wrong with exposing a boob and making some eats for our baby girl. If it'll make you feel better, we can all free-boob it together."

"Not necessary," I said with a laugh.

Jennifer had free-boobed it not too long ago since she was so proud of her breast augmentation. I had to admit, they did look fantastic. Missy, Amelia, Heather, Tory and June were also against free-boobing it. Candy didn't care and went to remove her shirt until Gram gave her a look.

"You keep your bosom undercover, girlie," Gram warned her. "If you flash your privates for no reason, you'd better give your heart to Jesus, cause your butt is mine!"

"Yes, ma'am," Candy said contritely.

Gram gave her a nod of approval that made her preen with delight. It still made me giggle that Gram could control one of the most powerful and destructive Immortals alive.

"Absolutely pump the girls, Sugar Pants!" Wally said as the queens all nodded in agreement. "It makes me a squeency bit jealous that my falsies can't feed a babe."

"Right?" Fred said, throwing his hands in the air dramatically. "I'm always amazed at the multipurpose usage of real bosoms!"

"So much more versatile than testicles, darlings!" Dirk added.

"Actually," Tim said, removing his notebook from the pocket of his uniform. "Men, in certain cases, can indeed breastfeed."

"Do tell," Carl said, fascinated.

"Please don't," Heather said at the same time.

Tim went with Carl and ignored Heather.

"A little background first," Tim said. "Since I have humbly and with great joy and anticipation volunteered my sperm to Missy and Heather so we can have a baby, I've researched all the ways I can be involved in a practical way."

"Oh my God," Missy mumbled under her breath, going a bit pale.

I just prayed Tim wasn't carrying around a turkey baster full of his little swimmers in one of his many pockets. I adored my odd and socially challenged friend, but there was only so much of him I wanted to see.

Tim cleared his throat then recited from his notes. "Male mammals of many species have been observed to lactate under strange or pathogenic conditions, such as excessive stress, castration and exposure to phytoestrogens or pituitary tumors."

"Thrilling!" Fred said. "Are you going to give yourself a pituitary tumor or lop off Tim Junior?"

Tim's brow wrinkled in thought. I was terrified.

"Your pecker would grow back," Candy Vargo pointed out.

"This is true," Tim agreed. "Not sure I'd be able to complete the deed, though. Self-mutilation isn't appealing."

"Thank God for small favors," Heather muttered, squeezing Missy's hand.

My BFF Missy's mouth just hung open. I was unsure if they'd accepted Tim's offer of sperm, but it was clear they weren't too keen on him getting castrated to breastfeed.

I truly couldn't believe where the conversation had gone.

"Not to worry," Candy assured her buddy. "I'd be happy to chop your johnson off. I've castrated quite a few over the years. Normally, it was because they were fuckin' assholes and deserved it. I've never ripped a wank off in the name of friendship and lactation." She picked her teeth with a toothpick, then pointed the chewed-up stick of wood at Tim. "I'm always up for somethin' new, jackass."

"Okaaay," I said, holding up my free hand. "No one is castrating anyone. If… and I mean, if Heather, Missy and Tim decide to have a child, they can figure out the logistics."

Charlie looked a little green around the gills. Missy and Heather were horrified. I didn't blame them.

"I'd like to point out that aside from sparkling, you guys are way crazier and more fun than vampires," Jennifer announced.

"I sparkle," Carl said, wildly offended. "My gown has ten thousand crystals on it."

"She's talking about *Twilight*," I offered lamely.

"Is that a brand I don't know about?" Dirk asked, confused.

"No," I said, wondering how in the heck everything went sideways all the time. "It's a book where the vampires sparkle in the sun."

"Fascinating," Wally said, delighted. "I must read that!"

Charlie was over the chitchat. "I do believe we need to discuss the messages from the Goddess Lilith," he said firmly. "I agree that Alana Catherine should be whisked away to safety. Heather and Tory made a solid point. I'd also suggest sending all who can't defend themselves with her."

I squinted at him. "Not following that one. I need people there who can defend her."

"Correct," he said. "I want June, Missy, Jennifer and Amelia safe as well. We don't know what we're up against. Who would you like to go to protect Alana Catherine?"

I inhaled and stopped pumping. With what we already had frozen and what I'd just produced, Alana Catherine would be full for a long time.

Glancing around the room, I tried to decide who we could spare with the impending shitshow. Gideon wouldn't hesitate to send the strongest among us to watch over our daughter. I was going to do the same.

"Charlie, I want you to go after we talk. I'd also like Carl, Wally and Fred to join you. Dirk will stay since he was there when we spoke to Lilith."

"As you wish," Charlie said with a curt nod.

That left me with Heather, Candy Vargo, Tim, Tory and Dirk. It was a badass army, and I was no slouch either.

"Let's go get our baby ready," June said, hopping to her feet. Jennifer and Missy followed her up the stairs.

Fingers crossed that I'd made the right call.

CHAPTER TEN

"Repeat," Charlie said, pacing the room.

I glanced down at the notebook Tim had loaned me to write down what Lilith said. Dirk had checked over my notes and added a few things. Tory didn't say a word. Her uneasiness and lack of participation made me wary.

Was she more involved than I'd thought? Had she lied? I pushed down the fury that rose in my chest. Keep my friends close and my enemies closer. It would be devastating to think she was playing us, but if she was, I wanted her with me.

Ending her wasn't in the plan, but plans changed. Could her hatred of Zadkiel and possibly of Gabe have led her to harm them? She'd be an idiot to have messed with the Grim Reaper, but Tory didn't seem to scare easily.

Half of me wanted to remove her from the room. The other half said to keep her here. The living room was filled with some of the most powerful Immortals in existence. If she had screwed us over, there was no hiding from what would come.

I did as Charlie requested and repeated Lilith's words. Tory had been there. She'd heard the same things I had. This was not new information.

I read from the notes. "She defined the word real—actual existing as a thing or occurring as fact… not imagined or supposed. She spoke of illusions hidden in plain sight and implied that the answers might be right under our noses."

"And she doesn't believe that Gideon and Gabe kidnapped Zadkiel?" Charlie pressed.

"She does not," I confirmed. "She said that he wouldn't aggressively go against the higher power by upsetting the balance."

"I have to say I agree with her on that," Heather said.

My sister's tattoos were in motion on her skin. It was riveting. Everyone was on edge. The queens' horns had popped out and their eyes were pools of black. Candy had a slightly menacing glow and Tim had the same. Charlie was doing his best to tamp back his power, but it was getting harder to breathe. Only Tory seemed nonplussed.

Again, that concerned me. Was she enjoying our confusion?

"More," Charlie demanded.

"Lilith told me to listen to the words of the Keeper of Fate," I added.

"The ass don't lie," Candy Vargo stated, slapping her bottom.

I almost laughed. I didn't. The conversation was far too serious. There was more to tell. "She insisted that I separate the head from the heart. Told me to collect the words and when the monster arrives… which it will… be ready to beat it at its game. Come not between the monster and its wrath."

"I find it interesting that the monster was called an it," Candy commented, more serious than usual. "Not a female or a male."

Charlie excused himself to walk outside for a moment. Five seconds after he exited the house, we heard an explosion. No one batted an eye. Charlie was far more polite than Candy Vargo. He took his frustration outside.

After another few minutes, he came back in looking more relaxed. Immortals were nuts.

"Did anything strike you as odd?" he inquired politely.

"All of it," I admitted. "However, she got two things wrong. She said the dead don't talk. They do. And she also misquoted King Lear. She said, 'come not between the monster and his wrath.'"

"The correct quote is, 'come not between the dragon and his wrath,'" Agnes Bubbala announced. "I use that beautifully written Shakespearian line as the theme for all my dragon romance novels."

I'd forgotten she was in the room with us. Candy hadn't let the poor ghost out of her sight.

I nodded at her. "Correct."

Charlie mulled over the conversation then excused himself once more. The next explosion was bigger and louder. I was tempted to join him, but didn't want to start an explosion competition. I didn't need Candy Vargo having free range to be destructive.

Charlie walked back in as if it was normal to blow craters in my front yard. I suppose it was...

"Lilith makes no mistakes. The errors were on purpose. I'd suggest focusing on those," he said.

Having a place to start was better than nothing. The dead and dragon's wrath... it made no sense at all, but like all the cryptic messages the Immortals liked to throw around, with some thought, they eventually made sense.

Agnes Bubbala floated over and hovered in front of me. "May I ask a question, Puddin'?"

"Sure," I replied.

"All of you here," she said, referring to the gathered group. "Are any of you human?"

"Umm…" I wasn't sure how to answer. She didn't seem freaked out. But then again, she was a deceased author who wrote about fantasy and magic. "No, not the people in this room."

"How wonderful!" she said, clapping her hands with delight. "Could you fill me in a little more on the issues at stake? There seems to be a lot of plot holes."

I stared at her for a long moment. A little zing went through me and I shuddered. She was dead and she talked… she also wrote about mythical dragons. Lilith had purposely brought that up. Maybe I was reaching for straws. Maybe this was supposed to be happening.

Whatever.

I was going to go for it.

It took an hour, but with nothing to lose and possibly something to gain, I made the time.

I explained who everyone was. She was shocked that Candy Vargo was the Keeper of Fate. I didn't blame her. Each person in the room, except for Tory, added information I was lacking. Agnes asked for specific details while we got her up to speed. The woman wasn't alarmed or put off by any of the story. In fact, she seemed to believe every bit of it. When I'd given her a synopsized version of Zadkiel, she put her hands over her heart and declared him the worst villain she'd ever heard of. She was correct. Some other time I'd tell her about Clarissa. She'd been a doozy of a villain but wasn't relevant to the story.

"Wait!" Agnes shouted when I'd finished. "I found an important plot hole, Puddin'!"

She zipped around the room so fast it created a wind.

"Agnes Bubbala is fuckin' brilliant," Candy Vargo yelled. "No plot holes in her books!"

I gently pulled Agnes out of the air when she flew past me. Ghosts didn't normally wear themselves out, but I was taking no risks. Hearing the plot hole was necessary. I felt it in my gut. While this was wildly unconventional, I didn't care.

Too much was at risk.

"Agnes, calm down, please, and talk to me," I said.

She was quivering with excitement. "You said that Gabe found Purgatory because he had shared blood with Tory thousands of years ago. Correct?"

I nodded and began to feel incredibly light-headed. Lilith had said answers were right under our noses… Could it be this easy? And why hadn't I thought of it? More importantly, why hadn't Tory?

"Correct," I said, standing up and striding over to Tory. I placed my hands on her arms. If she tried to transport away, I was going with her. "Find Gabe," I commanded.

She tried to wiggle out of my grip. That wasn't going to happen.

"Find him," I repeated. "If he found you through your blood bond, you can find him."

She glared at me. "I haven't tried to do it for a thousand years."

"Don't care," I replied flatly. "Do it."

"Get your hands off of me," she snapped.

I shook my head. "No can do. I can't risk you leaving."

For a brief moment she looked crushed. She tamped that down fast. Real emotion wasn't her thing. I felt bad, but I was separating the head and the heart like Lilith advised. Trusting Tory was difficult. I wanted to, but something held me back.

"Fine," she said in an icy voice. "But don't say I didn't warn you."

I had no clue what she meant until I did. She lit up like a flame. The air in the room grew frigid and her blue eyes turned as silver as her hair. The searing pain in the palms of both of my hands was intense. The blood pouring from them was shocking.

I didn't let go.

Tory bled from her palms as much if not more than I did. Her eyes rolled back in her head and I realized I was the only thing keeping her body upright. Her body shook like she was having a seizure and inhuman sounds came from her mouth. The silver glow around her was almost blinding. If I hadn't seen Candy Vargo get ass messages, I would have thought Tory was dying in my arms. I knew better. Immortals went through hell to do their magic.

As fast as it had happened, it was over. There wasn't a trace of blood anywhere, and Tory was as right as rain. Paler than usual, but fine.

That had sucked, but she'd warned me.

Tory shook her head in confusion. "It can't be," she whispered, looking around the room with wild eyes.

"What can't be?" I asked, still holding on to her.

"They're here."

My stomach knotted with fury. Sparks began to fly from my fingertips. The room was bathed in bright yellow light indicating my eyes had gone Angel-gold. I released Tory and glanced around.

She was lying.

"Bullshit," I snapped. "Tell me where Gabe is."

"He's here," she hissed. "In this house."

"Move," Charlie commanded. "Now."

Immediately Charlie, Heather, Candy Vargo, Tim and the queens raced out of the living room and began to search the house.

Were they trapped somewhere? None of this made a lick of sense. "Is Gideon with him? Is Zadkiel?"

"I don't know," she said, backing herself up against the wall. "I have no connection with them, only Gabe."

Again, I looked around the room. I even searched under the couch. It was beyond absurd to think they were hiding while we were freaking out. "Are you sure?" I ground out as I continued to tear apart the living room.

"I am," Tory insisted as she began to search. "It makes no sense."

"Ya think?" I said, upending the couch.

"Puddin'?" Agnes Bubbala called out as I ransacked the room.

"Now's not the time," I told her as politely as I could.

She was sweet and I liked her, but if Gideon and Gabe were in the house somewhere, that most likely meant that Zadkiel was as well. My blood pressure was sky-high.

"Can you pinpoint where he is?" I asked through clenched teeth.

"No," she said, sounding slightly hysterical. "It's not exact… but I know he's here."

"Motherfucker," I shouted as I continued to tip furniture over and search.

"Daisy girl," Gram chastised me as she flew like a ball out of a cannon into the destroyed living room. "Ain't no use for f-bombs."

I didn't agree. I wasn't one to often use crappy language, but the f-bomb was about the only word that fit the situation.

"I'm sorry, Gram," I told her as I looked under the rug. My laugh was scary as I came close to losing what little I had left of my shit. "Tory says that Gabe and Gideon are here. In this house."

"Well, I'll be. Dead folks," Gram yelled and then punctuated it with a loud whistle. "We got us a situation! Get your transparent rear-ends in here now!"

The gaggle of ghosts zipped into the room and excitedly hovered around Gram. Half of them held their appendages in their hands. My living room looked like the Haunted Mansion gone really wrong.

"Mission alert," Gram bellowed. "We're lookin' for two fine-lookin' gents. Both blond. Both big guys. One named Gideon, the other named Gabe. I need y'all to find 'em faster than a one-legged man in a butt kickin' competition. Faster than green grass through a goose!"

"Whhhaaaatha doooah weeeeeeee doooah wheeeeeeenah fiiiindah?" a huge specter holding his head asked.

Gram wasn't sure. "Daisy, you want to field that question?"

"Umm... call out to me," I said, thinking that Gram had lost it. "BUT, there's also a ghost—a very bad and evil ghost that might be here too. If you see a dead asshole, steer clear."

I blew a raspberry and pressed my temples. My mind raced and I felt slightly out of control. I had jobs—important jobs. One was taking care of the dead. Putting them in danger wasn't part of the description. "Actually, I don't want any of the dead around Zadkiel if he's here. Gram, new plan. Are you capable of taking the ghosts back to my farmhouse?"

I'd given my old farmhouse to Gabe, Rafe, Prue and Abby when Gideon and I had moved to the new house. They'd be safer there than here if Zadkiel was on the premises. I was still very unconvinced that any of them were in the house, but taking chances was stupid. Carl's words rang in my brain. *Let us not forget that a fact is information without emotion. An opinion is information plus experience. Ignorance is an opinion lacking information. Stupidity is an opinion that does away with fact.*

The facts were iffy, but I wasn't going to ignore that they might be true. Stupidity wasn't on the agenda.

"Can do," Gram said, still using her outdoor voice. "Alrighty, kids! We're gonna go on a field trip. Everyone grab 'em a flyin' buddy. Don't want anyone gettin' lost."

The dead seemed confused, but each found a buddy.

"Now, I know that some of y'all might be thinkin' that old gal don't know whether to check her ass or scratch her watch, but it's all good. There's a nice big TV at the farmhouse and *Jeopardy* comes on in twenty minutes! If we catch a good wind, we'll be there in ten."

At the mention of *Jeopardy*, the ghosts perked up. The obsession with the dead and game shows was real.

"Go, Gram," I insisted.

I had no real clue what I was doing, but dealing with one thing at a time was all I was capable of. In a gust of wind that felt like a mini cyclone, the dead went on their field trip. Tory stood as if she was frozen as I continued to ransack the room. My entire body felt overheated from the fear and anger simmering inside me. It took massive self-control not to blow something up to calm myself.

I stopped and turned to stare at Tory. Her utter lack of doing anything infuriated me to a point I'd never reached before. I'd dealt with horrid and deadly situations, but this was beyond personal. "If I find out you lied to me, I will end you."

"Do it," she hissed. "Nothing would make me happier."

I ran my hands through my hair and realized my sparking finger had set it on fire. Quickly slapping my curls, I put it out. On any other day, I would have laughed. Not today. "What is wrong with you?"

She glared at me. "I don't do this," she said, void of emotion. "I don't know how. I'm broken and heartless, but I do not lie. I follow orders, Angel of Mercy. No more, no less. My job is pain. It's all I understand. For a thousand years, I've watched over the Souls of the Martyrs. I have nothing left to give. If that doesn't work for you, end me. It would be a relief. I will not fight back."

She held her arms in the air in a sign of surrender. There was no expression on her lovely face and her silver eyes turned a dull and dead gray. I felt gut punched. All the air left my lungs.

"Separate the heart and the head or one of them will break," I whispered, repeating Lilith's warning. I closed my eyes, shame almost swallowing me. I was the Angel of Mercy, yet I'd shown Tory no mercy at all. My expectations of her were all wrong. She'd accused me of playing God. In this case, she wasn't wrong.

I wasn't God or some abstract version of an abstract concept. I was a fallible person with only forty years under my belt. My world had tilted upside down, and I was doing the best that I could.

It wasn't good enough.

Walking over to the woman who stood in a pose of surrender, I wrapped my arms around her. Her body stiffened, but she didn't push me away.

"I am so sorry," I said.

"Words are cheap," she replied.

"I agree," I told her. My words to her had been mean. In my

desperation, I'd damaged her more. It made me sick. "Thank you for finding Gabe. I don't understand how he's here, but I believe you. If you want to leave, you're free to go. You've helped, and I thank you for that."

"Fuckers aren't here," Candy Vargo shouted, jogging back into the living room with Alana Catherine in her arms.

"They are," I said, taking my baby from her and holding her close.

"You found 'em?" Candy demanded.

I shook my head. "No."

Candy Vargo squinted at me. "And everyone thinks I'm batshit crazy," she muttered.

"Puddin'?" Agnes said, appearing in front of me.

I almost screamed. It was unexpected since I'd sent the ghosts to safety.

"Agnes," I choked out, doing my best not to yell at her for scaring me. My nerves were frayed, but taking it out on everyone was a shitty plan. "You're not supposed to be here."

"We're going to have to agree to disagree on that one, Puddin'," she said with a smile. "You missed a plot point."

I waited. It was seeming more like Agnes was here to help me than the other way around.

"Illusions," she said. "Reminds me of the book I wrote called *Dragons Do It Drunk*."

"Great book," Candy commented. "Sisses, Eater of All got beheaded with a blender in that epic tome. Bloody as all get out. Bioterth, The Adorable wasn't all that adorable in that one. After she ate the hula dancers, I got phantom cramps." She popped a toothpick into her mouth and kept talking. "Eatin' grass skirts is rough on the digestive system. Last time I ate grass I got the shits for a week. Would have been much more realistic if Bioterth, The Adorable had explosive runs."

If Candy Vargo didn't stop talking, I'd be tempted to behead her with a blender. It was going to take therapy to get the images she'd just planted out of my head. I made a mental note never to read Agnes' books. While she was a lovely gal, her imagination was warped.

"My God," Agnes muttered, fanning herself. "Anyhoo, as I was saying before Candy unhelpfully chimed in…"

"Welcome," Candy told her, missing that she'd just been insulted.

"Yes, thank you, Cupcake," Agnes said with a wince.

"Agnes, can you make your point, please," I requested, hoping this wasn't a waste of time.

"Oh yes! In *Dragons Do It Drunk*, Parveit, Lord of the Red…"

"Total asshole," Candy added.

Agnes ignored her. "Parveit, Lord of The Red had excessive anger management issues and trapped Yrvat, The Warm and Ezires, The Stubborn on a different plane of reality. Yet, they were still in Zakuby-Walulu. He added them to his hoard and tried to abduct the entire thunder."

"A thunder?" I asked. I wasn't up on dragon mythology. I didn't touch Zakuby-Walulu. It was pretty clear that was the town they lived in.

"A thunder is a group of dragons," Agnes explained. "It's not out of the realm of possibility that the monster you seek has done the very same with Gideon and Gabe."

I let that sink in for a moment. Tory said she didn't lie. I believed her. My trust might come back to end me, but my gut was the only thing I could follow right now.

Charlie, Heather, Tim, and the queens had come back to the living room and had heard Agnes' theory.

"So, you're saying you believe they're here but on a parallel plane?" Tim inquired, fascinated.

"Yes," Agnes said, nodding enthusiastically.

Charlie approached Agnes. "And on the other plane, were Yrvat, The Warm and Ezires, The Stubborn aware of what had happened?"

"No!" Agnes said, clasping her hands together and lowering her voice to a whisper as if she was telling an important secret. "It wasn't until Xomru, The Kind was captured and added to the hoard that the truth came to light."

"And you say that Parveit, Lord of The Red was adding dragons instead of jewels and money to his hoard?" Heather asked.

"Absolutely," she assured my sister.

"Why?" Tory asked.

It was the first thing she'd said since I'd told her she was free to go. Apparently, she wasn't taking me up on the offer.

"Power," Agnes explained. "A dragon's hoard is a magical place. The owner of the hoard is all-powerful in the cave where he or she hides their treasures. Others have to bend to the will of the master in a hoard situation. He was stealing their magic."

Tim was writing a mile a minute on his pad. "Are you implying that the monster took Gideon, Gabe and Zadkiel and put them in his hoard to steal their magic?"

"It's a possibility," she said.

"This is positively wonderful, darlings," Dirk announced. "I say we look for cracks in the planes, find them and slay the dragon."

"Is that possible?" Carl inquired.

"Don't know," Dirk admitted. "But I say we have a quick kiki and make a plan!"

I wanted to scream. We were discussing fiction as if it were fact. This was nuts. But, then again, what in my world wasn't?

Shockingly, Agnes' plot was the only thing that made sense in an incredibly strange way.

When in Crazytown, it's best to bend to the crazy.

"How did Xomru, The Kind set them straight?" I asked.

"It was thrilling!" Agnes said as Candy Vargo burped and nodded her agreement. "When Parveit, Lord of The Red abducted Xomru, The Kind, the heinous dragon forgot that Xomru, The Kind could speak telepathically. He was able to let the others know they were trapped on a parallel plane without Parveit, Lord of The Red hearing him."

"And then they killed the motherfuckin' shit out of that slimy bastard Parveit, Lord of The Red," Candy shouted with glee.

She was way into the killing stuff. No surprise there.

"Yep," she went on cackling. "Burned that ugly fucker at the stake and then they ate him! Genius."

I gagged. I wasn't going to be eating a monster. Number one, I was a vegetarian. Number two, cannibalism wasn't in my future. Ever. Quickly reminding myself that *Dragons Do It Drunk* was a work of fiction, I was able to swallow back the bile in my throat.

However, I couldn't push away the plot point that had been made. Gideon and I could speak to each other via our minds. It was an incredibly handy trick. He might not be aware that we were technically in the same place, but I knew we were...

June, Jennifer, Amelia and Missy joined us. They were loaded down with all of the paraphernalia needed for Alana Catherine.

"June, can you hold Alana Catherine?" I asked.

"With pleasure," she assured me, taking the precious sleeping bundle from my arms.

Charlie glanced at me curiously. "What are you going to do?"

"Well," I said, pacing the destroyed room. "If Gideon's here, I might be able to reach him telepathically."

Agnes shrieked with delight. Heather whooped. Tim clapped his hands. The queens strutted around the room like they were walking a runway at New York fashion week, popping their tongues and waving their manicured hands. Candy Vargo tossed me a box of toothpicks.

I caught it and put one in my mouth.

Here went nothing.

CHAPTER ELEVEN

Inhaling deeply and crossing my fingers, I perched on the edge of the overturned couch. I wanted it to work so badly that I was terrified to try. It seemed like a final option. That was ridiculous. Nothing was final—not even death. I should know that. I dealt with the dead.

"Gideon, can you hear me?" I asked.

"Oh my God," he said, sounding frantic. *"Where are you, Daisy?"*

The sound of his voice almost undid me. All of a sudden, I felt stronger.

"I'm at our house," I replied carefully.

He was silent. I wondered if I'd lost the connection.

"Not funny," he finally ground out. *"Where are you?"*

Even a mad Gideon was better than no Gideon. I reminded myself that facts were information without emotion. I needed the facts if I was going to figure out how to free Gideon and Gabe… and as much as I didn't want to, Zadkiel.

"Is Gabe with you?" I asked, ignoring his anger.

"Yes."

"And Zadkiel?"

"Unfortunately, yes," he ground out. *"Tell me where you are. This is killing me."*

My lips compressed to a thin line. Before I explained the situation, which was pretty unbelievable, I needed a few more answers. *"Did you and Gabe take Zadkiel out of Purgatory?"*

"Of course, we did," he answered.

"Why?" I asked, confused. He didn't sound remotely guilty or remorseful. Maybe what Tory had seen was correct, and he hadn't given the higher power and the lack of balance any thought.

"Are you serious?" he asked.

"Beyond," I told him.

I could literally feel the man rolling his eyes. *"Games are beneath you, Daisy."*

"I'm not playing games, Gideon," I assured him as my heart pounded rapidly in my chest. Something was way the hell off, and I was pretty sure a puzzle piece was about to snap into place.

His sigh was loud. *"Fine. If you want to play it that way, I'll play. You came to the field and said you changed your mind about Zadkiel's afterlife. You wanted him in the darkness. Gabe used his blood bond with Tory to find Purgatory, and we went in and took Zadkiel. Somehow, and I don't fucking know how, we ended up at the house instead of in the darkness."*

His frustration was real. I didn't blame him. Mine was through the roof.

"I didn't follow you to the field."

"You did," he contradicted me. *"I was there and so were you. Gabe can confirm it."*

I shook my head. *"It wasn't me."*

Gideon's roar of fury made me shudder. His explosive

swearing was intense. It took him five minutes to gather himself. *"Explain."*

"It was an illusion," I told him. *"I don't quite understand it myself, but I'm in the house right now."*

"You're not."

"I am."

Again, he was silent. I wasn't sure how long our connection would last. We needed to figure out as much as we could in the time we had left. *"Talk to me, Gideon. Please."*

"How did you come to the conclusion that I was here as well?"

"Tory," I told him. *"She used the blood bond to find Gabe. We've searched every corner of the house looking for you. I even went to the darkness through Dirk to find you before I learned you were here."*

"And?" he asked, knowing there was definitely more. The Grim Reaper was no one's fool.

"And I ran into Lilith at a bar."

His furious reaction made the first one seem tame. I slapped my hands over my ears, but it didn't help.

"What do you owe her?" he demanded.

"To be determined."

His growl made it clear that he didn't like my answer. Debts were big in the Immortal world. Owing the Demon Goddess of the Darkness was not the best position to be in. However, I'd do it again for Gideon, and I knew full well he'd do it for me.

"Brief me," he snapped.

Ignoring his tone, I gave him the rundown of what was discussed. He listened quietly then spoke. *"Illusions. Interesting."*

"She kept harping on illusions. Agnes Bubbala thinks that you're on a different plane but we're in the same place."

"Agnes Bubbala?" he asked.

"A ghost," I replied.

"The ghosts are back?"

"About seventy-five of them."

The silence was long. I was taking advice from a dead paranormal romance writer. Telling him that might make him think I'd fallen off the cliff into insanity. I omitted Agnes' former occupation.

"Is Charlie with you?" he asked, all business.

"He is."

"Tell him to research parallel planes and find out if there's an Immortal who's capable of creating this particular hell," he instructed. *"I've never fucking heard of this."*

"Charlie, Gideon wants you to find out all you can about parallel planes and anyone who can create them," I translated.

The Enforcer nodded his head curtly. "It shall be done."

"Charlie's on it," I told Gideon. *"Should I send Alana Catherine back to the safe house where she was? Candy Vargo can transport her. I can send Charlie, Carl, Fred and Wally for protection. June, Jennifer, Missy and Amelia will look after her."*

"No," Gideon said. *"Keep her closer to home. Have them take her to your father's house and have Candy, Charlie, Tim and Heather put a ward around it. After she's safe, no one—not even you—will cross the ward until we understand what the hell is going on. If you weren't in the field with us, it means that someone is able to take on your physical body. If they can fool me, they can fool anyone."*

I wanted to puke. I glanced around the room and wondered if everyone was actually themselves or if the monster was with us. The thought was horrifying.

"We need a code word," I said, feeling shaky. God forbid I find him and find myself there as well. If he couldn't tell the monster wasn't me, we needed a way to recognize each other.

"Agreed. Choose it."

"Toothpick," I said, feeling the smooth cardboard of the box

in my hand. It was absurd and obscure. It was perfect. Candy Vargo for the win.

Gideon chuckled. The sound calmed my soul. *"Toothpick,"* he confirmed.

"Question. Do you think Zadkiel is behind this?" I asked.

I wasn't sure how he could be. If he'd had this power in life, he would have used it. However, no theory was off the table. We were searching in the dark with blindfolds on.

"No," Gideon said. *"He's literally falling apart. He's by the couch in the living room in pieces."*

I stood up immediately and moved. Even if it was a parallel plane, being near Zadkiel was repugnant.

"Can they leave the room they're in?" Tory asked.

It was an excellent question.

"My guess would be no," Agnes chimed in, sounding worried. "Or at least in my books they couldn't."

Her tone left me unsettled. Why I was equating fiction with fact verged on the ridiculous, but Agnes' clues had been the most accurate so far.

"Do you have free roam of the house? Can you leave?"

Gideon sounded confused and angry. *"We've tried. Every door leads back to the living room."*

"They can't leave the living room," I told the group. "If they try, it leads back to the living room."

"The hoard is here!" Agnes announced. "Right here where we are!"

That didn't sound good to me. At all. Why and how in the heck had a monster housed his hoard in my home?

"Gideon," I said, trying to tamp down the hysteria that was bubbling inside me. I didn't know how I was going to save him, but losing him wasn't an option. If I said the words, they had a better chance of coming true. Without goals, nothing could be

accomplished. It sucked that the goals were life or death. *"Just hold tight. We'll find a way to get you out of there."*

There was no answer.

"Gideon?" I tried again.

No answer.

The connection was broken.

"Pardon me," I said through clenched teeth as I briskly walked out the front door into the chilly and overcast afternoon.

It was the house or the yard. I chose the yard.

Donna and Karen accompanied me. My fur babies weren't disturbed when I pulled an enormous oak out of the ground and hurled it over a hundred feet from where it formerly lived. It was incredibly satisfying. The pups ran zoomies and barked with joy. Donna, as a Hell Hound, was in tune with the crazy. She was aware of the ghosts and my moods. Sometimes, I thought of her as a person. Karen was my lovable black lab who didn't have a clue to the strange world of the Immortals. I loved both of them to the moon and back.

I watched as they ran with abandon and was jealous. Running was my go-to when I was stressed out. When I was human, I jogged. As an Immortal, I could run at the speed of light. Right now, I had to settle for throwing trees. It was better than nothing. If someone had told me a year ago that I'd relieve stress by tossing trees, I would have told them they were nuts. Turned out, I was the nutty one.

"Puppers," I called out as they began to dig a hole where I'd uprooted the tree. "I'm going back inside."

They didn't look up. Digging was serious business. It didn't matter. Gideon had installed a doggie door that they used with great frequency. I'd been a little worried that we'd end up with a family of raccoons in the house, but so far so good—just people and dogs… and, apparently, a freaking monster's hoard.

"Shit," I muttered as I walked back to the house. "One thing at a time."

Lilith had said there was strength in stillness and that the monster would come to me. It gave me a sense of solace that Gideon was near me even if we couldn't get to each other.

If the monster was coming, I would be waiting.

And I would be ready.

CHAPTER TWELVE

THE PROTECTION WARDS HAD BEEN SET AROUND MY FATHER'S
house. Luckily, it was in the middle of nowhere. The magic
had been loud, intense and colorful. The thought of being
away from both my child and Gideon gave me physical pain.
But as Tory had bluntly put it, no pain, no gain. Separating the
head and the heart was imperative. My need to have my baby
with me was selfish. Loving someone more than myself meant
that her needs came before mine.

My mother had died for me. I'd do the same for my
daughter in a heartbeat.

In the end, Charlie had not stayed with Alana Catherine. He
needed to be The Enforcer. Gideon had tasked Charlie with
finding the Immortal who was capable of creating parallel
planes. The Enforcer had put no price on what he'd agreed to
do. Charlie never did. None of my Immortal friends put prices
on their favors. The species that seemed keen on exacting
payment were Demons. Gideon was a Demon, but he was very
different from his own kind.

Jennifer, Amelia, June, Missy, Wally, Carl and Fred were

with my little girl inside the mansion where my father had lived. For now, she was safe. They were all safe. That was what mattered.

It had taken all of twenty minutes to make it happen. My daughter was in my arms then she wasn't. A tiny and irrational part of me was worried that Alana Catherine wouldn't know I was her mom and would replace me with June, Missy, Jennifer or Amelia. It was silly since I was the milk machine, but rational thought wasn't in my wheelhouse right now.

Back at home, I glanced around the room. Candy Vargo had repaired all the damage with a wave of her hand. She, Tim and Dirk were playing cards. Candy was teaching the confused Horseman of the Apocalypse how to play poker. She was cheating. It was no wonder Dirk was perplexed. Charlie had vanished in a flash of sparkling blue light with a determined expression. It was kind of terrifying. If Charlie wasn't on my team, that would suck. He was a fearsome badass. I had no clue where he went and I didn't ask. If he'd wanted me to know, he would have told me.

Heather was in the kitchen making a late lunch for everyone. I was thrilled Tim didn't offer to help. It would be inedible and I was hungry.

Tory sat by herself on the bottom step of the stairs and stared into space. Agnes kept trying to engage Tory in conversation, but she ignored the ghost.

I was glad, relieved and surprised she was still here.

"So, what's the fuckin' plan, Stan?" Candy asked.

I assumed I was now Stan. "We wait. Business as usual, but we stick together. Lilith said the monster will come to us. And... if its hoard—so to speak—is here, I would hazard a guess that she's correct."

"And when it shows up?" Candy pressed.

I shrugged. "One step at a time. Main goal is to free Gideon, Gabe and Zadkiel."

"Well, hell," Candy griped. "We're saving that asshole too?"

"Unfortunately, we are," I told her. "Secondary goal… end the monster."

"Eat him?" Candy Vargo asked. "Like in *Dragons Do It Drunk?*"

I sucked my bottom lip into my mouth to keep from gagging. "Umm… no. We will not under any circumstance eat the monster."

"Fine point, well made. Cannibalism is gauche—very old school and wildly unappealing," Tim said with an approving nod of his head. "Also, I'd like to announce that Candy Vargo cheats at cards."

"I thought something was amiss," Dirk said with a giggle.

Candy threw her cards at Tim and flipped him off. "Fuck all you losers."

"No thanks," Tim said with a chuckle. "I'd prefer not to lose my appetite."

"We're goin' there, mail boy?" Candy asked with a wicked grin.

Tim shrugged and grinned back.

Dirk squealed. "I'll keep score, darlings! If we must wait for a monster, we should amuse ourselves in the meantime! Keeps the mind relaxed. Candy Vargo, you shall start and Tim will rebut. On your marks. Get set… GO!"

I shook my head and sighed. Tim and Candy going at each other normally ended in bloodshed. "Ground rules," I said quickly. "No decapitation. No removal of appendages. No biting. No punching. No loss of blood. Period."

"I can work with that," Tim agreed.

"Sucks," Candy grumbled. "But I can see how lack of arms

and legs might not be a good fuckin' way to go since we're waitin' for a jackass to show up. I'll save the violence for the fucker who has it comin'."

"Is she always like this?" Agnes whispered in my ear.

"This is mild," I replied.

Agnes' eyes grew wide. She floated over to Dirk and settled herself next to him for the best seat in the house. I sat down on the couch with my hands ready to electrocute them if they broke the rules. Honestly, this wasn't a bad idea. Nonsense, like weenus-squeezing, would stop my mind from racing to the worst possible scenarios. I'd tried again to reach out to Gideon with no luck. It made me uneasy and scared for his safety. The Grim Reaper was truly one of the most powerful Immortals in the Universe, but even he had never heard of parallel planes.

Waiting was awful. However, going against what Lilith had said was stupid. Awful was easier to handle than stupid.

Candy rubbed her hands together and popped a toothpick into her foul mouth. "I could eat me some alphabet soup and shit out smarter words than whatever you have up that fugly uniform sleeve."

Tim grinned. "Doubtful. But it's truly delightful to see you're not letting your education get in the way of your ignorance."

"Burn, darling," Dirk announced with glee.

"Me or mail boy?" Candy demanded.

"Point goes to Tim," Dirk announced.

"I call bullshit on that." She eyed Tim for a long beat then went for it. "Ain't it dangerous to use your whole fuckin' vocabulary in one sentence?" Candy Vargo countered with a raised middle finger.

Tim returned the favor. "Nice. However, I just love what

you've done with your hair! How do you make it come out of your nostrils like that?"

Candy slapped her thigh and cackled. "Gonna have to remember that one. Point to the mail boy! But I have to ask you to hold still. I'm tryin' to imagine you with a personality."

"Excellent!" Tim said, giving Candy a thumbs up. She took a bow. "I'll never forget the first time we met. But I shall keep trying."

Heather stood in the archway between the kitchen and the living room with a grin on her face and her arms crossed over her chest. Even Tory had the beginnings of a smile tugging at her lips. As silly as the release was, we all needed it. At least they weren't spouting gross facts.

"Got a question for ya, Timmy," Candy Vargo said.

"By all means, ask," he replied, thoroughly enjoying himself.

"If I throw a stick, will you leave?"

"Depends on the size," he shot back with a chuckle. "However, you are impossible to underestimate."

"Rude, darling!" Dirk sang.

"Thank you," Tim said.

Dirk put a check in the Tim column. "Point for Tim!"

Tim raised his hands over his head and pumped his fists in the air. "I'm winning!"

"Not for long," Candy Vargo informed him. "I thought about you earlier… reminded me to take out the trash."

Tim laughed. "Don't worry about me. Worry about your eyebrows."

Candy Vargo was loving it. "Try rollin' your eyes. You might eventually find a brain in that fat head."

"Ohhhhhhh," Dirk said, clicking his tongue and snapping. "Point to the Keeper of Fate."

"BAM!" Candy yelled, jogging a victory lap around an

amused Tim. "You're so annoying that you'd make a Happy Meal cry."

Dirk tsked Candy. "Darling, while that insult was lovely, you went out of turn. Point to Tim."

"Motherfucker," Candy bellowed and pointed her chewed-up toothpick at Dirk and Tim. "Rules are for pussies. Both of you are the human version of period cramps."

"Love it!" Dirk shrieked. "So very repulsive."

"So, I get a point?" Candy asked warily. She began to glow dangerously.

This was about to go south. It was time to end the game.

"Yep," I said, displaying my sparking hands in warning. "Game's over. Let's eat."

"Absolutely," Heather agreed. "Come and get it."

As I hopped up to grab some food, the loud knock on the front door stopped me dead in my tracks. I wasn't expecting anyone...

That was incorrect. I was expecting someone.

The monster.

For a hot sec, it felt like an episode of *The Three Stooges* in my living room. Some of the strongest Immortals in existence ran around the room like chickens with their heads cut off—me included. Everyone eventually got a hold of themselves except for Candy and Tim. It took Heather grabbing them and knocking their heads together to get them to calm down.

"Everyone, conceal yourselves," I directed quietly. "Get where you can see the front door, but don't let whoever it is see you."

"Roger that, jackass," Candy Vargo said as she quickly moved behind the curtains. Agnes joined her. That was good. If there was an Immortal monster at the door, he or she would be able to spot a ghost. I was thrilled I'd sent Gram and my other dead guests away.

Heather crouched down and hid behind the couch. Tim slipped into the foyer coat closet and left the door partially open. Dirk snapped his fingers and went from glorious gowned queen to boring guy in man clothes again. He was a huge person, but concealed himself completely behind the open door that led to the office. Tory walked over and stood next to me.

"I can go invisible and have your back," she said, not making eye contact.

"Badass," Candy Vargo said quietly. "You against cannibalism?"

"Zip it, Candy," I snapped. "We're *not* eating anyone."

"My bad," Candy muttered. "Just sayin', if we run out of options, I'll take one for the team."

"Oh my God." I wasn't touching that. "Tory. Yes, and thank you. Unless I get attacked, stay invisible."

"As you wish," she replied, slashing her arm in a downward motion and disappearing from sight.

"Where are you?" I asked.

I felt her touch my right arm. "Next to you."

The knock came again. My breathing felt labored. If the monster or dragon or whatever it was tried to take me, I had some shit-kicking backup. With a quick pinch to my weenus, I peeked through the peephole.

I went from close to freaking out to Buddha-Zen.

"False alarm," I whispered to the group. "It's Sheriff Dip Doody. Human."

"Are you sure?" Heather asked. "If the monster could pose as you, it could pose as anyone."

Thank God and every other deity imaginable that I had brilliant friends.

"Do you have any outstanding parking tickets?" Tim inquired. "Or any other crimes on your record that you'd like to confess? Knowledge is power. If you need defense, Heather can represent you. If you can't afford her services, I'd be honored to foot the bill."

Heather stifled a laugh from behind the couch.

I rolled my eyes but had to admit the conversation was on the funny side. "No. I do not."

"Good to know, friend," Tim said from the closet.

"You ever eat anyone?" Candy asked, totally serious.

"Good lord," Agnes Bubbala choked out. "I'm going to say, you could do with some therapy, Candy Vargo."

I didn't grace Candy's disgusting query with a verbal answer. I just flipped her off. She chuckled.

"There are two people on the other side of the door," Tory said.

I turned to look at her and, of course, she wasn't there. It was odd talking to air. "Immortal or human?"

"I can't tell until I see them and look for a footprint," she answered. "Open the door."

Inhaling deeply, I prepared myself to act normal. I wasn't exactly sure what the word meant anymore, but I was going to try.

"Sheriff Doody," I said as I opened the door with a smile that I prayed didn't look like a pained wince. "What can I do for you?"

Tory had been incorrect, which was surprising. Only Dip was here for a visit. He stood alone on the porch. His cruiser was parked in the driveway. My dogs raced over and sniffed him with enthusiasm. Dip patted their heads and gave me a warm smile. I used to judge people by the way they treated animals. Now that I was a mom, I'd added children to my judgment mix. Dip Doody passed both of those tests with flying colors, but today there were more criteria on the table.

I covertly glanced down at his feet and detected no magical footprint. That was a relief, but since Gideon had told me about the illusion that looked enough like me to fool him, I was wary of everyone.

Dip was a nice-looking man in his sixties. He'd been the local sheriff for as long as I could recall. As of the last few months, he'd also been Jennifer's new man-friend. He was solid and kind. Jennifer, having been divorced as many times as she had, decided living in sin with her new guy was the way to go. In her opinion, marriage screwed up everything. Dip was all in and worshipped the ground my buddy walked on.

I looked him right in the eye and tried to figure out if Dip was actually Dip. It seemed like it, but Gideon had mistaken the monster for me. I was taking no risks. Asking him a question that only the real Dip could answer was going to be every kind of awkward, but I didn't care. If Dip thought I was overstepping, it was a small price to pay to make sure he was who I thought he was.

"Did Jennifer get the mole removed off her left breast?" I asked, cringing inside with embarrassment. The mole was actually on her right breast. It wasn't cancerous. However, it looked like an extra nipple and pissed her off. I was banking that Dip would correct me. The man was a stickler for detail.

Dip's bushy gray brows shot up, and he turned a deep red. His reaction alone was enough to assure me he was him. But...

"Well, now," he stuttered, rocking back and forth on his feet. "It's umm... well... you know, actually the right one. And umm... yep. My gal had it removed last week."

The poor man looked like he wanted to make a run for it. However, he was spot on about the mole.

"Last Tuesday?" I inquired, knowing full well Tuesday was the wrong day.

"Wednesday," Dip corrected me in a hushed whisper.

I slapped my forehead. "Right. Wednesday. My bad."

There was one other thing that would help make the doubt in my mind disappear. Dip was never going to want to be in my presence again.

"How did the fuzzy blue handcuffs work out?" I asked. "Did they leave a mark?"

One, I knew they didn't. Two, they weren't blue. Three, Jennifer had overshared when she was tipsy last week. I'd tried to block out the images she'd described in great detail, but now I was delighted she'd blabbed.

Sheriff Dip Doody was gobsmacked. He wasn't delighted at all. He was mortified. He'd gotten the boob mole information correct. If he aced the handcuffs, he was definitely Dip.

He opened his mouth to speak, but nothing came out.

"They're blue, right?" I asked, knowing I was going to have to apologize to Jennifer for throwing her under the bus. Hopefully, she wouldn't mind. She'd talked about Dip's penis girth right in front of him when we'd all met for Mexican a few weeks back. He'd been flustered, but was a good sport. He knew what he'd gotten into when he fell hard for the nutty gal.

"Pink," he finally said, still rocking back and forth. "And... umm... no marks."

Dip was Dip.

"Awesome," I said, wishing I could erase what I'd just done. Actually, Tim could wipe the man's mind at a later date. That would be the kindest way to go. Plus, if we didn't erase this chat, I was sure Dip wouldn't ever want to be within twenty feet of me again in this lifetime. "Is there a reason you stopped by?"

Dip scratched his head and appeared confused. I'd knocked him sideways with my obnoxious questions.

He gathered himself quickly and put on his cop face. "I need to ask you a few questions, Daisy."

"Go right ahead," I replied, unsure where the conversation was headed.

"Officer Micky Muggles is no longer with the department," he began.

I forced an expression of surprise. Telling him that I already knew because Jennifer listened to his police radio wasn't going to land well. "Wow. Why?"

"I can't disclose the particulars at this time as it's still an ongoing investigation," he explained. "But his cruiser GPS indicates he was here earlier today. Can you tell me what that was about?"

"Sure," I replied. The heavy feeling that had settled in my chest eased. "He sold me some wrapping paper for the fundraiser at his kid's school."

Dip Doody wrote the information down. "Did he mention anything unusual?"

Gross would have been a more accurate description. "He talked about his girlfriends—multiple girlfriends," I admitted with a sour expression.

Dip shook his head with disgust. "Yep. Not surprising. Did he happen to mention the museum at all?"

Again, I knew where he was going, but couldn't reveal my source. It was rumored that the mullet-sporting dumbass had stolen a very expensive collection of Civil War coins.

"No. We chatted mostly about wrapping paper and his lady friends."

Dip closed his notebook. I thought we were done.

We were not.

A police officer I didn't recognize exited the cruiser. The man wasn't in uniform like Dip, but he had the 'tude. He ambled up to the porch with a superior expression on his handsome face. The man immediately reminded me of those people who relished their power with a vengeance. I didn't like the type. My chest tightened, and I was back in on-guard mode. I shoved my hands into my pockets just in case they started sparking. That would be difficult to explain. Something was way off here.

"Daisy, I'd like you to meet Detective Tar Basilisk. He's from Atlanta. Seems we might have a federal crime on our hands," Dip said, clearly uncomfortable with the big-city detective in his small-town territory.

I was uncomfortable for an entirely different reason. Was I face-to-face with the monster? "Nice to meet you, Tar," I lied, extending my hand.

The rude asshole didn't take it. Dip pressed his lips together in annoyance and shot the man a look. Tar ignored it and focused on me. When Tory squeezed my arm, chills skittered up my spine.

I wanted to glance down to see if the hard-ass left a magical footprint, but his eyes were glued to mine and being obvious wasn't smart. If Tar Basilisk—which I was positive wasn't his real name—was the monster, then I had to stay ready to fight. Having Dip caught in the middle of a shitshow was dangerous, but I didn't create the situation.

"You live here alone, Daisy?" Tar inquired.

I stared at him. I wanted to tell him to shove his question up his entitled ass, but knowing I could end up in handcuffs that weren't pink and fuzzy held me back. "No."

Tar raised a brow. I wasn't sure if he was impressed with my one-word answer or pissed.

"Husband?" he pressed.

Technically, Gideon and I weren't married, but our commitment to each other went far beyond a piece of paper.

"Yes."

"Name?" he asked as Dip grew angrier.

"Is this necessary?" Dip asked his new and unwanted partner in a tight tone.

"Just making sure that Daisy isn't one of Micky Muggles' girlfriends," he replied coldly. "She could be involved in the heist."

I laughed in his face. "I can assure you that I am not and never have been one of Micky Muggles' girlfriends. Mullets aren't my thing."

Again, Tar raised a brow a la The Rock. The idiot probably modeled himself after the wrestler-turned-actor. While I liked The Rock, I didn't like Tar Basilisk one bit.

"Husband's name?"

"Daisy's husband's name is Gideon," Dip said in a clipped tone. I was positive that Dip knew Gideon and I weren't married, but the sheriff had my back. It was obvious that neither of us liked Tar Basilisk. "Daisy just gave birth to their child. If you'd bothered to read the report, you wouldn't need to ask these questions."

Tar shot Dip a look that would have made a lesser man back down. Dip was human, but he was a badass human. I was worried that Tar was *not* human. The thought of Dip coming to harm sat like a lead balloon in my stomach.

"Not to worry," I said quickly. "I understand needing to get all the information. Any other questions or concerns, gentlemen?"

"Not at the moment," Tar said. "Stay in town. Do not leave."

Dip Doody rolled his eyes. I was wildly grateful that Tar missed that.

"I won't leave town."

"Can I see the baby and meet your husband?" Tar inquired smoothly.

"They're napping," I lied. His tone made me uncomfortable. "Some other time."

Tar stared at me. I stared right back. He was the first to avert his gaze. He knew I was lying. I didn't care. I didn't want the man within a mile of Alana Catherine. Gideon was technically missing, and I had a bad feeling he was aware of that fact. I wasn't precisely sure why, but I was going with it.

"If Micky Muggles shows up here, do not engage," Tar said coolly. He handed me a business card. "If you see him, call this number. Immediately."

The smile on the man's face did not reach his eyes. It left me feeling sick to my stomach. The idiot Micky Muggles didn't stand a chance against Tar Basilisk or whatever his name was. My gut told me Micky wouldn't live an hour in the presence of the smug bastard. Micky might be a stupid womanizer who didn't pay child support and may or may not have stolen the coins, but he wasn't a murderous criminal, and he certainly didn't deserve to die for being a jackass.

Hell, even Dip was staring at Tar like he'd lost it.

"Will do," I said, putting my hand on the door. "If there's nothing else, I have things to get back to."

"Thank you for your time, Daisy," Dip said. "Sorry about the intrusion."

"Not at all," I said. "Stay safe, gentlemen."

"You as well," Tar said in a tone that was hard to decipher. It was impossible to tell if he was being polite or handing out a warning. "It's a big bad world out there."

My mouth moved before I had time to think it through. "That's a shitty way to look at life."

His eyes narrowed, and I wanted to take back what I'd said. Lilith's words blasted in my brain. *Come not between a monster and its wrath.* Poking the beast—if he was indeed the beast— was ignorant. Right now, my stupidity level felt on par with Micky Muggles.

"Reality bites," Tar commented before he turned his back on me and walked back to the police car.

Dip Doody shook his head and sighed. "Atlanta cops are assholes," he whispered.

I agreed except I was pretty sure he wasn't a cop at all.

"Look," Dip continued. "Micky's a dumbass, but he's not a killer. Still, if you see him, give me a call. That boy is in a heap of trouble."

"I will," I promised.

I highly doubted I'd be seeing Micky Muggles anytime soon, but if I did, I was calling Dip, not Tar.

"Have a good day, Daisy," Dip said.

"You too, Dip."

I closed the door, pressed my back against it and slid down the smooth wood until my butt hit the floor. "What the hell was that?"

Everyone came out of hiding. No one looked relaxed. Candy glowed and Dirk's horns had popped out. Of course, he was back in his fabulous sequined gown. Tim was subdued and paced the room. Tory materialized next to me and shuddered. Heather walked over and pulled me to my feet.

"Was that the monster?" I asked.

141

Heather shook her head. "I don't know, but he's definitely Immortal."

"Angel? Demon?" I wanted specifics.

Heather shrugged. "I can't pinpoint his species."

Candy Vargo chimed in. "Neither can I, which is fuckin' weird."

"He's possibly a dragon," Agnes said, fluttering her hands in distress.

The fact versus fiction angle was starting to stress me out. That was tough shit. With so little to go on, everyone's input was valuable—even if it came from a ghost who'd titled her book, *Dragons Do It Drunk*.

"Please, tell me why you think that?" I requested.

Agnes zipped around the room frantically. It made me dizzy, but I let her do her thing.

"His name," she said, wringing her hands. "Both of the words tar and basilisk are terms used for dragons."

"Problem one," Candy Vargo shouted with ten toothpicks hanging out of her mouth. "Dragons don't technically exist. I don't think we're looking for a dragon."

I wondered how she'd kept the toothpicks in her mouth while she yelled. However, I was going on her word. She'd been around for a heck of a long time. Plus, both Tim and Dirk nodded in agreement.

"Correct," Tim confirmed. "However, a dragon is a monster, mythically speaking. I think labeling the monster is unimportant. What I do find important, if we're going with the suspicion that Gideon, Gabe and Zadkiel were taken as part of a hoard, then the name the Immortal chose has meaning."

"Would he be so bold as to walk up and out himself?" Heather inquired, running her hands through her sleek pixie cut and making it stand on end. "It's too obvious."

"Unless the fucker enjoys playing games," Candy grunted.

"Interesting points, darlings," Dirk said, putting on bright red lipstick with expertise. "I'm perplexed if the Demon is a friend or foe. It's a possibility that he's looking for the same thing we are. His presence here could have been a warning of sorts. Felt very territorial."

Confusion didn't begin to cover all the emotions running through me. I had half a mind to ward this house the way we'd warded my father's, but that would be stupid. I wasn't doing stupid. If I kept the monster out, there was no way to get Gideon and Gabe back. Of course, once I let the monster in, I still had no clue how to get to them. As powerful as I was, I felt helpless.

"Nothing is impossible," Tim reminded me gently, putting his hand on my shoulder. "You just have to believe."

"In what?" I asked him.

He smiled. "That we will succeed."

"It's that simple?" I asked, desperate for someone to tell me that I would succeed.

"Nothing worthwhile is simple or easy," Tim said. "But it's also not impossible."

That was going to have to be enough for now. If it took believing, I could believe enough for all of us.

And then the weird got weirder.

CHAPTER THIRTEEN

MY SIBLINGS WERE BACK AND LOOKED LIKE THEY'D BEEN IN A
vicious bar fight where they'd lost badly. Prue had gotten the
worst of it. Both of her eyes were swollen and dark purple. She
had oozing lacerations on her face and neck and was limping.
Abby had a split lip, a bruised cheek and what looked like a
broken arm. Rafe's nose was broken. The dried blood all over
his face and clothing made it appear far worse than it was. He
had deep cuts on his knuckles, and he, too, was limping.

Their haunted expressions were concerning.

We sat at the kitchen table. Heather had insisted that
they eat.

No one said a word. Not even Candy Vargo. Dirk tried to
fuss on them, but they were having none of it. Tim had gone
ashen when he saw them. He walked out of the kitchen and
was sitting in the living room by himself. Their coldness and
shitty attitude reminded me of when I'd first met them. They'd
been God-awful, but they'd still been under Zadkiel's control
then.

They were no longer under Zadkiel's control. I'd made sure

of that. They had not had it easy, and it saddened me to see them in the state they were in. The only words spoken had been from Rafe when he asked where Amelia was. The answer satisfied him, and he went back to eating.

They ate fast and barely chewed. It was like they hadn't seen food in a month.

Heather reloaded their plates and sat down. All eyes were on them. They ignored us.

When Abby went to lick her plate, I swiped it out of her hands and gave her a look. "Dude, you are not going to lick a plate. If you want more to eat, fine. But no licking."

"I lick plates," Candy Vargo volunteered.

Abby blanched. Candy wasn't one of my siblings' favorite people. In a mind-numbing situation that had happened hundreds of years before I was born, they'd had an altercation —and that was putting it mildly. They'd attacked Candy on the orders of Zadkiel. Candy Vargo was down both legs and both arms. So, she did what any batshit-crazy Immortal would do in that scenario... she ate them. Honestly, I hoped she was the only Immortal who would have chosen that route. If there were others, I didn't want to know about it. Ever. She also crapped them out. The logistics were so freaking bad, I rarely, if ever, tried to work that one out in my head. Suffice it to say, they had a wary and somewhat friendly truce.

The upside was that if Candy licked plates, there was no way in hell Abby would do the same. One problem solved. A buttload more to go.

"Are you going to tell me where you were?" I asked.

Prue, Rafe and Abby exchanged glances.

Rafe shook his head. "It's safer if we don't."

I didn't like the sound of that and neither did Tory by the

snort of disgust she made. Abby narrowed her eyes at the silver-haired Immortal and hissed. It didn't faze her.

"Okay," I said, respecting their choice not to share. "Was it successful?"

"What do you think?" Tory demanded harshly, pointing at the trio. "If they look like this now with their ability to heal, they looked worse an hour ago—like almost-dead worse." She glared at them. "I didn't think you had it in you."

Tory clearly knew where they'd gone and was unimpressed.

Prue's furious stare was enough to make me want to leave the room. I stayed. We were allies even if no one was behaving like it.

"We have it in us because we understand love, bitch," Prue snapped. "Unlike you."

Tory's mask slipped for a millisecond. Prue didn't notice, but I did. My heart broke for the poor woman who only understood pain.

"Accurate," she said flatly. "How much? What was the price?"

"Immaterial," Rafe shot back.

All of a sudden, the carrot I was munching on tasted like cardboard. What had they done?

"This isn't working for me," I stated. "How about an exchange?"

"Of?" Prue asked.

It was difficult to look at her without wincing in pain. I sucked it back and went on in a pleasant and conversational tone as if it was par for the course to be sitting and chatting with people who were angry and covered in blood.

"Information," I replied. "I tell you what we've learned, and then you tell me where you went and what you've learned."

Again, they exchanged glances. It was worth a shot. I would

have told them everything anyway. If I got what I wanted, win-win.

Rafe nodded at me.

I told them about the trip to the darkness. They were as stymied as we had been about the bar. They paid close attention to Lilith's words. Prue grabbed Abby's hand when I mentioned illusions. I told them about the parallel planes and talking to Gideon. Abby even gave Tory a small smile when she learned that she'd used her blood bond to find Gabe. They growled in unison and began to glow when I'd gone over the exchange with Tar Basilisk.

"I'd like to meet Agnes Bubbala," Abby said.

"After you tell me where you were and what happened," I reminded her.

The three sat tight-lipped and refused to talk.

"We had a deal," I reminded them.

They stayed silent.

"I can tell you where the cagey motherfuckers went," Candy Vargo said, staring daggers at them. "Can't believe you dumbasses are that fuckin' stupid."

"Would you go to the ends of the Earth for someone you love?" Prue demanded.

Candy was silent.

"I didn't think so, Keeper of Fate," she hissed. "You can't even begin to understand what a real bond is."

"Fuck you," Candy snarled. "You have no clue what I can understand and what I can't. I know where you were because I've been there myself. I can smell it on you... and it stinks like death."

I'd had enough of being left out of the conversation. The Immortals were cryptic, but I wasn't. They were going to spell it out or I was going to electrocute the living daylights out of everyone until they did. Gideon, Gabe and even my mortal enemy Zadkiel were at risk. Zadkiel was simply a job that needed to be done. Gideon and Gabe were a huge part of my heart. That being said, we were all at risk if we didn't figure out how to get to them.

There were puzzle pieces scattered all over the place. Everyone seemed to have a different piece. If we didn't work with each other the full picture wouldn't come together.

"Here's the deal," I said. A wind picked up around me as my magic bubbled up to the surface. My hands sparked and my eyes spit gold sparks. I was the Angel of Mercy, but the last thing I felt at the moment was merciful. "I don't have time for this crap. If your bond with Gabe is as strong as you say, you'll talk. If you don't, then you're liars. Your bond is nothing."

Abby stood up to go at me. Prue grabbed her and held her back. She'd be a fool to attack me. It wasn't on my to-do list in this lifetime or any other to end her, but if it was me or her, I was coming out on top. Period.

Abby swore and tried to escape our sister's grip. Prue was clearly smarter and stronger than Abby and didn't let go.

"Enough," Rafe bellowed. "Stop. Daisy is correct. Sit down."

Abby was crying. Prue shoved her into the chair and sat on top of her. Rafe observed them then closed his eyes for a brief moment. They'd come a long way after being freed from the hell that had been their existence for thousands of years, but they still fell back into violence when up against a wall.

My compassion for them was real, but there was only so far I was willing to bend when Gideon was in danger.

"The Oracle," Rafe finally ground out. "We went to the Oracle."

Tory pressed her temples and paled considerably—which was difficult since she was already pale. Dirk put on so much lipstick, his teeth were covered and it looked like he was bleeding profusely from the mouth. I heard Tim groan from the living room. Candy Vargo bit her toothpick in half and used the F-bomb in a sentence so many times, I didn't even know what she'd said. Although, the sentiment was clear.

Only Heather was calm. "That was foolish."

Rafe stared at her for a long beat then shrugged. "No pain, no gain."

He'd repeated the words Tory had said. I was getting really tired of the pain. It sickened me to think about what Tory, Rafe, Prue, Abby and Gabe had gone through at the vicious will of Zadkiel. And now... after the bastard was dead, he was still at the root of our problems. If I could kill the man again, I would. Mercy be damned.

"Okay," I said, sighing and preparing myself to be freaked out. "What or who is the Oracle?"

Tim had come back to the kitchen and sat down next to Candy Vargo. He put his hand on her shoulder and gently squeezed. Candy put her hand over his and held on.

Tim cleared his throat twice before he spoke. "Do you know what a diviner or a soothsayer is, Daisy?"

"A fortune-teller," I replied.

"Of a sort," Tim said, staring with pity at my siblings. "It's not as linear or succinct as that. It's more of an abstract concept—similar to God and Satan or Heaven and Hell."

I waited for more. There was always more.

"One only goes to the Oracle as a very last resort. Often-times it ends up being the last thing a person does."

"Not following," I said.

"They don't survive it," Heather explained. "The price the Oracle demands is high."

I grabbed a carrot stick then put it back on my plate. The

bile had risen in my throat and I wasn't sure I could swallow food. "How do you go to a nonlinear concept?" I asked. I couldn't wrap my mind around the logistics.

"I've never been," Tim admitted. "I can't tell you."

Candy Vargo slammed her fists on the table. "You go to the Oracle when there are no fuckin' options left. The fucker can take any form it wants—male or female. The price to be in the Oracle's presence is flesh." She stared at Rafe, Prue and Abby. "You see what those idiots look like now?"

I nodded.

"Well, a few hours ago, they would have looked like bones and organs. No skin, no fuckin' faces. And that ain't all," she snarled. "That's just the price to get in. For the next hundred years, these dumbasses are gonna owe the bastard. Bein' a bag of bones is mild compared to what will come. Get ready, fuckers."

I gagged and tried not to throw up.

Rafe held her furious gaze. Abby and Prue stared at the table.

"Hindsight is twenty-twenty," Rafe said coldly. "And why would you care, Keeper of Fate? We mean very little to nothing to you."

"Was it worth it?" Candy demanded, ignoring his question.

Rafe ran his hands through his hair. "I don't know."

"Goddammit," Candy shouted. "What the fuck were you thinking? I don't particularly like you, but I wouldn't wish the hell you've brought on yourselves on my worst enemy."

Prue looked up at Candy with an expression that was mixed. I couldn't tell if she admired Candy or if she was grateful for the profane woman's compassion.

"Who did you go to the Oracle for?" Prue asked quietly.

"None of your damned business," Candy snapped.

Prue wouldn't stop. I was curious too, but setting Candy Vargo off was unwise. If she blew up the house, I wasn't sure if it would affect Gideon and Gabe.

"It had to have been someone you loved," Prue pressed as Candy's breathing grew erratic. "Someone you would die for."

Candy stood up and flipped Prue off. "Not sure what part of none of your damned business you didn't understand." She grabbed her box of toothpicks and walked out of the kitchen door after she punched a hole in the wall.

The silence in the kitchen was loud. The reality of the Oracle exacting payment from my siblings for a century was horrifying.

Tim stood up and looked out the window at his friend. "She went for me," he said, still staring out of the window.

"Why?" I asked.

He shook his head and kept his back to me. His eyes were on Candy. "It's ancient history now and too difficult to relive. Suffice it to say, I owe my friend my life many times over."

The statement was loaded. The reality was that it was none of my business. I would not push. Ever. Some stories were best left buried. The more I learned about the Immortals, the more it broke my heart. It was hard to comprehend how long they'd lived.

I used to think it bizarre that Tim was a mailman and Candy Vargo worked at the Piggly Wiggly. But it made sense. The desperate need for normal kept them from losing their minds in the dangerous world we lived in. Charlie's delight with his kids and his grandkids made all kinds of sense. Heather being a public defender and, more often than not, representing people for no charge wasn't a surprise. The fact that they'd gathered in a small, sleepy Southern town wasn't happenstance. It was necessary for their survival.

From the looks of it, I was going to live a very long time. I prayed that my sanity would stay as stable as my friends'. Gideon was my touchstone. I needed him.

I looked Rafe in the eye. I wasn't going to let them play any more cryptic games. "Tell me what the Oracle said."

He sighed and gave me a tight, humorless smile. "I'm unsure if it will make any sense. I didn't understand most of it."

"Let me be the judge of that," I told him, reaching my hand across the table to him.

He took it and gave it a squeeze. I was careful to avoid the painful-looking cuts as I gently squeezed back.

"Illusions were mentioned," he informed me. "Three times, so I believe that to be important. It makes sense now that we know the monster took on your visage."

Both Lilith and the Oracle had spoken of illusions.

Tim turned away from the window and pulled his notebook out of one of his many pockets. For the first time since I'd known him, he looked old. His appearance hadn't changed —he still looked to be around forty-five, but his eyes told a very different story. His eyes, Candy's eyes, Gideon's eyes, all of the Immortals' eyes had seen things that could destroy a mind. Hell, I'd even witnessed things that would have sent the human me over the edge.

But I was still here and I planned to stay that way.

My need to comfort Tim was overwhelming. I stood up, crossed the kitchen and wrapped my arms around my friend who enjoyed sharing random gross facts, x-rayed people's packages and created culinary disasters. He was beautiful to me.

"I'm so sorry, Tim," I whispered in his ear as I held him tight.

He kissed the top of my head and smiled. It was a sad smile, but it was also filled with kindness. "Thank you, friend. It means much to me."

He kept his arm around my shoulders and read from his notepad. "Several different definitions for illusion. However, they all seem to fit—a thing that is wrongly interpreted or perceived by the senses. A deceptive appearance."

I took it in, then turned my attention back to Rafe. "What else was said?"

"The Oracle said not to let the dead take their secrets to the grave. The dead hold the key."

My knees buckled. Tim held me up. Rarely in our world did things happen without reason. It made me ill that Rafe, Prue and Abby owed the Oracle. However, I would not let their sacrifice for Gabe be in vain. The dead had come home, so to speak. The only one of my guests that I'd gotten to know so far was Agnes Bubbala… and she had been wildly helpful. I was also suspicious of her death. Something didn't sit right. There was a secret there.

Now it was time to help her.

"Agnes," I called out, hoping she was still here.

"You rang, Puddin'?" she sang, floating into the kitchen.

I smiled at her. Her teased hair alone was enough to make me happy. It was horribly lovely.

I took her hand in mine as she floated. It was fifty-fifty if a ghost was corporeal enough to touch. Sometimes my hands went right through them. Other times, like now, we could have a physical connection. Only Death Counselors could feel the touch of a specter.

Wait, that wasn't true. Tory had been able to touch Gram. I pushed the thought away and would deal with it later.

"Would you be okay if we talked about your death?" I asked.

Agnes patted my head with her papery hand and smiled. "I would be just fine, Puddin'."

"Thank you," I told her.

If what the Oracle said was accurate, Agnes held a secret that was imperative to freeing Gideon and Gabe. I couldn't for the life of me figure out what it was, but I was going to find out.

CHAPTER FOURTEEN

I'D CONSIDERED A MIND DIVE BUT DECIDED AGAINST IT. AGNES spoke clearly and was in good shape. A mind dive could take me out of action for over twenty-four hours. I didn't think it was a good move to be gone so long with a monster on the loose.

We'd gathered in the living room. Prue, Abby and Rafe still looked rough, but were healing. Tim had coaxed Candy Vargo back inside after a long discussion. She was still stewing and refused to look at my siblings. Thankfully, Heather had a huge container of June's peanut butter cookies in her bag. Tory squealed with delight and grabbed a handful. The sound of happiness coming from her was foreign, but it was also beautiful. June's cookies were magic. Even Candy had taken a few and inhaled them. I'd indulged in six and felt happier, too.

Dirk had insisted on singing a song to lighten the mood. He'd chosen "The Thong Song" in the key of Z. It was bad, but his enthusiasm and joy made up for his terrible voice. Agnes was thrilled with the impromptu performance. It got iffy when

Dirk lifted his gown and displayed his thong and bare ass, but the stunt made Candy Vargo laugh. Seeing the Keeper of Fate more herself was a relief and lightened the heavy load on my heart. My stress level was high. Seeing Dirk slide into the splits at the end of his number made it soar higher.

His scream as he crushed his balls made everyone cry out in phantom pain. I didn't own testicles and *my* crotch hurt.

"OH MY GOD!" Dirk shrieked. "I've flattened my nuggets."

It took Rafe, Tim and Heather to get Dirk back to his stiletto-clad feet. The man was sweating and cupping his balls.

"Need ice," he gasped out.

"On it," Abby said, jumping to her feet and running to the kitchen.

After settling Dirk on a comfortable armchair with a bag of frozen peas on his privates, we were ready to begin.

I took Agnes' hand in mine and smiled at her. "Okay, let's start with why you believe you had a heart attack," I suggested.

While Agnes had said she was willing to talk, I didn't want to overwhelm or upset her. This was not my usual MO with the dead. I usually waited until they made it clear that they wanted to talk. I never pushed and the ghosts were welcome to stay as long as they wanted. However, I never knew how long a ghost would stay. If Agnes had secrets—which seemed likely—I couldn't afford to let her take them to the grave.

Agnes floated in front of me with a worried expression. Not a good sign.

"Pain in my left arm, shortness of breath," she said, getting agitated. "Lightheadedness."

Tory got to her feet, crossed the room and stood next to Agnes. She lightly touched the ghost's cheek and smiled. "It's okay Agnes. I'll stay right here."

Agnes calmed immediately. It was similar to what Tory had

done for Gram. Gram had been flickering away from the spell Zadkiel had cast, keeping the dead from finding me. It had been terrifying. Tory's presence had calmed Gram and kept her from fading away. For that, I would owe Tory for the rest of time. She'd also taken my pain when Tim had healed me after I'd let the wraiths take some of my happy memories to ease their suffering. I was still unsure of how she had done it.

"May I be so bold to inquire how you calm the dead?" Tim asked politely.

Tory tensed for a moment. She was one to keep everything close to the chest, but she turned to Tim and nodded slowly. "I can take the pain, fear and uncertainty away. I learned the skill when the Souls of the Martyrs came to me. Necessity breeds ingenuity."

Her voice was casual. What she'd shared was not. Tory was a vessel for other people's torment. It was tragic and humbling.

Candy Vargo dropped an F-bomb, got down on her knees and bowed to Tory. "You're a badass bitch. You ain't very friendly, but that don't bother me. Ninety-nine percent of the fuckers I know don't like me. I've decided we're going to be best friends. You sure as hell need one and I'm your gal."

Tory looked horrified. Candy Vargo didn't notice. She wasn't the best at reading a room.

"That's right," Candy continued. "You just need some socialization. I can get you a bagger job at the Piggly Wiggly and you can work your way up to cashier in no fuckin' time. Daisy gave me her dad's old house cause I'm takin' in a bunch of foster kids. There's plenty of room for you. Amelia's gonna live there too. She's girlier than I am, so that's a bonus if you wanna shop and shit like that. As far as moolah goes, you don't have to worry. I'm fuckin' loaded. So, Silver, what do you say?"

Tory was speechless. I didn't blame her. That was a lot. It

ROBYN PETERMAN

was pretty clear Candy Vargo wasn't going to take no for an answer.

"I… umm… have to go back to Purgatory," Tory stuttered. Even she was careful not to piss off the Keeper of Fate.

"Bullshit," Candy grunted. "Livin' where you work is gonna make you lose what's left of your mind. I'm older than dirt and the only reason I haven't gone batshit nuts is because I stay in touch with humanity. When you lose that, you're fucked. Now, you're on the young side only bein' a few thousand years old. Gideon's the Grim Reaper. You don't see that dumbass livin' in the darkness. Daisy—who hasn't read the bible—is the Angel of Mercy and she ain't livin' in the light."

I rolled my eyes at the mention I hadn't read the Bible. It was on my very long to-do list. And as to whether she was batshit nuts was debatable. However, the part about staying in touch with humanity was wise.

"Anyhoo, as I was sayin'," Candy went on. "Rules are made to be broken—especially bullshit ones made by sons of bitches like Zadkiel. You feel me, Silver?"

Tory didn't know how to respond.

Candy Vargo eyed the broken Immortal for a moment then smiled. She pulled an unchewed box of toothpicks from her pocket and gave it to her. "Repeat after me. Yes, Candy Vargo, you badass bitch, I'll take you up on your offer."

Tory opened her mouth to speak, but no words left her lips. Candy laughed and slapped her on the back, sending her flying across the room. Dirk expertly caught her before she slammed into the wall.

"Darling," he said as he righted her and set her on her feet. "I think it's a fabu plan! The Keeper of Fate is a profane, disgusting and bossy bee-otch, but she has a heart that is true.

Plus, the digs are spectacular. I say do it! What have you got to lose?"

Tory ran her hands through her silver hair and groaned. She glared at Candy. "I don't play nice with others."

Candy shrugged and grinned. "Neither do I."

"This is true," Tim commented with a giggle.

"Thank you," Candy told Tim.

"Welcome, friend," he replied.

Tory tried again. "I've never done housework and I don't know how to cook. I don't enjoy conversing with people. I have no desire to rectify any of those things. I'm violent. I'm rude and if you piss me off, I'll electrocute you without hesitation."

"Same," Candy shot back. "We'll get along just fine. If you say no, I'll electrocute your ass so hard you'll taste metal for the next five centuries."

Tory's mouth hung open.

Agnes leaned into her and whispered, "Say yes, sweetie. Cupcake means business. I should show you the letters she wrote me for several decades—horrible stuff. But I can say she's committed and loves hard. With a friend like Candy Vargo, you don't have to worry about much. She's ferocious and will be happy to eat anyone who tries to harm you."

Prue, Rafe and Abby visibly winced.

"Umm... I'll think about it," Tory finally said.

"Roger that," Candy replied. "But you ain't gonna get a better offer, jackass."

Strangely, I agreed, but kept it to myself. That was their business not mine. Talking to Agnes was my business and I needed to get back to it.

"Agnes, can you tell me about your morning before the heart attack?" I asked.

Tory reached out to Agnes and touched her. Agnes smiled her thanks. "Well, me and my handyman were eating breakfast while I read to him what I'd written the night before."

"Tell me about your handyman," Heather said, staying very conversational and neutral.

It was the manner she used in court. My sister the lawyer got people to admit things they never intended to due to her kind delivery and mild tone.

Agnes let out a nervous giggle. "Well, he was *much* younger than me…"

This was getting interesting.

"Were you more than employee and employer?" I questioned.

"Don't I wish," she said with a sigh. "But alas, no. He wasn't interested in me that way."

"What was his name?" Heather inquired, cleaning up cookie crumbs so the weight of the question wasn't heavy.

"Mr. Handyman," Agnes replied, much to everyone's confusion.

Heather laughed. Agnes joined her.

"You're so silly," she told the ghost. "I meant his real name."

"Silly I may be," Agnes agreed. "But that's what he went by for years. When I tried to get it out of him, he would laugh and laugh. It became our little joke."

It wasn't funny. It bordered on creepy. "Umm… how did you pay Mr. Handyman for his work?"

"Cash," she told me. "He only took cash. Most of the time the dear man wouldn't take any payment at all. We were friends."

Heather shot me a look. I received it and shot one back.

Tory intercepted the exchange and dove right in. She

caressed Agnes and pulled her close. "Did you love Mr. Handyman?"

Agnes nodded and began to sniffle. "I did."

"That's lovely," Tory told her in a gentle tone. "Did you provide for him in your will?"

"No," Agnes said. "I should have though." She sighed with sadness. "Mr. Handyman was instrumental in many of my dragon plots. He had such a brilliant mind for dastardly deeds."

"I bet he did," I muttered under my breath.

Tim spoke up. "Agnes, my friend, tell me more about your potassium deficiency, please."

I wasn't sure why he asked the question, but Tim rarely made mistakes. If he inquired, there was a reason.

"Oh dear," she said to Tim. "Do you think you might have one too?"

Tim nodded. "I might. Not sure the bananas are helping enough."

"Ohhhh, Sweet Pea," Agnes said, floating over to Tim. Her voice was filled with concern. "Tell me your symptoms."

I was fairly sure Tim was fibbing. Immortals didn't get sick as far as I knew. They could also grow back appendages. Tim having a potassium deficiency was absurd.

"Weak muscles, leg cramps, some twitching, a few tingles here and there, and the occasional numbness," he explained.

His wide range of knowledge about practically everything was coming in handy.

"Yes," Agnes yelled. "You most definitely have a potassium deficiency, Sweet Pea. You must go to your doctor and have blood work done. TODAY!"

"Excellent advice," Tim said. "What did your doctor put you on?"

Agnes was perplexed for a moment then threw her hands in the air. "It was a liquid supplement. Orange flavored. Used to drink it in my Tang every morning."

"Fascinating," Tim said, jotting notes as Agnes shared her medicine regime. "And the taste?"

Agnes cocked her teased blonde head to the side as she considered her answer. "Salty. I suppose I could compare it to Epsom salts. But don't eat Epsom salts!" She slapped her thighs and giggled.

Tim joined her. "I promise I will not ingest Epsom salts."

"Sweet Pea is a smart man!"

Candy Vargo might be a toothpick-chewing nightmare, but she wasn't stupid. She was following along and on the same page as Heather, Tory, Tim and me.

"Did Mr. Handyman make your breakfast for you?" Candy asked.

Agnes giggled. "He did. He'd been around on and off for a few weeks. I broke my dishwasher, dryer and trash compactor on purpose so he'd have more things to fix."

"And you ate breakfast together often?" Heather pressed.

"Absolutely!" Agnes said. "We'd nosh on some cake and Tang and discuss the dragons' adventures. Mr. Handyman is the very one who came up with the plot for *Dragons Do It Drunk*."

"Remind me of the plot," I requested. I thought it was the one with the parallel planes, but wasn't positive.

"I've got this," Candy told Agnes. "It's the brilliant one where Sisses, Eater of All—who's modeled after me—got beheaded with a blender. Bloody as all get out. Bioterth, The Adorable was a dumbass in that one and ate the hula dancers. Agnes Bubbala should have given her explosive shits, but she fucked that up."

"Okay," I said, pressing my temples. "Was *Dragons Do It Drunk* also the book where the bad guy put his hoard on a parallel plane?"

"Yes, Puddin'!" Agnes said. "Parveit, Lord of The Red trapped Yrvat, The Warm and Ezires, The Stubborn on a separate plane of reality and stole their magic to increase his power."

I looked at Heather and Tory. Both had their brows knitted in surprise. Was Mr. Handyman the monster? Or was it Tar Basilisk? It would be as random as all get out if Mr. Handyman was the monster, but I wasn't knocking anyone out of the lineup.

"Well, fuck a duck," Candy Vargo grunted, clearly thinking along the same lines as me. "Agnes Bubbala, did you happen to get a peek at the fucker who was questionin' Daisy at the door?"

I held my breath. Could the identity of the monster be this easy?

"I did," she said. "I much preferred the nice sheriff to the movie-star-good-looking but rude detective."

I expelled my breath loudly. Nothing was easy. If Mr. Handyman had been at the door, Agnes would have said something. Of that, I was certain.

"So, neither of the lawmen at the door were your handyman?" Heather asked.

"Don't be silly," Agnes said. "Of course not! Mr. Handyman lives in Ohio where I'm from. And while the mean one was handsome, I prefer someone more in touch with the '80s. Hence, my out-of-style hair-do that I just love!"

"And you wear it well, darling," Dirk assured her, much to her delight.

A compliment from a gorgeous drag queen was a compliment indeed.

Candy Vargo walked over to the wall and punched both fists through it. I understood the impulse but refrained from joining her.

"When the fuck is it going to get easier?" she grumbled.

Again, I agreed. I'd been ninety percent sure that Tar Basilisk was the monster. He still might be, but the connection to Agnes was getting thinner. I didn't know if her secret was the key. However, my job as the Death Counselor was to help her. If she wasn't the dead person who held the *secret that couldn't go to the grave*, then it meant it had to be one of my other guests who had arrived. The Oracle's warning didn't seem to fit with Agnes. But I still needed to aid the lovely woman. It was looking likely that she'd somehow been poisoned by Mr. Handyman. From Tim's line of questioning, my guess was that the potassium was the culprit.

For the umpteenth time, I was wildly grateful for my friends. I wasn't well versed in the Bible, and I'd gotten a C in chemistry. However, my posse could cover my weaknesses. Amen to that.

"Agnes," Tory said. "Can you give me your address?"

"Already got it," Candy said, pulling a piece of paper from her pocket. "I'm goin' up to steal her laptop so we can finish *Call Me Daddy Dragon*."

"Excellent," I said. "Does anyone have a background in chemistry?"

"I do," Rafe replied. "I was tasked with poisoning Immortals by Zadkiel. Prue and Abby are well-trained too."

That left everyone speechless for a hot sec. I made a mental note never to eat anything they cooked.

"Tim, you and I are going to transport to Agnes' house. I want to check out a few things. Rafe, Prue and Abby, I need you to set up a lab in my office."

Candy handed Tim the piece of paper with the address. Rafe looked confused. "Here? Now?"

"Yep," Heather answered before I could. "I can transport into Charlie's lab at the hospital and get what you need."

"You mean pilfer, Miss High and Mighty Law and Order?" Candy asked with a naughty grin.

"I prefer borrow," she told Candy, flipping her off.

I stepped in between them so no one threw a punch.

"I'll come with you," Rafe told Heather. "It will be easier than making a list or trying to describe it."

"Perfect." Heather gave him a thumbs up.

"Puddin'," Agnes said with a sad expression on her sweet face. "Do you suspect foul play?"

Honesty was always the best policy. Most of the time the dead felt a serene peace about the cause of their deaths, but Agnes had only died yesterday and didn't seem to have that tranquility.

"Agnes, do you have any unfinished business?" I asked.

She appeared confused. "I'm not sure what you mean, Puddin'."

I held my hand up for everyone to stop what they were doing and stay still. I gently led Agnes to the couch and beckoned Tory over. Tory moved swiftly and sat down on the other side of our 1980s-loving new friend.

"When a ghost sticks around and comes to me, it's because they need me to help them with something," I explained. "It can be something simple—like when my friend Sam was worried that his wife wouldn't be able to find her reading glasses—or something more complicated. I help them find peace so they can move on."

Agnes kissed my cheek. Her semi-transparent lips felt dry and papery, but her kiss had touched the happy part of my soul.

"That is beautiful, Puddin'," she whispered. "Such a beautiful gift you have."

"Thank you. Can you think of anything you might like my help with?"

She shook her head and wore a perplexed expression. "I can't."

I wasn't sure if it was because I pushed for it, or if she truly had no unfinished business. If that was the case, I didn't know why she was still here. "Not to worry," I assured her. "It'll come to you. And you're welcome to stay with me for as long as you'd like."

She fluffed her '80s hairdo, then pursed her lips. "You know, it is a little odd I keeled over from a heart attack. I got an A+ on my physical exam just last week other than my potassium."

"Which is why I'm kind of concerned," I told her. "Was there anyone else in your life besides Mr. Handyman who came in and out of your house? A cleaning person, maybe? Or possibly your literary agent?"

"No," she said, getting fidgety. "No one."

Tory wrapped an arm around her, and she grew calm.

"But I can assure you that Mr. Handyman would never hurt me," she said. "He was my friend."

"And friends are lovely things to have." I gave her a warm smile even though my insides were not feeling warm and fuzzy.

I wasn't sure if figuring out her manner of death was going

to help or hurt her. It was also risky to spend time away from finding the monster.

"Everything happens for a reason," Tory reminded, as she watched me war with myself. "Deal with what's in front of you, and it will lead you to where you're supposed to be."

"From your mouth," I muttered. I looked around the room. What was right in front of me was Agnes and the issue of how she passed. I couldn't for the life of me figure out how learning if Mr. Handyman had murdered her would lead me to where I was supposed to be, but Tory's words felt very right. Again, I was going with my gut. "We move and we move fast." Without any solid clues, we had nowhere to go but up. "Heather and Rafe will go. Be back in no more than a half hour."

In a flash of golden glitter, my brother and sister disappeared.

"Candy, you're in charge. Protect the house with your life. Do not destroy it or let it get destroyed. Prue and Abby, clear out the office and set up the area for the lab. Tory and Dirk, you'll back up Candy Vargo."

"Roger that, Jackass," Candy said, saluting me. "And if the monster shows up?"

I stared at her for a long beat. I didn't think all hell would break loose in a half hour, but stranger things had happened. "Find out how to get to Gideon, Gabe and Zadkiel."

"And then?" she demanded with a raised brow.

I couldn't believe what I was about to say, but desperate times called for repulsive measures. "Once Gideon, Gabe and Zadkiel have been secured… eat the monster."

"FUCK TO THE YES!" Candy shouted.

"Do you realize what you just said," Tim inquired, looking a little squeamish.

"Yep. I'm done with this shit. If Candy Vargo wants to be a

169

cannibal, then so be it. We need a little downtime and some peace and quiet around here. You feel me?"

Tim choked back his bile and nodded. "I do, friend. You ready to go to Ohio?"

"Born ready," I said.

CHAPTER FIFTEEN

"DUDE, WE'RE IN A CAR," I WHISPERED TO TIM. HAD HE transported us to the wrong place? I was positive Agnes Bubbala hadn't lived in her car. Granted, it was a nice car, but it was a *car*.

"Yes, I know," he replied.

It was dark outside and much colder than Georgia. Snow blanketed the grass and a full moon was rising on the horizon. Since I hadn't eaten much lunch, I was starving. Thankfully, I'd had the smarts to shove some cookies into my pocket. I was tempted to eat all of them but that was rude. I was Southern. Rude wasn't in my DNA. I handed Tim two of the cookies and saved two for myself.

"We have a half hour," I reminded him. Sitting in a car wasn't going to cut it. "Are we even in Ohio?"

Tim took a bite of his cookie and smiled. "We are, my friend. We're sitting in Agnes' car in her driveway."

"Because?"

"Because transporting into her house if it happened to be filled with humans would be a terrible plan. Candy Vargo talked in great detail with Agnes about her house and the surrounding area. She shared it with me. Knowledge is king."

"Sorry," I mumbled with a mouthful of peanut butter cookie. In my haste, I was being stupid. Stupid wasn't on the agenda.

"Not to worry," he said, eyeing the cute craftsman house in front of us. "The house is dark and I detect no heartbeats within."

He opened the car door and got out. I did the same.

"Are we breaking in?" I asked, looking around at the neighboring houses.

The homes weren't all that close to each other. Each sat on a property of approximately two acres. Even if we had to break a window and crawl through, there was a good chance we wouldn't be seen. Agnes' yard was filled with trees and rose bushes. The branches were naked and bare in the frigid winter. Come spring, the yard would be lovely.

The house was older and sat sure in its foundation. There was a welcoming warmth to it that was similar to its former owner.

Tim looked at me like I'd lost it. "No, friend, there's a key hidden in the flowerpot to the left of the front door."

I heaved a sigh of relief. I'd broken into a house before for a ghost. I'd do it again if I had to, but I wasn't a very skilled criminal. Nervous wreck would aptly describe me when I'd broken into Sam's house to find his wife's glasses in the cookie jar. I used to be a paralegal before my Immortal jobs consumed me. Breaking and entering had never been in any of my job descriptions... until now.

"Ready?" Tim asked.

"No, but that's never stopped me before."

He squeezed my hand and giggled. The key was easy to

find. The door opened right up. What we saw broke my heart.

The house was dark, but moonlight streamed through the windows and washed the charming abode in an eerie glow. The décor was kitschy and comfortable. It was done in bright florals mixed with lots of warm peaches and cream. While the color scheme and furniture were inviting, the overall scene was not.

Agnes' lifeless body was slumped over her desk. Her eyes were wide open and stared unseeingly at me.

I put my hand over my mouth so I didn't scream, but tears of sadness ran down my cheeks. It was heartbreaking that her body hadn't been found yet.

I was used to dealing with the dead in ghost form. They could communicate and I had grown to love them. Initially, I was terrified. However, they were all lovely people who needed my help. It was a job that gave as much to me as I gave to them. Dealing with deceased human bodies wasn't my thing.

"Oh my," Tim said with his hands on his heart. "This is tragic."

"What do we do?" I asked, swiping at my tears. Agnes was dead, there was nothing I could do to change that. Her body might be here, but thankfully, her soul was safe at my house.

Tim snapped his fingers, and a phone appeared in his hand. "When we're done taking what we need, I shall put in for a wellness check as a concerned friend." Tim handed me a pair of rubber gloves. "Put these on. Leaving fingerprints is bad form."

That was an understatement. Doing criminal things and having a criminal record were two entirely different situations. As sad as the scene was, I almost laughed at the thought that I was going to have to brush up on illegal skills. God, my life had changed.

"Plan?" I asked. I was going to follow, not lead, in this instance.

Tim approached Agnes' body and closely examined her and the area for a good ten minutes. The man didn't miss a detail and took notes on everything. I stood quietly and watched. After he was satisfied, he took plastic bags from one of his many pockets and handed me a few.

"Get the laptop. I'll take samples of the cake, Tang and her blood."

"You believe she was poisoned?"

He nodded solemnly. "Yes. Agnes' description of the potassium she took led me to believe she was taking prescription strength. High doses of prescription-strength potassium can cause a heart attack. It's called hyperkalemia. Normally, to kill someone with potassium, it would have been injected into the body, but Agnes has no recollection of being stabbed with a needle, and I see no evidence of that having happened. This leads me to believe that Mr. Handyman was putting high doses in her food and drink for a period of time."

"Wouldn't her physical last week have shown that?" I asked.

"Excellent observation, Daisy," Tim said. "My guess is that Mr. Handyman went for it after the exam. Depending on dosage, he could have done it in a few days without Agnes being aware she was being poisoned."

While Tim's praise made me feel ten feet tall, the way Agnes had died made me feel ill. "Mr. Handyman is a monster," I hissed.

Tim paused then sighed. "Sadly, monsters take many forms and are in many places in this world. There is no sense to be made sometimes."

Reality could really bite. I carefully removed the laptop from the desk while doing my best not to make eye contact with the cadaver of my dead friend. It was freaky and uncomfortable. Tim worked quickly and precisely as he took samples of the food, drink and Agnes' blood. He left a mark and some blood on the skin of her neck where he'd drawn the sample. He was so meticulous, his sloppiness surprised me.

"Should we clean her up?" I asked, holding up a tissue.

Tim shook his head. "No. I did it on purpose. Since it appears to be a heart attack, the human authorities will take the easy way out and look no further. Agnes has no family and no criminal record. It looks cut and dry... unless it doesn't. A neck wound will have to be pursued and changes the parameters of the investigation. It screams foul play. Agnes Bubbala deserves justice and if I can do a little something to help her get it, I'm honored."

My mouth made a perfect O. Tim never failed to impress me with his ethics and sense of morality. He was a good man and I was proud to be his friend.

"Thought," I said as Tim finished up.

He looked at me quizzically.

"The phone call for the wellness check. Won't it lead back to you?"

He winked at me. "Fine point, well made. However, it's a burner phone. Can't be traced and it will disappear after use."

"Brilliant and handsome," I said with a wide smile.

Tim blushed a deep red. "Your vision must be impaired, friend."

"Not one bit," I assured him. Tim was handsome in a quirky, nerdy way. The mail uniform he wore 24/7 was iffy, but he made it work. It was his goodness from the inside that shone brightly and made the man beautiful.

Tim chuckled and took one final look around. "I believe we have what we came for."

I checked my watch. We had five minutes to spare before our half-hour was up. "Make the call, and let's get out of here."

Tim disguised his voice and called the local authorities. My buddy sounded like a British woman. It was bizarre. He requested a welfare check for Agnes Bubbala and gave her address. He identified himself as a freelance editor who worked with the author and hadn't heard back on a deadline for a week. He explained she lived alone with no family to speak of and he was concerned. After getting a promise that they would send someone out, he thanked them and hung up. With a wave of his hand, the phone disappeared.

"Our work here is done," he said.

That was correct. Unfortunately, there was a lot more work in front of us.

Whatever. Anything was possible as long as I believed.

I believed we'd get justice for Agnes.

I believed I would find Gideon and Gabe and bring them home.

I believed it with all my heart.

IN THE HALF HOUR WE'D BEEN GONE, CANDY VARGO DIDN'T HAVE to eat anyone. The monster hadn't shown up. Rafe, Prue, Abby and Heather had set up a lab in the office that looked like it belonged at NASA. I had no clue how they'd gotten everything here, but not much surprised me lately. Rafe had taken the samples and chatted briefly with Tim. Tim turned over his notes. My siblings were wildly impressed with the details. The Courier between the Darkness and the Light was a stickler and missed very little. They'd quickly gone to the lab and closed the door behind them.

Agnes had been full of questions. I wasn't sure how to answer them without hurting her. Tim stepped in. He kindly and without lying explained what we'd found.

"I just don't understand," Agnes lamented.

Even Tory couldn't calm her distress.

"What don't you understand?" Tim asked her.

She flew around the kitchen in tight circles. "Mr. Handyman was with me when I died. Why did he leave me there?"

Tim didn't have an answer. Neither did I.

Candy Vargo did. "Agnes, I hate to tell you this, but Mr. Handyman is a motherfucker."

Agnes paused her erratic flying and squinted at Candy. "You think?"

"I know. That asshole used and abused," Candy snarled. "When I find him, he's gonna pay."

Agnes calmed down and floated in front of an irate Candy Vargo. "You'd do that for me, Cupcake?"

Candy nodded jerkily and wiped the tears falling from her eyes with the sleeve of her shirt. "Damn straight," she grunted. "I love you, Agnes Bubbala. I know my letters to you might have been a little harsh."

"That's an understatement," Agnes pointed out. "I'd have to call them profanity-laden threats."

"Thank you," Candy said, again not reading the room.

Agnes laughed. "Welcome, Cupcake."

"You saved me," Candy said softly. "Your books took me away from reality for a few hours and gave me hope. I related to the violence and the hopelessness, but the happily ever afters made me realize if Qylzrog, The Skinny One can get laid, I can too. I'm gettin' sick and tired of vibrators. I've got fuckin' carpal tunnel from whacking myself off. You know what I mean?"

Agnes nodded in commiseration. The rest of us cringed. Candy had just made one heck of a horrible pun. It was one thing to use sex toys, it was another thing altogether to admit you got carpal tunnel from using sex toys. The visual was not good. Candy Vargo was the queen of TMI. Second place went to Jennifer. Although, it might be a tie...

"I do know what you mean, Cupcake," Agnes said. "I didn't get any nookie for years... only my battery-operated boyfriend. Just lived through my characters. I'd hoped Mr. Handyman was going to be my knight in shining armor, but he turned out to be a real son of a bitch, didn't he?"

"Word," Candy said, offering Agnes a toothpick.

Agnes tried to take it, but it fell right through her hand. It was the thought that counted.

"You know what?" Agnes shouted, zipping around the room and creating a wind. "I'm pissed—really pissed. I gave the best years of my life to Mr. Handyman. And what reward did I get? Nada. The man killed me. So incredibly rude! But how ironic... my demise sounds like one of my novels." She tried to run her hands through her hair, but being that it was a teased helmet of hairspray, it didn't quite work out. It took her a full minute to get her hands unstuck from her head. No one commented. That would be mean. We all adored the woman. "Do you have any idea how many appliances I purposely broke to keep that murderous bastard around? I'm such an idiot."

"You ain't no idiot," Candy Vargo bellowed. "You're Agnes Bubbala, the greatest author alive."

"Dead," Agnes corrected her.

"Sorry, my bad," Candy said.

Agnes floated down from the ceiling and sat her ghostly body on a kitchen chair. Well, kind of. Her bottom went right through it, but she didn't notice. "I know why I'm still here, Puddin'."

I did too.

"I want you to bring Mr. Handyman down," she said in a matter-of-fact tone. She'd found the peace that the dead do about dying. The truth, or what we believed to be the truth, had set her free.

I seated myself next to her. "While I believe that you were poisoned, let's wait for the results. And I promise you, we'll find Mr. Handyman."

"And tear him from limb to limb," Candy Vargo huffed. "But before I rip off his appendages, I'm gonna feed that jackass a bunch of potassium just for fun. Then comes the removal of his entrails. Those slimy bits will be shoved down his throat then I'll decapitate the fucker and wedge his head into his ass. After that, I'm gonna—"

"Pretty sure he's dead by that point," Heather chimed in with a pained expression.

"Not dead enough," Candy growled. "After that, I'm gonna spread his parts all over the world so that murderous fuck can't have an afterlife. No ghostly fun for him."

Agnes was delighted. I was appalled and a little queasy. Tory, Dirk, Heather and Tim were on my team.

"Ohhhhhhh!" Agnes gasped out. "That's how we'll end Parveit, Lord of The Red in the novel! It's genius!"

Candy blushed with delight. "Really?"

"Absolutely, Cupcake," she gushed, flying circles around a preening Candy Vargo. "I especially like putting his head in his ass."

"Face first," Candy told her.

"Wouldn't have it any other way," Agnes assured her with a giggle.

"My God," Dirk cried out, fanning himself. "I must read the tome when it's done. Sounds positively dastardly! Love it!"

I was going to take a pass on that one.

"Results are in," Rafe said, coming out from the office slash lab with Prue and Abby behind him.

That was fast, but that was how Immortals worked. The expressions on their faces already told the story, but the words needed to be spoken.

"And?" Agnes inquired. She was no longer frantic about it. The ghost was composed and resigned.

"You were poisoned with an overdose of potassium," Rafe explained. "The levels found in the cake were so high I'm surprised you didn't taste it."

"Mr. Handyman wasn't a great cook," she said flatly. "I ate it to be polite."

"And that right there is why I'm as rude as shit," Candy chimed in.

"Zip it," I chastised her. "Not the time or place."

She did as told, but quickly apologized to Agnes first. The Keeper of Fate was getting softer. Gram's influence was working wonders on Candy.

"Rafe, would you mind explaining the mechanics of how that worked?" Agnes asked.

My brother wasn't quite sure how to react. My guess was that the particulars weren't pretty.

"Umm... are you sure?" he asked hesitantly.

"I am," Agnes replied. "Need it for research for a book. Cupcake," she pointed at Candy, "I want you to take notes. We need the realism. I might have been off with Bioterth, The Adorable not getting the explosive shits, but I will not screw up Parveit, Lord of The Red's grisly demise."

"Hell to the yes!" Candy shouted, borrowing a notebook and pen from Tim.

"How about taking the discussion to the lab," I suggested. While I was greatly relieved that Agnes wasn't devastated over her death, I didn't want to hear the gritty details.

"As you wish," Rafe said.

Abby, Prue, Rafe, Candy Vargo and Agnes went back to the lab and closed the door behind them.

"Thank you for that," Heather said with a yawn. "Not sure my stomach could have handled it."

"Word," Tory muttered. "Not real sure how we're going to find Mr. Handyman and avenge Agnes' death, though."

I wasn't either.

"I did dust for prints at the house," Tim volunteered. "There were several. I can hack into the national database and do a cross-check, but if Mr. Handyman doesn't have a criminal record, it won't be helpful."

"Not that I want to get anyone else involved here," Heather said. "But rumor has it that Abaddon can memorize a scent and find the person."

I considered it. It would be a last resort. Owing a Demon wasn't a great way to roll. Plus, I already owed Lilith a to-be-determined price.

"Good to know," I said, feeling pretty exhausted myself. It was only nine at night, but it had been a long day. "I'd like to suggest that everyone sleep here. There's plenty of room, and we can take turns guarding the house."

"Agreed," Dirk said. "I shall take the first shift. When Agnes and the crew have finished the discussion, I shall send them to bed posthaste."

"Sounds like a plan," I said, giving the queen a hug.

Just when the thought of sleep was forefront in my head,

my body jerked to a halt and my fingers began to spark. Donna and Karen growled low in their throats. I was pretty sure Dirk did the same.

The light knock at the front door felt ominous. Sleep was going to have to wait.

"Hide," Heather commanded quietly. "Tory, go invisible and stay with Daisy. Dirk, go to the lab and warn the others. Everyone, stay out of sight unless necessary."

Quickly and silently, everyone did as Heather ordered. I willed my hands to stop sparking. When I looked through the peephole, no one was there. Had all of us imagined the knock?

That was absurd. There was someone out there, and they didn't want to reveal the surprise.

My stomach roiled. I turned and glanced around the room. Everyone was out of sight.

"I don't see anyone there," I said in a hushed tone.

"There's someone there," Tory replied, touching my arm so I knew where she was.

"Well, there goes my fantasy that we all heard nothing at the same time."

"Fantasies are often rooted in truth, but more often, truth isn't rooted in fantasy," she shared.

While cryptic, I got what she'd said.

"Candy?" I whispered.

"Over here, jackass," she replied from behind the office door.

"I hope you're hungry."

She laughed. "I'm always hungry."

"No cannibalism until Gideon, Gabe and Zadkiel are safe," I reminded her.

"Still can't believe we're saving that nasty fucker," she muttered.

"It's the right thing to do," I said.

"If hating that son of a bitch is the wrong thing to do, I don't wanna be right," she sang. It was a bastardized version of the song, but it made me laugh.

In the face of possible death, I could still laugh.

"Darlings, pinch your weenuses," Dirk called out softly. "Does wonders for the mind."

My mind was a racing mess. I pinched my weenus and felt clearer. Who knew? I spotted Agnes floating near Candy. Her arm had fallen off. My gut said to get her out of here. If the monster destroyed her, she had no chance of an afterlife.

I quickly sprinted to the kitchen, grabbed a tube of superglue and glued her arm back on. Agnes kissed the top of my head. I'd done the entire operation in less than thirty seconds. However, there was more to do before I opened the door.

"Abby and Prue, can you transport Agnes to the farmhouse? Then stay and protect Gram and the other ghosts? I also want you to take the dogs."

"Will do," Prue said. "Agnes, try and hold on to me, please."

Agnes floated right into my sister. Prue put her arms around Donna and Karen. They wagged their tails with excitement. I crossed my fingers and hoped it would work. In a blast of glittering gold, they disappeared—even Agnes and my fur babies. It was a load off my mind to know everyone was safe. Especially Agnes. She'd been through enough.

"We ready to rumble?" I asked.

A whispered round of yesses was the reply. Tory gripped my arm and held tight. Having her with me was a blessing. I was a badass. She was a badass. Together we were lady-balls on fire.

Good luck to whoever was on the other side of the door.

CHAPTER SIXTEEN

THE GUST OF CHILLY WIND RUSHED INTO THE HOUSE AS I OPENED the door. I leaned out and looked both left and right. No one was there.

Tory squeezed my arm. I understood. Someone was definitely there, but I couldn't see him or her.

"Hello," I called out.

"Over here," came a muffled reply.

The voice came from behind the porch swing. My eyes narrowed as I detected the frame of a man squatting low.

"Who are you?" I demanded, holding up my cell phone. "Come into the light or I'm calling the police."

"Awwwww, hell no," he whimpered. "Don't do that."

I recognized the voice. What the hell was he thinking? "Micky?"

He stood up with his head hanging low. "At your service," he said, giving me a pathetic salute. Even though the man had been fired, he was still wearing his police uniform. On top of all his troubles, I was sure impersonating a cop was a crime.

"What are you doing here?"

He came out from behind the swing and glanced around. The man was terrified. "I'm in a little trouble," he whispered.

"I heard," I replied flatly. He shouldn't be here. I didn't want to turn the dumbass in, but if he insisted on staying, I didn't have a choice. Of course, I'd call Dip Doody and not Tar Basilisk. I didn't trust the Atlanta detective as far as I could throw him. Although, that wasn't a great analogy since I could throw trees... Plus, I was leaning toward Tar as the monster. I didn't under any circumstances want Micky in the middle of an Immortal smackdown.

"Daisy, I didn't steal them coins," he said. "While I would have loved to add 'em to my collection, I didn't take them."

I shook my head and groaned. "Micky, I'm not sure why you thought it was a good idea to come here late at night."

"I ain't got nowhere to go." He was close to tears. "My ex threatened to mace me blind if I set one foot in the house. Don't know if you heard I was banging women in the cruiser."

"Unfortunately, yes. You told me earlier."

"Right, my bad. Not my best idea, but it really did impress the ladies."

Clearly, the *ladies* were *easy* to impress on top of having no taste whatsoever.

"Oh, I've still got that box of condoms you gave me. You want it back? The unused ones?"

"Umm... no." I was close to electrocuting the pig. The only thing that stopped me was knowing it would kill him. "Micky, this is a super bad idea on your part—even worse than the cruise banging. The sheriff stopped by earlier looking for you. Your GPS had proof that you'd been here."

He went ashen. I actually felt kind of sorry for the mullet-sporting dummy.

"What did you tell him?" he asked with a quiver in his voice.

I blew out an audible breath and pressed the bridge of my nose. "I told him that you were selling wrapping paper."

"Shoooowheee," he said, gaining back a little color. "Thanks for coverin' for me, Daisy. I really appreciate it."

My eyeroll was as tiny as I could make it. He was missing a few important brain cells. I wasn't sure how he'd passed the tests to become a cop in the first place. "Micky, I wasn't covering for you. You were here selling me wrapping paper. No lying or covering necessary. I'd suggest turning yourself in. If you didn't steal the coins, you're not in trouble. The longer you hide, the worse it's going to be."

"Can't do it," the idiot said, shaking his head so hard the combover on the top of his head got loose and fell into his face.

It was a terrible look. He licked his hand and put the three hairs back. It took all I had not to gag.

"There's a guy lookin' for me," he said as his voice rose high in distress. "A cop from Atlanta. Bad business. Out to get me."

I agreed with his assessment of Tar Basilisk, but it wasn't my problem. I already had tons—Tar Basilisk potentially being one of them, but not for the reason Micky took issue with him. However, as always, my curiosity got the best of me. "Why?"

Micky leaned in. His breath was rancid. "I banged his woman. Banged her better than he ever did."

I found that incredibly difficult to believe unless she was blind. Tar was absurdly handsome. Micky was gross.

I backed away. I didn't want to throw up on him, but if I had to smell his breath, that was exactly what was going to happen. "You can't stay here, Micky. I'm sorry."

First of all, I wasn't going to harbor a fugitive. Secondly, when the monster showed up, Micky Muggles didn't stand a chance. I didn't have the time to protect the cheating human asshole from dying. Getting rid of him was the way to play it. I didn't like the man, but I didn't want to see him dead. And I certainly didn't want to have to host him as a ghost.

"Please, Daisy? For old time's sake? We were quite the thaaang in high school." He waggled his brows. He had more hair in his brows than on the top of his head.

"Micky, we were *never* a thing," I corrected him.

He had the audacity to wink at me. When he went to cup his nuts, I gave him a withering glare that stopped his repulsive action in its tracks. I wasn't sure if this was how he wooed the ladies, but it wasn't working on me. The little dude was abhorrent.

"Coulda, woulda, shoulda," he said.

"Nope. You need to leave now. If you don't, I'm calling Dip," I warned him.

"I'll be dead by morning," he said with a shudder. "That detective means business. Please, Daisy, have mercy on me."

Crap. The word mercy cut straight to my heart. I was the Angel of Mercy... not just for Immortals but for the human race as well. My compassion was probably going to bite me in the ass, but I had a very bad feeling about Tar Basilisk. Yes, I suspected he was the monster. No, I didn't buy that Micky had slept with his gal, but stranger things had happened. If Micky had, he picked the wrong guy to mess with. The monster wouldn't hesitate to destroy a human and Tar had quite the hard-on for Micky Muggles.

"Did you drive here?" I asked, feeling wildly unsure about what I was about to do.

"Yep, hid my car in the field over yonder," he said, pointing to the field where Gideon and Gabe had disappeared from.

I inhaled slowly and blew it out on a woosh. Normally, I

didn't break the law, but I was going to make an exception for the man. "Sleep in your car. You need to be gone by sunup. If you're not, I'm calling you in."

I planned to tell Dip tomorrow regardless, once Micky was gone. I'd omit that I'd given him permission to stay.

Micky Muggles was so relieved, he cried. His distress pulled at my heart, but I couldn't help him any more than letting him stay in his car on the property. Without a doubt, I would call Dip in the morning and let him know all of it—that he said he hadn't stolen the coins and that he was sure Tar was out to kill him. After talking with Dip earlier, it was clear he had a soft spot for the idiot.

"Thank you, Daisy. Thank you so much. The Draaagoon thanks you!"

He gave me another salute and jogged away into the dark night. The nickname was as pathetic as he was. Although the *goon* part was fitting.

TIM THOUGHT LETTING MICKY STAY WASN'T MY BEST DECISION. Candy Vargo disagreed and said she would have done the same. Dirk didn't believe for a second that Micky had banged Tar's gal, but he too would have given the deplorable little human refuge. Tory, who was always for the underdog, said she would have let him stay as well. Rafe had no opinion on the matter. Heather was of a different view altogether. She thought it was shady.

"Why shady?" I asked.

Heather had popped a few frozen pizzas into the oven for everyone. No one was ready for bed after the latest development. It was a smart move on Heather's part. A bunch of hungry Immortals was an explosion waiting to happen.

She shook her head and handed out napkins. "Why would he come here—to your house—instead of leaving town?"

"Fine point, well made," Tim said, still not happy that Micky was on the property. "He made quite a few bold assumptions."

"Like?" I asked, starting to feel wonky about my decision.

Tim was quick to list them off. "Like that you wouldn't immediately call the authorities. He treated you as if you were a trusted friend, which you are not. It also rubbed me wrong that he asked you to have *mercy*."

"That was a little odd, darling," Dirk said, digging into a pepperoni pie. "But there is no way for a human to know that Daisy is the Angel of Mercy."

"That fucker's porch light might be on, but ain't no one home," Candy added with a mouthful of pizza. "You've got tree stumps in the yard with higher IQs than Micky Muggles."

"While I'm still iffy on letting him stay, I agree with Candy Vargo's assessment of the man's intelligence. Quoting Gram, I'd have to add when the Lord was handing out brains, Micky Muggles thought God said trains and passed because he doesn't like to travel."

"Ohhhh!" Dirk squealed. "I've got one. He's so lacking in brain matter he could throw himself on the ground and miss!"

I held up my hands to put a stop to the Micky Muggles bashing. Yes, he was dumb, but being mean didn't feel right. "Guys, enough. He's not the sharpest, but I kind of feel sorry for him."

"Well, shit," Candy said. "Daisy's right. I don't always have both oars in the water either."

"My apologies," Tim said. "None of us should throw stones at glass houses."

"Agreed," Dirk said remorsefully. "I'm a proud bitch, but I'm not mean. So sorry."

"I have an opinion on the situation," Rafe said.

"What is it?" I asked.

"I agree with Heather," he replied. "Something is off."

The slice of cheese pizza I was eating no longer tasted good. "I can walk out to the field and tell him to leave."

"Desperate people can do desperate things," Tory said, standing up, walking over to the front door and locking it. "I'd suggest leaving it alone. We lock up the house, and if he's still here in the morning, let the human police handle it."

"Human police?" Tim questioned. "As opposed to what?"

"Non-human," she replied, checking the windows and making sure they were securely locked. "Tar Basilisk, if that's even his name, should not be alerted about the human with the appalling hair. For some unknown reason, I believe the Immortal wants the human dead."

As I mulled over what everyone had said, I felt a jolt of energy rush through my body. My body tensed noticeably and tears pooled in my eyes.

"Daisy," Gideon called out.

"Oh my God. Gideon, I can hear you."

"What's happening?" Tim asked alarmed.

"It's Gideon. He's talking to me."

The room went silent. No one, not even Candy Vargo, made a peep.

"Are you okay? Has anything happened?" I asked.

"We're fine... for now," he said in a terse tone. *"Something is drawing on our power."*

"What do you mean?" I asked, feeling frantic. If they couldn't defend themselves, they could be destroyed. *"How do you know?"*

"Another Immortal has been added," he said. *"A woman. She's in bad shape. We tried to help her. We failed."*

"Do you know her?" I asked. The question was absurd, but Gideon was older than dirt. He knew lots of Immortals.

"No, but she won't last long," he replied. *"My guess is that her power has been drained to a degree she can't survive."*

"You can't do anything for her?" Gideon was able to heal others. He should be able to heal the woman. Gabe could heal as well.

"We tried. That's how we know our magic has been compromised. Shockingly, Zadkiel is the only one with power, but he's literally in pieces and falling apart fast. His jaw is gone. He can't speak."

My gut tightened at the news. If Zadkiel had power, did that mean that he was the one stealing it from the others? He was a vile abomination of a man. Was my mortal enemy the monster we were searching for?

"Stay away from Zadkiel," I told him. *"He might be behind all of it."*

Gideon was quiet for a long moment. *"While normally I'd agree, the bastard was able to infuse Gabe with some magic. Gabe used it to ease the woman's pain for a brief time. I don't think it's him. Soon, he'll be nothing but dust."*

A feather could have knocked me over. *"Did you get a name from the woman? Was she able to communicate at all?"*

"Barely," he replied. *"It sounded like she said cat, but there was more to it we couldn't understand."*

"Okay," I said, pushing myself to sound more confident than I felt. Worrying Gideon wasn't going to help anything. *"We'll have you out of there soon. I promise."*

"Daisy, I don't..."

"Gideon?" I cried out. *"Talk to me. You don't what?"*

There was no answer. The connection was broken.

I felt like I was floating above myself. My body worked on its own accord. My feet walked me over to the wall. I put my right fist through it, then my left. My knuckles were bleeding and my hands throbbed. I did it again. No one said a word. It made me feel alive when part of me felt dead. I stared at the blood and watched it run down my arms.

People who were alive bled. I was alive. I was going to make sure Gideon stayed alive.

Turning slowly, I addressed the occupants of the room. "To see the full glory of the sun, one has to weather the storm first. Candy said, treading lightly is the best plan. We've done that. Actually, we've done nothing. And for that, we've gotten nothing. Gideon's and Gabe's powers are being siphoned off. There's a female Immortal with them who doesn't have much longer. Treading lightly is no longer the answer. Since the monster won't come to us, it's time to wake the monster. *I* will be the storm that gets me to the sun."

Again, silence.

I didn't blame them. Candy's ass didn't lie. However, the message she'd received was cryptic, with no actionable information. Waiting wasn't working. I believed I knew who the monster was, and I was going to draw him out. He may not technically be a dragon, but he'd created a hoard, and power was his goal. I refused to let Gideon die when there was something I could do.

"You're all free to leave," I said. My hands sparked. My eyes glowed and bathed the room in a golden light. A magical wind swirled around me. The tension I felt caused a rumble of thunder to roll through the house. "I'm making an executive decision that could end badly. And when I say badly, I mean *badly*. I don't expect you to back it. There will be no hard feelings if you disagree. Illusions are hidden in plain sight—right under our noses. The clues are there. It's a matter of following them. I'm going to do that."

"I ain't goin' nowhere, jackass," Candy grunted. The Keeper of Fate was glowing. She shoved an entire piece of pizza into her mouth and kept talking. "I think you're fuckin' nuts, but I'm in. That whack job Lilith said that the words might be as much of an illusion as the answers we seek. My ass might have said not to wake the monster, but from where I stand, the fucker is already awake."

Tim got to his feet. He was not socially awkward at all. He glowed, as well. The fury in his eyes was difficult to look at. For all Tim's kindness and goodness, he was a terrifying badass in his own right. "I am not going anywhere. I will fight by your side, Daisy. Candy Vargo is correct. The monster is awake. It's time to draw him into the storm."

Heather joined the standing duo and made it a trio. "We've collected the words as Lilith suggested—the words of Agnes, the words of Gideon and the words we've shared with each other. We're ready for the monster. I'm in."

"Darlings," Dirk said, jumping to his feet and throwing his hands in the air. His horns popped out, and his eyes were deep pools of jet black. "The boys and I have never had friends until now. No one wants to hang with the Four Horsemen of the Apocalypse. But you people? You people are my people now. You have my word I will kill the shit out of anyone who means you harm. And just a heads up… I'm *fabulous* at the killing thing. I'm with you till the end."

Rafe stood up and gave me a tight smile. "It should go without saying that I'm with you, sister. However, I will say it.

Your mercy gave Prue, Abby, Gabe and myself a chance at life —a real life. There's nothing I can do to repay that. It's but a small gesture to stand with you, and I shall do so until the end of time."

I kind of felt like crying, but sucked it back. I would continue to separate the head and the heart. I refused to let one of them break. There was too much on the line.

Tory was the last one to stand. I had no idea if she would stay or go. Either way, she had become dear to me. She'd been through a life of agony. If she'd had enough, that was fair. There would be no judgement if she chose to leave.

She stared at the floor for a moment then raised her silver eyes to mine. "I wanted to hate all of you. You've made that very difficult. I can't say I like any of you, but I can say I don't hate you. New for me. While what Gabe and I shared is dead, I choose to fight for his life. It will be a final thank you for the years he made me whole."

"He still loves you," Rafe said.

"Irrelevant," she shot back harshly. "Love is not meant for people like me. However, loyalty I understand. Daisy helped the wraiths. She gave them mercy." Her unusual eyes bored into mine. "I owe you. I don't leave debts unpaid. I will stand with you."

"I require no repayment," I told her.

"But I do," Tory said. The grayness around her grew almost black. "My payment for staying will be that Zadkiel is returned to Purgatory. He deserves to live with the pain he wrought on the Souls of the Martyrs until Judgement Day. His ears will hear every scream of the innocents he betrayed. His eyes will observe the suffering and anguish he caused. His heart will break as the misery and trauma embeds itself in his lifeless organ. Zadkiel will live in the Hell that he created. There will be no refuge from the anguish—nowhere to hide from his sins. From now until the end of time, he will be tortured with the wretched decisions he made. The punishment fits the crimes."

"I like your fuckin' style, bestie," Candy commented. "That gal has some gnarly big lady-balls."

Tory ignored her and kept her intense gaze glued to mine.

I nodded. "Zadkiel will be returned to Purgatory. You have my word."

My army was assembled. It was time to walk headfirst into the storm. I had no clue where Charlie was or if he'd learned anything, but the waiting game was over. The sun would rise in the morning and I wanted Gideon by my side to watch it.

"Daisy," Rafe said in a worried tone, staring at his phone. "Prue just texted."

"And?"

"And there's an Immortal who has been casing the farmhouse for the last ten minutes."

"Tar Basilisk?" I demanded.

He shook his head. "Don't know. We've never seen him." He texted her back quickly then waited for a response. "They can tell he's male, but can't see his features in the dark."

"Fuck," Candy shouted, glowing dangerously. Tendrils of fire flew from her mouth with each word she spoke. "Get the ghosts back here now. I can't protect Gram if she's not here."

Adrenaline pumped through my veins. My vision blurred for a hot sec and my heart beat like a jackhammer in my chest. "Separate the head and the heart," I muttered to myself as I paced the room. Prue and Abby couldn't defend seventy-five ghosts against someone who had trapped Gideon and Gabe in a parallel plane. Candy was right. "Can Prue and Abby transport that many, including my dogs?"

Rafe texted and asked. The reply was immediate. "Yes. Without a doubt, they can."

"Do it," I commanded. "Now."

He texted. We waited.

Shortly there would be no more waiting. I was about to come between a dragon and his wrath.

CHAPTER SEVENTEEN

THE ARRIVAL OF THE DEAD COINCIDED WITH THE RETURN OF Charlie. My relief at seeing him was enormous. The Enforcer was one of the deadliest and most powerful Immortals in existence. While I was thankful the ghosts were home, their behavior was out of control. They were frantic. They flew around the house and created a wind that ripped curtains from the rods and upended furniture. The pile of body parts accumulating in the kitchen was absurd. The more frenzied they became, the more legs and arms dropped to the ground.

"FREEZE!" I bellowed as a ghost flew right through me, causing me to double over in pain. It felt like an icy knife had pierced my chest. I glanced down to make sure I wasn't bleeding out. I wasn't. My clothes weren't even torn. It took me a minute to gather myself and be able to speak without saying something awful. The ghost, whichever one it was, didn't mean to hurt me. However, a few ground rules needed to be set immediately. "I need everyone to calm down."

My dead guests were still wild-eyed, but they were no

longer wrecking the house. They floated en masse in front of me.

"Here's the plan," I announced. "First off, let's refrain from flying through people who are alive. It smarts." It was a woeful understatement, but I didn't want to hurt anyone's feelings. "And secondly, in an orderly manner—which means quietly and without destruction—I want you to grab a body part from the kitchen and head upstairs. It doesn't matter if the arm, leg or head belongs to you. We'll figure that out later." I had a tube of superglue in my pocket and about seven cases in the pantry. I wasn't sure that was enough to put everyone back together, but I'd cross that bridge when I got to it. "There's a TV in the master bedroom." I turned to Heather. "Can you put on the game show channel?"

"On it," she said, racing up the stairs.

"You will pick up your pieces and in a single file line, you'll go upstairs," I instructed the hovering crew. "You'll be safer there."

"We can go with them," Prue said, referring to her and Abby.

I looked over at my sisters. They had come so far. "Excellent. If I need you to get them out of here, I'll send word."

"Liiiiiikah Pruuuuuuah," a gentleman who had to be in his eighties informed me, doing flips in the air. He was missing half of his head and his left foot. "Shhhhheeeeah fuuunnneeeeeee!"

"Mr. Jackson, behave yourself," Prue said with a chuckle. "He likes knock-knock jokes."

I smiled for real. The simple amidst the crazy was welcome. "Knock-knock," I said to a grinning Mr. Jackson.

"Whoooooosah theeeereah?" he asked, quivering with excitement.

"Goat."

Goooatha whoooooooooooooo?"

"Goat to the master bedroom and find out," I replied with a grin.

The ghosts went nuts. Their laughter sounded like a roomful of people choking to death, but it warmed my soul.

"Knooockah-knooockah," Mr. Jackson said, returning the favor.

He was so darn sweet, I played along. "Who's there?"

"Haaatchah!"

I already knew this one. However, far be it from me to ruin a good knock-knock joke. "Hatch who?"

"Bleeeesah yooouah!"

Again, the dead loved it. They were a very easily amused audience. "One more. Knock-knock."

In unison, all seventy-five answered. It was eerily beautiful. "Whooooooosah theeeereah?"

"Anita," I replied.

"Annnitaaah whooooooooooooo?" they demanded in a fit of giggles.

"Anita you to grab your parts and skedaddle," I told them.

I didn't have to ask twice. In a mostly orderly manner, they grabbed feet, hands, arms, legs, heads and even a few rear ends, and floated up the stairs. Prue, Abby and my fur babies followed them up.

"Gram and Agnes, please stay," I requested.

"I ain't goin' nowhere, Daisy girl," Gram said, zipping over with Agnes on her transparent heels.

"Right here and at your service, Puddin'," Agnes added.

They hovered next to me silently. I smiled at both of the gals.

Charlie approached with a grim expression. Even if he

hadn't learned anything, having him with me made me feel stronger and more confident.

He hadn't come back empty-handed. He rarely did.

"We're searching for an Immortal known as the Collector," he said, taking a slice of pizza from Tim with a grateful nod. "He's been off the grid for centuries. Most thought him dead. A few thousand years ago, he abducted Immortals and drained their power. He was known as the dragon. Basically, kept a hoard and systematically destroyed everyone in it. He increased his power tenfold. It's rumored he's the Immortal who can create parallel planes."

"How?" I asked.

"I don't know," Charlie ground out. "No one knows. He was hunted for hundreds of years by some of the most powerful... including your father. When he wasn't found, he was assumed to be dead. Never assume..."

"I think the Collector has been here already," I told Charlie.

He squinted at me in confusion. I was a little confused as well. Why had he left? If his hoard was here, why hadn't he claimed it? I wouldn't think Dip's presence would have mattered. A human was easily dispensable to someone who was draining and killing Immortals for their magic. However, I couldn't shake the feeling the man was deeply involved somehow. If he wasn't the monster, he was working with him. He had to be.

"An Immortal showed up pretending to be a detective from Atlanta. He came with Dip. They were looking to arrest Micky Muggles."

Now Charlie was very confused. "Micky Muggles is a cop, as far as I knew."

"Was," I told him. "He got caught having sex in his cruiser, and they believe he stole some expensive coins from the museum. But he said he didn't steal them."

"I am not following this at all," Charlie said. "Why would they think Micky Muggles was here of all places, and how do you know he didn't steal the coins?"

"He's sleeping in his car in the field," Candy Vargo volunteered. "Pled his innocence and asked Daisy for mercy."

Charlie stared at me with a raised brow and waited for an explanation.

I ran my hands through my hair and dove right in. With each word I shared, including the wrapping paper sale earlier in the day, letting Micky stay in the field until morning sounded stupider and stupider. When I got done, Charlie inhaled deeply and blew it out slowly. It felt like I'd disappointed my dad. It sucked.

"My opinion of you showing the strange man mercy is irrelevant," Charlie stated, making his view quite clear by not commenting. "What I'm more interested in is why you believe the Collector was here?"

"Gut feeling," I replied. "He's Immortal. He was terrifying and seemed to be aware that Gideon wasn't here."

"The Collector's gonna be a dead motherfucker shortly," Candy Vargo growled.

Charlie gave her an irate glare. "Not until he returns Gideon, Gabe and Zadkiel," he admonished her sharply.

"And another," I said quickly. "There's a woman there too."

"Name?" he demanded.

I shook my head. "She said the word cat, but there was more they couldn't understand. Gideon doesn't think she has much time left. When they tried to help her, they realized their magic was somehow being siphoned."

Charlie banged his fist on the coffee table and split it right down the middle.

Agnes floated over with a serious expression on her normally carefree face. "I know how a parallel plane is created, or at least how I created them in my stories."

Was I really going to take fictional advice from a dead romance writer?

Yes. Yes, I was.

She'd been more right about the shitshow than anyone else. There was nothing to lose and possibly everything to gain.

"How?" I asked.

No one looked at me like I was crazy. I took that as a good sign.

"Parveit, Lord of The Red would choose a ley line to house his hoard," she explained. "Because of the strength of the magic, he was able to use an ancient spell to create the parallel plane and hide his treasure."

"Which consisted of other dragons," Candy added.

I glanced over at Tim. He pressed his temples and sighed. "Your house is on a ley line," he confirmed.

"What in the ever-lovin' heck is a ley line?" Gram asked.

"A ley line in layman's terms—no pun intended," Tim said, "is a place where the magic is stronger. In a more specific explanation, a human amateur archaeologist by the name of Alfred Watkins made an interesting discovery in the year 1921. He argued that different historical sites—both man-made and natural—fell into somewhat of a line. The man believed the lines had power. He coined the term ley lines and opened up a whole world of supernatural thinking and superstitions. Of course, Immortals are aware of and have used ley lines since the beginning of time. Often, you'll find many of us living near or within a stone's throw of the magical areas. We don't call them ley lines, though."

Tim's knowledge never ceased to amaze me.

"Parveit, Lord of The Red called them enchanted thaumaturgy bands," Agnes piped in.

Tim's mouth fell open in shock. Candy Vargo dropped an F-bomb that made the house shake on its foundation. Charlie's eyes spit icy-blue sparks. Heather's tattoos began to race over her skin. Rafe and Tory looked at Agnes like she'd grown an extra head. Dirk dropped a piece of pizza on his gown and screamed. I wasn't sure if it was because his pink-sequined gown was covered in red sauce and ruined or if it was Agnes' words.

"Repeat," Charlie said, holding on to his composure with great effort.

Tim carefully put his hand on Charlie's arm and waved his other in front of his mouth and nose to indicate it was hard to breathe. Charlie tamped back his power. I sucked in a huge breath of air just in case Charlie slipped up. Breathing was necessary.

Agnes looked worried and began to wring her hands. Tory moved to her and touched her face. She calmed immediately.

"Did I say something wrong?" she whispered. Charlie could be terrifying and Agnes was scared.

"No, friend," Tim said. "You said something right. Something you have no way of knowing. Did you make up the term enchanted thaumaturgy bands for your novel?"

She shook her head and kept her eyes on Charlie. "No. Mr. Handyman came up with it and I loved it. He took a real liking, almost an ownership, to Parveit, Lord of the Red—came up with all sorts of things I used in the stories."

"Oh my God," I choked out, dropping onto the couch and

putting my head in my hands. "Do we have the wrong monster? Do we have to start back at square one and find the freaking handyman?"

"We might have screwed the pooch," Candy Vargo stated flatly.

I didn't like the saying, but I agreed.

"What did Mr. Handyman look like?" Tory asked Agnes.

Agnes had seen Tar Basilisk. He was not the handyman.

"A few days ago, before I knew the bastard killed me, I would have said tall, dark and handsome," Agnes admitted sheepishly. "Love can blind people. Today, I'd describe him as short, stinky and stuck in a time warp. I mean, some might say I'm a fashion faux pas with my big hair and all, but Mr. Handyman takes the cake—a big, fat, heinous, ugly cake."

She wasn't making sense. I also had to stop myself from commenting that a cake filled with prescription-grade potassium killed her along with her Tang. Agnes already knew that. She was dead and getting more transparent. Upsetting her unnecessarily wouldn't help. The fading of a ghost was always the first thing to happen as they prepared to move on. After that, speech became difficult to understand, followed by the loss of body parts. I knew it would distress Agnes to fall apart. I didn't want that for her, but it was beyond my control.

It was also becoming increasingly clear that her books weren't exactly fiction...

"We're fucked," Heather muttered.

My sister wasn't one to F-bomb it. I was pretty sure I was going to puke. Time was now of the essence since I knew Gideon and Gabe were losing power.

"Darlings!" Dirk said, wiping at the stain on his gown with a napkin and making it worse. "Illusions. Don't discard the illusions."

"Keep talking," Charlie insisted.

"What I'm saying is that the monster took on Daisy's form. He's adept at illusion. Tar Basilisk could be yet another illusion or possibly the real visage of the beast… or simply an uninvolved asshole with an authority complex. Or Mr. Handyman is the true visage. Doesn't matter." Dirk gave up on trying to clean his dress. He snapped his fingers and went from a pink-sequined gown to a peach silk number trimmed in marabou. "I do believe that is how he evaded everyone for so many centuries—he just changed faces and bodies. All of these people—Mr. Handyman, Tar and the clone of Daisy—could be one in the same… I think. Maybe. Or maybe not. I'm such an indecisive queen."

I closed my eyes and tried not to lose my shit. It would be bad form for the gal in charge to curl up into a ball on the floor and spew out a few primal screams. My gut instinct might be letting me down for the first time.

Nothing lasts forever.

"The name, the aggressive behavior, the fact that he's Immortal… all important," Tim pointed out. "If Tar Basilisk is not the monster—which I'm leaning towards he is—I feel like he could lead us to him."

"Fuckin' A," Candy Vargo agreed, handing out toothpicks to all. "Jackass?"

I wasn't crazy about her term of endearment for me, but discussing it could end in electrocution. "Yes?"

"You still have that motherfucker's card?"

I pulled it out of my pocket and showed it to her. "I do."

"Use it," she said.

I stared at it. The storm would come on its own eventually. We didn't have time to wait for it. The poor woman who was close to death didn't have time to wait. I had no clue how much longer Gideon and Gabe would last. I even worried about Zadkiel. He didn't deserve my compassion, but it was mine to give as I wanted.

"Is everyone ready for a storm?" I asked, pulling out my cell phone.

"A regular one or a shitstorm?" Candy inquired with a grin.

I grinned back. "A shitstorm. Definitely a shitstorm."

CHAPTER EIGHTEEN

THE CALL TOOK ALL OF TWO MINUTES. I'D PUT TAR BASILISK ON speaker so everyone could hear. Every second of it was unnerving. He was expecting my call. It was clear from the arrogant and condescending tone of his voice. When I'd suggested he wasn't who he said he was, he laughed.

He insinuated I had something that belonged to him. I pressed for what it was, and he refused to answer. I assumed he meant his hoard. However, Charlie had pointed out earlier that it was not smart to assume... made an ass out of you and me. I could only go on what I knew. While I didn't know much, I knew enough to be dangerous and on the defensive.

I accused him of casing my old farmhouse. He denied it. He inquired if my partner in crime would be present. I told him I had no clue who he was talking about. Again, he laughed. The laugh was vicious. When I asked him to come over to talk, he immediately inquired how many other Immortals would be present.

I lied.

He knew, I suspected. He said he would arrive in half an hour.

I found that strange since the man could clearly transport and be here in seconds. It made me wary.

The storm was rumbling, and it would unleash its full strength shortly.

"Not sure lyin' was the way to go, Daisy girl," Gram said. "Truth is easier to remember."

"He knows she's lying." Tim confirmed my suspicion. "For all we know, he is as well."

"Who is my partner in crime?" I asked.

Candy shrugged. "Don't know. Maybe me. I'm not real well-liked."

Charlie paced the room. "We're going to need more backup. If Tar Basilisk is indeed the Collector, we can't let him get away this time."

Candy Vargo narrowed her eyes. The Keeper of Fate was not one to trust easily. "Who?"

Charlie paused in thought, then sighed. "Abaddon," he finally said.

"That Demon is whacked," Candy grunted.

Charlie eyed her for a long moment. "As are you. As am I. As are all of us. What is your point?"

Candy laughed. "No point. Just an observation."

"Abaddon and Gideon have a bond. He and I have a bond," I said. "I can call him. He'll come."

"Not so fast. You already owe one Demon. I'm not sure it's prudent to owe two," Heather said. "More importantly, I believe you're forgetting about someone."

"Who?" I asked.

"Me, darling!" Dirk squealed. "You've never seen me turn it on! I've been compared to the Tasmanian devil on crack but with far more style. Oh, and I make an African wild dog look like a sweet puppy. And honey badgers? Forget about them. I could take on a thousand without mussing my wig. Of course, I was created to kill... I am Death, after all."

Dirk's teeth extended grotesquely to razor-sharp points, and his manicured nails became deadly claws. His black eyes glittered ominously, and his horns spewed fire. Not surprisingly, his dress and wig were pristine and perfect. It was a horrifying look and the peach marabou made it even more scary.

"I stand corrected," Charlie said, bowing his head in respect to the queen. "We need no one else."

"Fabulous!" Dirk sang as he pranced around the room, swishing his peach frock with his claws. "I shall not let you down."

"And don't forget, in a pinch, I can eat the fucker," Candy Vargo reminded everyone.

No one commented. I truly hoped it didn't come to that. The visual could not be unseen.

"Shit," Tory cried out. "Daisy, help."

I whipped around and my stomach sank. The timing was not good. It was terrible.

Agnes was no longer a transparent corpse. She was still dead. An ethereal and somewhat blinding golden glow surrounded my friend, and her body was restored to what it was before she'd passed. She was adorable. Agnes' eyes twinkled, and her silly grin would stay etched in my memories.

I smiled at the romance writer who'd provided most of the clues to our deadly puzzle. She waved back. Reaching out, I touched the golden glow surrounding her. It was warm and inviting and, as always, felt like silky liquid.

"I think it's time for me to leave, Puddin'," she said with a giggle.

Candy Vargo was openly crying. It made me sad. Candy worshiped Agnes Bubbala.

"I'm not sure I've helped you enough," I said, concerned I hadn't done right by her with everything going on.

I wasn't God, nor did I have a God complex like Tory had accused me of. I didn't make the timetable for the dead to move on. When they were ready, they left me. It was always heartbreaking. I'd only known Agnes a short time, but she was truly delightful. I'd miss her and I'd grown awfully fond of being called Puddin'.

Agnes waved her hands and fluffed her 1980s hairdo. "I disagree, Puddin'. I believe knowing how I died and who did it was my unfinished business. And do you want to know what else I think?"

"I do," I told her with a wide smile.

"I think I might have stuck around longer than I was supposed to just so I could help you." She clasped her hands together and winked at me.

I approached the sweet gal and put my hands over hers. They were no longer papery and cold. They were warm and soft. Her cheeks were rosy and her hair, in all its blonde glory, was a sight to behold. It had to have taken a full can of hairspray to make it so big.

"I think you're correct," I told her. "Thank you."

"Right back at you! Can I share a few more tidbits that might help?" she asked.

"Absolutely," I said. She was beginning to fade. "I would be ever so grateful, Agnes Bubbala, famous romance writer."

"Don't forget *New York Times* Best-fuckin'-seller," Candy choked out through her sobs.

"And *New York Times* Bestseller," I added. I omitted the fuck. It wasn't the way I rolled.

Agnes leaned toward me. "The reason Parveit, Lord of The Red was able to get away with being such a shit for so long was that he was able to hide his essence. He hid in plain sight."

"His essence?" I asked, not quite getting it. I reminded myself Parveit, Lord of The Red wasn't a real person... or even dragon, since they didn't exist, but I listened carefully. Lilith had said words were important and to collect them.

"His stank," Candy chimed in, still sniffling.

Agnes winced. "Umm... no. Not exactly. He was able to disguise who he was. He got others to trust him. That's when he struck. He was able to slide under the radar for many moons."

"That's decades in dragon-speak," Candy added. She was a hardcore Agnes Bubbala fan until the very end... which was fast approaching.

"Was that your idea or Mr. Handyman's?" I asked.

"Mine and Mr. Handyman's, Puddin'."

It seemed as if the factual parts of her fiction came from Mr. Handyman. It was possible Mr. Handyman was a lonely Immortal who'd found a friend in Agnes... who then turned out to be a murdering asshole. Maybe he wasn't one of the monster's facades. Figuring that one out might take some time. Although, the man could have very well been a human. It was just too coincidental that he knew the term "enchanted thaumaturgy bands". The shocked reaction from my family and friends had been very telling and unsettling.

"Thank you, Agnes, for everything," I said. "You're free to move on now."

Most of the ghosts went into the light rather quickly. Not Agnes. Nothing about the lovely gal was ordinary.

"You know," she mused aloud. "I think I'll stick around a little longer."

"Umm… okay. Not sure that's how it works," I told her.

She laughed. "I'm a rule-breaker, Puddin'."

Candy Vargo walked over to Agnes and slapped her hands on her hips. "How in the fuck am I supposed to finish writing *Call Me Daddy Dragon* without you?"

"Whoops! Forgot about that, Cupcake," she said, scrunching her nose in thought. "Wait! I have an idea of how you can do it alone."

Candy stopped crying and wiped her nose with her sleeve. She went from devastated to thrilled. "Fuck to the yes!"

"In my desk at home, there's a folder labeled Shit Pile," she explained.

Tim pulled out his notebook and wrote down what Agnes was saying. Candy patted her friend on the back in thanks.

"Shit Pile, you say?" Tim inquired, unsure if he'd heard correctly.

"Yes, sweetie. When I get stuck on a story at the computer, I write long hand. The folder contains deleted scenes from different stories and, for some silly reason, I ended up putting a semi-fleshed-out plot outline for *Call Me Daddy Dragon* in there. Go to my house and get the folder. It will guide you, Cupcake!"

Candy curtsied to Agnes. It looked like she was taking a dump. But with Candy, it was substance over style. "It would be my honor."

Agnes eyeballed Candy then gave her a warning. "No excessive violence. No castration or cannibalism. Do not use the word stank. And take it easy on the F-bombs, please."

Gram floated over and said her piece. "Agnes, I'll make sure our gal follows the rules. If she don't, she'll get a whoppin' that will make her rump hurt for a year. You don't worry your head about it."

"Thank you," Agnes told Gram with relief. "I know Cupcake has the passion. I'm just a bit concerned about the performance."

"No worries!" Candy promised, so excited she was bouncing on her toes. "Gram ain't joshin'. She'll kick my fuckin' ass into the next century if I don't obey. I've got this, Agnes Bubbala. I'll do you proud."

Agnes smiled at her biggest fan. "I know you will, Cupcake. I believe in you."

Candy turned around and faced all of us. "Did you mother-fuckers hear that?" she yelled. "Agnes Bubbala believes in me!" She elbowed Tim. "Write that in your notes too."

"But of course, friend," he replied with a smile.

"Darlings, we have a potential snafu," Dirk said with an expression of what I thought was concern on his face. I wasn't positive. The sharp fangs made it hard to tell.

"What?" Heather asked.

"The dirtbag in the field," he said. "Not sure he'll make it through the storm."

"Oh my God," I muttered. I'd forgotten all about Micky Muggles. Yes, he was gross. Yes, he was an idiot. However, he didn't deserve to die for something he had nothing to do with. Plus, Tar Basilisk had made it very clear he wanted a piece of the creepy ex-cop. "He has to leave. Now."

"On it," Charlie said. "Tory, will you join me?"

Tory's brow arched in surprise. "Me? You want me to come with you?"

"I do," he replied. "I trust you."

Tory's pale skin blushed pink. It was an honor indeed to

have the Enforcer believe in you. Charlie's reputation was legendary, and he didn't suffer fools. Ever.

"Of course," she said, pulling herself together.

Charlie also wasn't stupid. Showing respect, gained respect. He'd shown his publicly for a reason. It worked. Tory stood taller and had a difficult time hiding her joy.

"Go," I said, checking my watch. "Tar Basilisk will be here in ten."

In a shimmering mist, they disappeared. My relief was visceral.

They were back in thirty seconds. My relief was replaced by tension.

"Umm…" It should have taken a little longer to convince Micky Muggles to vacate the premises. He was an idiot and needed everything spelled out.

"He's gone," Tory said. "There are tire tracks and no car."

"He's been gone for a while," Charlie added. "I detected no recent exhaust fumes in the air. They last for about an hour. He's been gone at least that long."

"You can smell gas fumes?" I asked. I don't know why anything surprised me anymore.

"See," he corrected me. "I can see the residues of gasses and poisons."

"That's a handy trick," I told him.

He smiled. "I have many."

I was sure he did.

"Five minutes, kiddos!" Gram said, darting around the living room.

"Gram, I want you to go upstairs with the other ghosts. I can't keep you safe and I don't want to worry about you."

Gram hesitated. Candy Vargo stepped in.

"You recall that whoopin' you threatened me with?" she asked with a sly grin.

"I do, little missy," Gram told her with a smile pulling at her lips.

"Well, I love your crazy ass so much, that I will whoop the heck out of it if you don't listen to Jackass."

I rolled my eyes. Puddin', I liked. Jackass, not as much. But it did the trick. Candy could call me jackass till the end of time —which I was pretty sure she would do—as long as she kept Gram safe.

"Fine," Gram said with a cackle as she floated over to the stairs. "I'll go on up, but you youngins be careful. You hear me? If you don't, there's gonna be a round of whoopin's none of y'all will forget anytime soon!"

A chorus of yes, ma'ams came from the crowd. It satisfied Gram and she left the room.

"And so it begins," Dirk said in a much deeper voice than usual.

He was correct. The storm had arrived.

CHAPTER NINETEEN

THE STORM CREATED ITS OWN EERIE SONG IN THE BRANCHES OF the leafless winter trees. It was a warning to stay inside. That wasn't an option. If I wanted to see the sun, I had to weather the storm. The storm wasn't allowed in my home. Period.

"I'm going outside," I said, quickly pulling on a jacket. "I want a ward put around the house. Charlie, Candy, Heather and Tim, can you do that?"

I hoped the ward would protect the house in this plane and in the one that held the love of my life. Gideon, Gabe, Zadkiel, the unnamed woman who I'd mentally named Cat, and the ghosts needed to stay safe. If the house went down, I wasn't sure that was possible. It also had the potential of keeping the monster from his hoard. If he wasn't able to get to them, he might not be able to destroy them.

"Yes," Charlie said, putting on his coat and barking out instructions. "Everyone outside. Candy, go to the back of the house. Tim, right side. Heather, left. I'll stay toward the front but hidden from sight." He checked his watch. "In two minutes from now, cast the spell. We must do it at the same time. Leave about six feet of buffer. When the house is warded, go to the front yard."

"Roger that," Candy said, sprinting out of the back door.

Tim and Heather used the same exit.

"Tory and Dirk, flank me," I said, moving to the front door as Charlie used the kitchen door.

"Always, darling," Dirk said with his horns on fire.

For a brief moment, I wondered if the rain would extinguish the flame and ruin his dress. It was a random thought and made me chuckle. In the midst of war, the little things that made me think helped me stay calm. I pinched my weenus for extra piece of mind. It wasn't great since I was wearing a coat, but it helped.

"What are you doing?" Tory asked.

"Squeezing my weenus," I replied.

"Brilliant!" Dirk squealed, as he pinched his own. "The magic of the weenus cannot be denied!"

Tory rolled her eyes, but pinched her weenus. It was absurd. We were some of the most powerful people on the planet, yet, we were gripping our elbow skin like it was a magic bullet. Whatever. It certainly couldn't hurt.

I opened the door and walked into the storm.

"Gideon, I'm doing this for you. I love you."

There was no answer. I'd hoped for one, but hadn't expected it. My words held true whether he could hear me or not.

The nighttime sky was blacker than usual. The stars had hidden and the moon wasn't visible. The wind was as furious as a hurricane. It tore through the landscape with a frenzied high-pitched screech. Trees uprooted as the gales screamed a tune that would visit my nightmares. The gorgeous oaks and willows twisted in the violent gusts and shattered into kindling.

I felt a jolt of energy as the ward dropped around the house. My sigh of relief was momentary when I realized Agnes had not stayed inside.

"Agnes," I shouted over the storm. "Go into the light. NOW."

The thought of her being destroyed terrified me. She still had a chance. The blinding yellow glow surrounded her and kept her safe from the vicious weather. However, I didn't think it would keep her safe from the monster. Tory turned and pushed against the ward to find a spot to shove Agnes back in. It was futile. Charlie, Heather, Candy and Tim didn't screw around. It was impenetrable.

"Puddin'," Agnes said far too calmly for what was going down. "I can't. I need to see how the story ends."

There was no time to fight with her.

With the storm overhead, it was difficult to be heard. I glanced wildly around for Tar Basilisk. He wasn't there. Or at least not where I could see him. The crashes of lightning and the booms of the thunder were so loud, I put my hands over my ears. It didn't help. Being in the middle of the raging storm seemed like a stupid plan, but it was also the only plan we had.

Candy, Tim, Charlie and Heather had joined us in the front yard. Everyone scanned the turbulent landscape, searching for the monster.

"Where is the fucker?" Candy bellowed.

No one had an answer.

The rain came down in torrents, soaking us to the skin. I barely felt it. My most fervent wish was that it would wash away the vile situation we were in. That wasn't going to happen. That wasn't the job of the rain. It was my job.

Charlie touched my back and pointed. "The field," he shouted. "I think the field is the eye of the storm."

Cupping my hands above my eyes so I could see through the downpour, I looked in the direction he pointed. He was correct. It appeared that the field where Gideon and Gabe had disappeared was the quiet eye of the deadly storm.

"Follow me," I shouted to my small but powerful army. We stood a better chance without the wind blowing us around like rag dolls.

I was faster than everyone and made it to the field in seconds. Tar Basilisk appeared in an explosion of black and golden glitter. He glanced around in shock and fury. When his gaze landed on me, his eyes narrowed to slits.

I was struck by the unusual colors of his eyes—one glowed gold, one was sparkling blood-red. He was a mix of species, Angel and Demon... just like my daughter. The man's outer beauty was undeniable. However, his pretty exterior belied his putrid insides.

"Was this necessary?" he demanded, waving his hand at the storm raging all around the outer rim of the field.

"I could ask you the same question," I ground out.

He appeared confused. I wasn't buying it. The monster had gotten away with his evil for thousands of years. Playing games was in his nature. I was going to beat him this time.

"Stop the storm," he growled.

I rolled my eyes. "I didn't start it, asshole. That's on you."

Where were the others? I didn't want to take my eyes off of the dangerous prize, but it was odd they weren't here yet. I took the chance of glancing over my shoulder and gasped. They were about forty feet away and unable to reach me.

The monster had dropped a bubble around us. I no longer had backup to fight the evil man. I was on my own. The only positive was that the storm was outside of the bubble. I had a better chance of defeating him if I wasn't blinded by the rain. I slid out of my coat. It was soaked and weighing me down.

Tar Basilisk glowed dangerously as a fire of his own making licked up his large body. I'd never seen anything like it. The red and orange flames danced over his jeans and parka but didn't come close to setting him ablaze. His power was evident. It was massive.

So was mine.

The man appeared unhinged. That was fine. I could use it to my advantage. If he lost control, he'd be sloppy and emotional. Being emotional and sloppy equated to being dead. Lilith said to separate the head and the heart. It was exactly what I was going to do.

I gauged the bubble around us to be about the size of half a football field. A grove of pine trees was behind the enemy. A slight movement in the tree line caught my eye—and my heart sank.

Micky Muggles had not left the property. He'd obviously moved his car. I didn't see it anywhere. He shook like a leaf and had an expression of terror on his face.

I didn't blame him. This was a lot for an Immortal to handle. To a human's mind, this had to be a living nightmare. The only solace I had was that if Micky Muggles lived, Tim could erase his memories.

Micky waved. I ignored him. Tar wanted the human dead. That wasn't going to happen on my watch. Maybe Micky *had* banged his gal pal. I couldn't wrap my mind around that, but beauty was in the eye of the beholder.

I just hoped the idiot had the smarts to stay out of sight.

"Where's your partner in evil?" Tar bellowed.

My fingers sparked and I could feel a destructive magic

bubbling inside me. It was dark. Abaddon had given me some of his Demon blood to fight Zadkiel. I was told the effects would wear off, but I could still feel it entangled with my own energy. My desire to end the monster warred with every compassionate tendency I owned.

I squinted at the Angel/Demon. "I have no evil partner, asshole."

His roar of fury set the tree line behind him ablaze. Out of the corner of my eye, I saw a deathly scared Micky Muggles relocate behind a large rock. I wanted to save the dummy, but there was too much to lose if I tried. The bubble around us was unbreakable. All of the Immortals on the other side were trying to get through, to no avail.

Candy circled the barrier and threw fireballs every several feet. They bounced right back at her. That didn't stop the Keeper of Fate. Dirk flew above the bubble and tried to tear his way through with his fangs and claws. It was useless. It was also horrifying to glance up and see him in is full badass glory. No movie or book had ever created a being as fearsome as what Dirk had become. The delightful queen was nowhere to be seen. My friend personified Death and then some.

"Give me what's mine, or you will die, you scum," Tar shouted.

"Pot, kettle, black," I shot back.

He didn't like that. Too bad, so sad.

I swallowed back all the other ugly things I wanted to yell. I needed something from him. I needed it badly. To get it, he had to stay alive… for a little while. As much as I wanted to turn him to dust, I needed the ancient spell he had used to create the parallel plane. Without it, I couldn't get to Gideon. Of course, I was working off a piece of fiction, but it was all I had, and I was going for it.

Tar thought I had something of his. Maybe I could make a trade… Although, if it was his hoard, then it was a no-go. That didn't make sense, though. If he'd hidden his hoard here, he should be able to get to it. Maybe the ward around the house posed a problem. If so, that was very good news.

"What do I have that's yours?" I asked calmly, holding my sparking hands out in front of me as a warning.

"Playing stupid is beneath you," he snarled. "But I should have expected it. It's shocking that you've been able to hide your true age. How did you do it?"

"What the hell are you talking about?" I hissed.

"You're not forty. More like forty thousand," he said icily. "How did you fool the Grim Reaper?"

This dude wasn't working on all cylinders. He was nuts. I looked damned good for forty. My brain raced with all the ways I could handle the bizarre situation. Gram had said that lying wasn't smart and that the truth was easier to remember, but that was when one was dealing with a sane individual. Tar Basilisk wasn't sane. He was the opposite.

I decided to play along. Although, I stayed just vague enough not to enrage him. He was already a loose cannon. "Age is just a number. Unimportant."

I hadn't even lied. Gram would approve.

He laughed. It was ugly.

I rolled my eyes. I shouldn't have.

In the millisecond that I took my eyes off the man, he sent a zap of magic my way that threw me against the side of the bubble like a ball out of a cannon. I was sure a few of my ribs were broken. Getting air into my lungs was a chore. However, two could play his game.

I jumped to my feet and ignored the searing pain in my torso. I wiggled my fingers. A massive tree came down on the monster with a sickening thud and trapped him beneath it. I wasn't a fool. He wouldn't be down for long. Slashing my hands through the air, I sent a bolt of electricity that exploded when it hit him.

He slammed the ground with his fists and caused a massive crater beneath my feet. As I fell in, I threw another electrocution his way. He roared his displeasure and dove into the crater.

This wasn't going to end well. He advanced on me like a rabid animal. Snapping my fingers, I levitated out of the hole. The monster was right behind me.

My fury bubbled up to the surface. The hideous man was trying his best to end me. He'd taken Gideon and Gabe. He'd destroyed so many over the centuries. I wasn't going to be part of the Collector's collection.

I froze for a moment. A strange déjà vu came over me, but I couldn't pinpoint what it was. The keyword was collection. However, a fireball the size of an SUV was headed my way and needed to be avoided. Figuring out a déjà vu wasn't on the agenda. Staying alive was.

We were both bleeding profusely. The banging and shouting on the other side of the bubble was loud. Understanding it was impossible. It was garbled. I couldn't spare a glance. Looking away from the monster would be the last thing I did. I was sure of it.

Blow after blow was traded. We both gave as good as we got. I pictured Gideon and Alana Catherine in my mind. They were who I fought for. The monster couldn't win.

My exhaustion was real. My body felt sluggish. Tar Basilisk was as strong as I was, if not stronger. Out of the corner of my eye, I saw Agnes Bubbala losing her shit. She was screaming and crying. She should have stayed in the house. This was too much for a human mind to take in.

The shot of magic Tar sent hit me in the stomach. I leaned forward and threw up.

He laughed.

I was done.

Slashing both hands through the air, I envisioned razor-sharp blades of fire. As if on command, they appeared in my waiting hands. With a scream of fury and fatigue, I threw them, aiming for his arms. They sliced right through and lopped the appendages off. The shocked expression on his bloody and bruised face would have been funny if the situation wasn't so deadly serious. I conjured up two more of the fiery weapons and removed the monster's legs.

Tar Basilisk was now a stump with a head.

He was pissed.

The appendages would grow back. He was Immortal.

Right now, it was information time.

Limping over to the bastard, I stopped a few feet away. I wasn't taking any chances.

"Give me the spell," I said flatly.

He writhed on the ground in pain. It was hard to watch and I didn't like knowing I was responsible. However, it was me or him, and I preferred me.

"I'll trade myself for her," he begged. "I'm far more power-ful. It's me you want."

Was he delirious? What was he talking about?

"Who?" I asked, wildly confused.

He glared at me. Even without arms and legs he was terri-fying. I took a cautious step back.

"Catriona," he snapped. "Trade me for my sister. You don't need her in your hoard if you have me."

It felt as if I was having an out-of-body experience. Gideon had said the woman had uttered the word cat. Was she trying to say Catriona? Was this man not the monster? Was he trying to do the same thing I was doing? Had I royally fucked up, as Candy Vargo would say? I moved quickly to Tar Basilisk and squatted down next to him.

"You're the Collector," I whispered.

He shook his head. "*You* are the Collector."

"I'm not," I said, unsure whether to trust him. "On my life, I'm not." My gut said he was also telling the truth, but my gut had been on the iffy side lately. "Your name—Tar Basilisk—it means dragon. A dragon collects hoards."

"My name is Zander," he said. "I used the name to draw the monster out. I felt its presence here."

"The hoard is here," I confirmed. "On a parallel plane in my home. My mate and my brother are in it. I'm trying to get them out."

We stared at each other in silence, trying to figure out if the other was lying.

"Break the bubble," I told him.

"I didn't create it," he said.

I inhaled deeply. If he hadn't—which I wasn't sure I believed—who had? Who was screwing with us? Or was I being naïve? The Collector was an excellent actor and liar.

I backed away from the man who called himself Zander and kept my eyes on him. He couldn't throw magic since he had no arms, but trusting him completely could easily be my final mistake.

When I got to the side of the bubble and took a quick look, the light around Agnes Bubbala grew almost blinding. All of my friends and family pointed and gestured frantically at her. She was talking a mile a minute, and I wasn't a terrific lip reader. I used my hands to indicate that she needed to slow down.

She did. And what she had to say changed everything.

"Mr. Handyman," she mouthed, pointing to the far side of the bubble.

My head whipped around, and my eyes landed on Micky Muggles. He stepped out from behind the rock and waved. My stomach lurched, and I shuddered with disgust. All the words I should have collected but missed came roaring to the forefront of my brain. The déjà vu hit me like a ton of bricks. Collections were the key. He was a collector. He'd told me himself.

Micky Muggles smiled. It was oily and triumphant.

I'd hurt someone badly who wasn't the monster. Granted, he'd hurt me too, thinking I was the monster. It was so incredibly senseless it was hard to absorb.

I'd sworn I wouldn't be stupid, but I had been. I'd been very stupid. All of the clues… the words I should have collected had been right under my nose in plain sight. The illusion had tricked me. And I'd dismembered the one Immortal who the Collector feared.

The words I'd missed danced in my head and mocked me. I didn't blame them. My lack of awareness could end some of those I loved the most.

Micky Muggles had laid it all out. *Nickname, the Draaagoon.* The sadistic man had told me he was the dragon. *Thank you, Daisy. Thank you so much. The Draaagoon thanks you!*

I'm a collector, he had said. *Beer cans, rabbits' feet and beautiful chest-blessed women, among other things. Can't call me stupid even though my ex-wife does.* The "other things" were what I should have paid attention to.

Agnes' words held more weight now as well… *Love can blind people. Today, I'd describe him as short, stinky and stuck in a time warp. I mean, some might say I'm a fashion faux pas with my big hair and all, but Mr. Handyman takes the cake.* The time warp was the 1980s. Micky Muggles' mullet was as bad as Agnes' teased and sprayed hairdo.

Tim's words were prophetic. I just didn't know at the time. *The name, the aggressive behavior, the fact that he's Immortal... all important. If Tar Basilisk is not the monster—I feel like he could lead us to him.*

My stomach roiled, and my body shook with rage. Without Zander, I wouldn't have found the Collector.

According to Agnes, the reason Parveit, Lord of The Red was able to get away with being such a shit for so long was that he was able to hide his essence. He hid in plain sight. He was able to disguise who he was. He got others to trust him. That's when he struck. He was able to slide under the radar for many moons.

Micky Muggles had slid under the radar for far more than many moons.

"Well, now," Micky Muggles said, walking across with field with a pep in his step and an evil glint in his eyes. "Have you figured it out, Angel of Mercy?"

My title on his lips made me want to hurl.

"You're the Collector," I stated flatly.

"Bingo," he replied gleefully, pulling a quarter out from behind his ear and offering it to me.

When I didn't take it, he dropped it on the ground and sneered. "Thought you had better manners than that, Daisy. You sure did back in high school."

"You thought wrong," I ground out, wondering if I could take him.

He grinned. "I've been waitin' on you to come into your

power for a long time. It's simply delicious." He licked his lips and winked.

He still seemed human to me—repulsive and human. I detected no Immortal footprint and couldn't gauge his power. The word illusion had come up with both Lilith and the Oracle. Its importance wasn't lost on me. The Collector was a master of illusion. He'd hidden who he was, and he'd somehow hidden his footprint.

The imbecile I'd known since high school stared at me. It occurred to me the Collector might not have any power at all. It could be why he continually stole it from others. However, he'd created the storm and the bubble. Was that his power or had he used up what he'd stolen from Catriona, Gideon and Gabe?

I wished I knew.

If wishes were horses, beggars would ride.

If I wanted something to happen, I had to make it happen. Micky was a talker. I'd get him to talk and pray that his arrogance would reveal what I needed.

"Why did you kill Agnes Bubbala?" I asked.

The Collector/ Mr. Handyman shrugged and waved at Agnes. She spat on the ground from outside the bubble and flipped him off. "She killed me. I returned the favor."

"From where I'm standing, you're unfortunately alive."

His chuckled. It was a hollow and obsequious sound. "I'm Parveit, Lord of the Red."

I couldn't help it. I rolled my eyes. "He's a fictional character."

"Was he?" the Collector inquired with an arched brow. "I think not. Agnes should never have killed him. I told her over and over it was wrong. She said the bad guys have to lose, and the good guys have to win. The bitch also said that love conquers all. She was incorrect. And now she's dead. Funny how the good guys tend to lose in real life…"

"Hilarious," I snapped. It was difficult to take an asshole with a combover seriously. However, I had to. He'd somehow abducted the Grim Reaper and the Archangel.

Over Micky's shoulder, I could see that Zander was healing. It wasn't fast enough to make a difference. If I kept the idiot monologuing, maybe Zander could be my second. Our goal was the same.

"How do you do it?" I asked, trying my damnedest to feign real interest.

The Collector cupped his crotch and leered at me. "Read the book. It's all in there. Every single bit."

Hubris mixed with stupidity was a scary combo. I was still unsure if he was truly simple-minded or if it was an act. I was going with an act, there was no way he was as brainless as he presented himself.

"Seriously," I said, ignoring his comment. It was a risk, but I was going for the dumb girly angle. He'd bought it at the scene of the crime when the queens had stolen the horses, he might buy it now. I already felt dirty and I hadn't even started. Flirting with people who sported mullets and killed Immortals wasn't my forte, but tonight it was going to be. The Collector's ego was enormous. My goal was to be a better actor than him. "It's just brilliant. I don't know another Immortal who can do what you do. I'm in awe."

The scrawny jerk puffed out his chest. "It's nothing," he replied in an "aw shucks" tone.

I swallowed my bile and kept going. Zander had regenerated one leg and part of an arm. I didn't know how much longer I could keep Micky talking, but I was going to try to make it long enough for Zander to grow back his appendages. Backup would be welcome right now.

"No," I said with a giggle. "It's not nothing. Tell me! I'm so impressed."

The Collector morphed from Micky Muggles into me. There was no fanfare. No sparks, just a quick blink of his eyes. I was looking at an exact replica of myself. It was surreal. He then morphed into Zander. From Zander, he became Tory. And he finished it off as Agnes.

"Easy as pie," he crowed as he morphed back into Micky Muggles.

"Wow!" I squealed, clapping my hands, much to his delight. "Is Micky Muggles the real you?"

The Collector grew perturbed and angry. Shit, what had I said that pissed him off?

"What's wrong with Micky Muggles?" he shouted.

I held up my hands. "Nothing. Nothing is wrong with Micky Muggles. Micky's a great guy—very handsome."

The lie stuck in my mouth like sandpaper. A gaslit Collector was better than a furious one. Flipping my hair like I'd seen the queens do multiple times, I giggled again. "Was that you at my old farmhouse? Were you checking out my old digs, you dirty old man?"

Micky recovered quickly from his tantrum and flexed his muscles. "Yep! I was gonna take your grandma hostage for collateral. But them ghosts just up and disappeared."

It took all I had not to dive at the bastard and rip his head off with my bare hands. Separate the heart and the head, I reminded myself. "Ingenious," I said with a little shimmy that made me feel like an ass, but the Collector bought it hook, line and sinker.

"I thought so, too," he said with a pleased nod. "Didn't know you'd be so amiable, Daisy... and so hot to trot."

I shrugged and batted my eyes. "I guess you don't know me."

"Sure would like to," he replied, grabbing his crotch again.

I was going to need to shower for a week if I came out of this alive. "I want my own hoard, Micky. Tell me how to make my own hoard."

"It's easy," he said with a boastful grin. "But you're gonna have to get naked for that info."

I threw up a little in my mouth. "Too cold out here," I said quickly.

"My car is parked over there," he said, pointing beyond the still-smoldering pines. "We could get in a quickie before I need to skedaddle."

This was headed in a seriously bad direction. "Tell me the spell, and I'll take off my shirt."

"I sure do like 'em horny," he said. "But I'm gonna need more than a titty shot to share my secrets."

If I agreed to go to his car, he'd have to disintegrate the bubble. I'd have my army back. Was he thinking with his dick or his brain? It certainly appeared that his little head was in control of his big head. I was about to find out. Zander was fully regenerated and standing about twenty feet away.

Maybe the army wasn't needed. Candy Vargo would eat Micky Muggles without thinking. She was literally spewing fire. I had no intention of banging the Collector, but I needed the spell. If I had to do a strip tease and remove a single piece of clothing for each word of the spell, I'd do it, and then end him. I was mad at myself for removing my coat. Quickly picking it back up, I put the soggy down-filled mess back on.

Wait...

Words. Collect the words. I hadn't done it right yet, but there was no time to start like the present. The Collector had just said I needed to read the book... it was all in there. It was a risk, but he was so damned conceited, he'd most likely given it all away to Agnes. It was perilous to believe that the actual spell was in the book, but if he'd used the term enchanted thaumaturgy bands, there was better than a 50/50 chance that he'd revealed all.

"Full disclosure," Micky said, unzipping his pants and adjusting his erection. "I ain't gonna show you my hoard. That one is pretty much dead. In fact, if it ain't dead now, it will be by sundown tomorrow."

Not often in my life had I seen red, but Micky's words undid me.

I'd bank on the book. It was time for the Collector to die. Violently.

Unfortunately, Zander had the same plan. His roar of fury shook the bubble and caused a five-alarm fire to explode to life. Before I could even move, Zander had the Collector by the throat and was ready to rip it out.

"I will kill you like you killed my sister," he snarled, shaking Micky as if he weighed only a pound.

Zander snapped Micky's legs and arms. The disgusting little man screamed in agony. Zander was just getting started.

"I will make you suffer before I end you," he shouted as he head-butted the broken man.

Micky flew across the field like a paper doll in the wind. His terrified shrieks were unsettling. I couldn't find it in me to care. He was never going to share the spell. It didn't matter if he was dead. The spell was in the book. He'd said it himself.

Zander ran at him so fast that he disappeared from sight

for a second. His fists connecting to Micky Muggles' face were sickening.

"No," Zander shouted in horror. "Oh my God, no!"

I ran as fast as he had. I stopped short and screamed. On the ground was a beautiful woman. She looked almost identical to Zander. Her legs and arms were broken. Her face was bloodied from being punched. She was moaning and crying. She held her hands in front of her face and begged for her life.

"Zander," she gasped out, coughing up blood. "It's me, Catriona. Please stop. Please. Don't kill me."

Zander tried to crawl to his sister. I stepped in front of him and blocked him. "Separate the head from the heart or both will break," I said harshly. "It's not her."

"How do you know?" he demanded with tears running down his handsome face. "Tell me you're sure. Tell me you would bet your daughter's life that she is not my sister. Tell me," he bellowed.

I couldn't. I wouldn't bet my daughter's life on anything. And the truth was that I wasn't sure. Had the Collector screwed with us and tricked Zander into beating his sister to within an inch of her life? Or had he simply morphed into Catriona?

"I don't think it's her," I finally said in a whisper.

"Help me, Zander," she begged. "Please, help me."

Zander shoved me aside. I hit the wet ground like a sack of potatoes. "*Think* is not good enough, Angel of Mercy," he hissed at me.

My heart felt like it was lodged in my throat as I watched Zander gently pick up his sister and cradle her close. If it was Gideon on the ground, I wasn't sure if I'd have the strength to stay back, but the word illusion had been beaten into my brain by multiple powerful entities.

Catriona sobbed in her brother's arms. It seemed so real…
until it didn't.

In the blink of an eye, the woman in Zander's arms disappeared, and the Collector was in her place. Zander was so
filled with self-hatred and remorse, he hadn't noticed that he
was lovingly rocking Micky Muggles in his arms.

"Zander," I screamed.

His head jerked to the left, and he glared at me with fury.
He still didn't know.

It wasn't until the Collector laughed that he realized his
fatal mistake. Micky chanted a spell, and they disappeared in a
flash of green mist. In the wind after they were out of sight, I
heard Micky whisper, "See ya. Wouldn't wanna be ya. You're
next, Daisy."

I dropped to my knees as the bubble disintegrated. Dirk
and Candy Vargo were the first to get to me.

"Motherfucker," Candy shouted. She waved her hands and
put out the fire.

Dirk carefully helped me to my feet and hugged me close.
He was still in his terrifying form, but his arms around me
made me feel safe and loved. "I've got you, darling."

"Agnes," I muttered against his chest. "Is Agnes still here?"

"Barely," Heather said as she looked me over for wounds.
"Tim," she called out. "We need some healing over here, please."

"Not now." I extracted myself from Dirk's embrace and
glanced around wildly. I spotted the golden glow immediately.
It was fading fast and taking Agnes with it. "Don't go, Agnes," I
yelled. "I need you."

Grabbing a still-cussing Candy Vargo by the neck of her
sweatshirt, I dragged her over to where Agnes was growing
fainter by the second. Candy had read the books. All of them.
"Was there a spell in *Dragons Do it Drunk*?" I asked her.

"What are you talkin' about, jackass?" Candy asked.

My head felt like it was going to explode. Nothing was going right. I had one more chance, and that chance was about to vanish.

"Agnes, did Mr. Handyman ever share the spell with you? The ancient one he used to create the parallel planes?"

"Spell. Yes!" she said.

Her voice sounded so far away. She kept talking, but I couldn't make out the words. The light was wrapping her in its warm embrace. For the first time since I'd become the Death Counselor, I despised the golden light. It was about to take away the information I needed to save Gideon.

"Yes," I said as tears of frustration and fear ran down my cheeks. It felt like I was having a panic attack combined with a nervous breakdown. My legs no longer wanted to hold me up. I held onto Candy Vargo, so I wouldn't fall. "Do you know the spell? Can you tell me the spell?"

Agnes' lips were moving. I tried to read them since the sound was muffled, but like before, she was talking too fast. As the glorious light closed in around her in her final moments, I heard three words as clear as day.

"PILE OF SHIT," Agnes bellowed.

And then she disappeared.

I let go of Candy and hit the hard ground. I had no one to blame but myself. Lilith had given me guidance and I hadn't recognized it when it was under my nose. My gut had told me that it wasn't Catriona on the ground, but I didn't trust it. Now Zander was part of the hoard. I could have stopped it. I hadn't. If the Collector had been telling the truth, then Gideon, Gabe and Zadkiel only had until sundown tomorrow.

"We're fucked," I said, glad that Gram was inside. She might let Candy get away with the F-bomb here and there, but she wasn't fond of me dropping the foul word.

Tim seated himself next to me on the ground and pulled out his notebook. "I beg to differ, friend."

I wasn't following. "Okay, I'll bite and beg you to differ."

Charlie, Heather, Tory, Rafe, Candy and Dirk formed a circle around us.

"Nothing is impossible," Tim reminded me as he took my hand in his. "You just have to believe."

I nodded. I couldn't speak. If I did, I would cry. Right now, separating the head and the heart wasn't working. My heart was breaking, and I was sure my mind would follow. I didn't know what to believe anymore. I knew I needed to stay strong for Alana Catherine, but without Gideon, I felt like half of me was missing. I yearned for his laugh.

"Candy Vargo," Tim said, looking up at her. "Are you positive that the words of the spell are not contained within the pages of the novel, *Dragons Do It Drunk?*"

"Positive," she said. "I've read it about fifty times. No fuckin' spell. I mean, the spell is cast, but the actual spell ain't in there."

If asking Candy was why Tim had begged to differ, I was sticking with my profane prediction of us being fucked.

"The words," Tim said. "It's all in the words."

He stared at me for a long beat and waited. I loved him, but if he was about to dole out something cryptic, I was going to punch him.

He didn't speak. He simply waited.

It hit me as hard as I'd hit the bubble wall when Zander had blasted me. The words… Agnes' words. My body had been through the ringer. I was covered in dried blood, and my ribs were definitely broken, along with a few other bones.

I'd never felt better in my life. There was nothing quite as euphoric as hope renewed.

"Pile of shit," I said with a grin.

Tim's expression matched mine. "Keep going, friend."

"The spell is in the deleted scenes in the Shit Pile folder in Agnes' desk."

"Oh my!" Dirk screamed. "So exciting! Better than an orgasm!"

I stood up and brushed the mud off my pants. There was nothing I could do about the blood. I needed a shower, but that would have to wait.

"Who's coming with me?" I asked.

"Where you goin', jackass?" Candy Vargo asked, handing me a toothpick.

The question was redundant. The Keeper of Fate knew exactly where I was going.

I put the toothpick into my mouth and flipped her off. "Ohio. You in?"

"Hell to the fuckin' yes, I'm in," Candy bellowed, handing out toothpicks to everyone.

"I'm in," Tory said with a stick of wood hanging out of her mouth.

It was all wrong and oh so right.

Charlie took over. "Heather, Rafe, Dirk, Prue, Abby and I will stay here and protect the house. I'd suggest Tim goes to Ohio with you, along with Candy and Tory."

I nodded at the Enforcer and hugged him. "Nothing is impossible. I just have to believe."

Charlie hugged me back. "You're correct, Daisy. You must believe in the outcome you want and more importantly, believe in yourself."

His words were wise. Over the past few days, I'd been

running for my midlife. I'd keep running until Gideon, Gabe, Zander, Catriona and even Zadkiel were back safe and sound. That was the outcome I wanted, and I'd accept nothing less.

I looked up at the sky. The storm had subsided, but the stars were still hidden by the clouds. I'd weathered one storm, but there were more on the horizon. I'd take the rain, the wind, the lightning and the thunder gladly. I believed that I would indeed see the full glory of the sun.

Tory, Tim, Candy and I joined hands. The power between us was intense. It was as glorious as the sun. Nothing worthwhile was easy. If it was easy, it wouldn't be worth it. I'd go to the end of the world and back for Gideon. As for now, I was going to Ohio.

"Shit pile, here we come."

The End... for now

Ready for the next one???
ORDER It's A Hell of A Midlife NOW!

NEXT IN THE GOOD TO THE LAST DEATH SERIES

ORDER BOOK 10 TODAY!

ROBYN'S BOOK LIST

(IN CORRECT READING ORDER)

<u>HOT DAMNED SERIES</u>
Fashionably Dead
Fashionably Dead Down Under
Hell on Heels
Fashionably Dead in Diapers
A Fashionably Dead Christmas
Fashionably Hotter Than Hell
Fashionably Dead and Wed
Fashionably Fanged
Fashionably Flawed
A Fashionably Dead Diary
Fashionably Forever After
Fashionably Fabulous
A Fashionable Fiasco
Fashionably Fooled
Fashionably Dead and Loving It
Fashionably Dead and Demonic
The Oh My Gawd Couple
A Fashionable Disaster

GOOD TO THE LAST DEMON SERIES
As the Underworld Turns
The Edge of Evil
The Bold and the Banished

GOOD TO THE LAST DEATH SERIES
It's a Wonderful Midlife Crisis
Whose Midlife Crisis Is It Anyway?
A Most Excellent Midlife Crisis
My Midlife Crisis, My Rules
You Light Up My Midlife Crisis
It's A Matter of Midlife and Death
The Facts Of Midlife
It's A Hard Knock Midlife
Run for Your Midlife
It's A Hell of A Midlife

MY SO-CALLED MYSTICAL MIDLIFE SERIES
The Write Hook
You May Be Write
All The Write Moves
My Big Fat Hairy Wedding

SHIFT HAPPENS SERIES
Ready to Were
Some Were in Time
No Were To Run
Were Me Out
Were We Belong

MAGIC AND MAYHEM SERIES

Switching Hour
Witch Glitch
A Witch in Time
Magically Delicious
A Tale of Two Witches
Three's A Charm
Switching Witches
You're Broom or Mine?
The Bad Boys of Assjacket
The Newly Witch Game
Witches In Stitches

SEA SHENANIGANS SERIES
Tallulah's Temptation
Ariel's Antics
Misty's Mayhem
Petunia's Pandemonium
Jingle Me Balls

A WYLDE PARANORMAL SERIES
Beauty Loves the Beast

HANDCUFFS AND HAPPILY EVER AFTERS SERIES
How Hard Can it Be?
Size Matters
Cop a Feel

If after reading all the above you are still wanting more adventure and zany fun, read *Pirate Dave and His Randy Adventures*, the romance novel budding novelist Rena helped wicked Evangeline write in *How Hard Can It Be?*

Warning: Pirate Dave Contains Romance Satire, Spoofing, and Pirates with Two Pork Swords.

EXCERPT: THE WRITE HOOK

BOOK DESCRIPTION

THE WRITE HOOK

Midlife is full of surprises. Not all of them are working for me.

At forty-two I've had my share of ups and downs. Relatively normal, except when the definition of normal changes... drastically.

NYT Bestselling Romance Author: Check
Amazing besties: Check
Lovely home: Check
Pet cat named Thick Stella who wants to kill me: Check
Wacky Tabacky Dealing Aunt: Check
Cheating husband banging the weather girl on our kitchen table: Check
Nasty Divorce: Oh yes
Characters from my novels coming to life: Umm... yes
Crazy: Possibly

Four months of wallowing in embarrassed depression should

be enough. I'm beginning to realize that no one is who they seem to be, and my life story might be spinning out of my control. It's time to take a shower, put on a bra, and wear something other than sweatpants. Difficult, but doable.

With my friends—real and imaginary—by my side, I need to edit my life before the elusive darkness comes for all of us.

The plot is no longer fiction. It's my reality, and I'm writing a happy ever after no matter what. I just have to find the *write hook*.

CHAPTER 1

"I didn't leave that bowl in the sink," I muttered to no one as I stared in confusion at the blue piece of pottery with milk residue in the bottom. "Wait. Did I?"

Slowly backing away, I ran my hands through my hair that hadn't seen a brush in days—possibly longer—and decided that I wasn't going to think too hard about it. Thinking led to introspective thought, which led to dealing with reality, and that was a no-no.

Reality wasn't my thing right now.

Maybe I'd walked in my sleep, eaten a bowl of cereal, then politely put the bowl in the sink. It was possible.

"That has to be it," I announced, walking out of the kitchen and avoiding all mirrors and any glass where I could catch a glimpse of myself.

It was time to get to work. Sadly, books didn't write themselves.

"I can do this. I have to do this." I sat down at my desk and made sure my posture didn't suck. I was fully aware it would suck in approximately five minutes, but I wanted to start out right. It would be a bad week to throw my back out. "Today, I'll write ten thousand words. They will be coherent. I will not mistakenly or on purpose make a list of the plethora of ways I would like to kill Darren. He's my past. Beheading him is illegal. I'm far better than that. On a more positive note, my imaginary muse will show his ponytailed, obnoxious ass up today, and I won't play Candy Jelly Crush until the words are on the page."

Two hours later...

Zero words. However, I'd done three loads of laundry—sweatpants, t-shirts and underwear—and played Candy Jelly Crush until I didn't have any more lives. As pathetic as I'd become, I hadn't sunk so low as to purchase new lives. That would mean I'd hit rock bottom. Of course, I was precariously close, evidenced by my cussing out of the Jelly Queen for ten minutes, but I didn't pay for lives. I considered it a win.

I'd planned on folding the laundry but decided to vacuum instead. I'd fold the loads by Friday. It was Tuesday. That was reasonable. If they were too wrinkled, I'd simply wash them again. No biggie. After the vacuuming was done, I rearranged my office for thirty minutes. I wasn't sure how to Feng Shui, but after looking it up on my phone, I gave it a half-assed effort.

Glancing around at my handiwork, I nodded. "Much better. If the surroundings are aligned correctly, the words will flow magically. I hope."

Two hours later...

"Mother humper," I grunted as I pushed my monstrosity of a bed from one side of the bedroom to the other. "This weighs a damn ton."

I'd burned all the bedding seven weeks ago. The bonfire had been cathartic. I'd taken pictures as the five hundred thread count sheets had gone up in flame. I'd kept the comforter. I'd paid a fortune for it. It had been thoroughly saged and washed five times. Even though there was no trace of Darren left in the bedroom, I'd been sleeping in my office.

The house was huge, beautiful… and mine—a gorgeously restored Victorian where I'd spent tons of time as a child. It had an enchanted feel to it that I adored. I didn't need such an enormous abode, but I loved the location—the middle of nowhere. The internet was iffy, but I solved that by going into town to the local coffee shop if I had something important to download or send.

Darren, with the wandering pecker, thought he would get a piece of the house. He was wrong. I'd inherited it from my whackadoo grandmother and great-aunt Flip. My parents hadn't always been too keen on me spending so much time with Granny and Aunt Flip growing up, but I adored the two old gals so much they'd relented. Since I spent a lot of time in an imaginary dream world, my mom and dad were delighted when I related to actual people—even if they were left of center.

Granny and Flip made sure the house was in my name only —nontransferable and non-sellable. It was stipulated that I had to pass it to a family member or the Historical Society when I died. Basically, I had life rights. It was as if Granny and Aunt Flip had known I would waste two decades of my life married to a jackhole who couldn't keep his salami in his pants and would need someplace to live. God rest Granny's insane soul. Aunt Flip was still kicking, although I hadn't seen her in a few years.

Aunt Flip put the K in kooky. She'd bought a cottage in the hills about an hour away and grew medicinal marijuana— before it was legal. The old gal was the black sheep of the family and preferred her solitude and her pot to company. She hadn't liked Darren a bit. She and Granny both had worn black to my wedding. Everyone had been appalled—even me—but in the end, it made perfect sense. I had to hand it to the old broads. They'd been smarter than me by a long shot. And the house? It had always been my charmed haven in the storm.

Even though there were four spare bedrooms plus the master suite, I chose my office. It felt safe to me.

Thick Stella preferred my office, and I needed to be around something that had a heartbeat. It didn't matter that Thick Stella was bitchy and swiped at me with her deadly kitty claws every time I passed her. I loved her. The feeling didn't seem mutual, but she hadn't left me for a twenty-three-year-old with silicone breast implants and huge, bright white teeth.

"Thick Stella, do you think Sasha should wear red to her stepmother's funeral?" I asked as I plopped down on my newly Feng Shuied couch and narrowly missed getting gouged by my cat. "Yes or no? Hiss at me if it's a yes. Growl at me if it's a no."

Thick Stella had a go at her privates. She was useless.

"That wasn't an answer." I grabbed my laptop from my desk. Deciding it was too dangerous to sit near my cat, I settled for the love seat. The irony of the piece of furniture I'd chosen didn't escape me.

"I think she should wear red," I told Thick Stella, who didn't give a crap what Sasha wore. "Her stepmother was an asshat, and it would show fabu disrespect."

Typing felt good. Getting lost in a story felt great. I dressed Sasha in a red Prada sheath, then had her behead her ex-husband with a dull butter knife when he and his bimbo showed up unexpectedly to pay their respects at the funeral home. It was a bloodbath. Putting Sasha in red was an excellent move. The blood matched her frock to a T.

Quickly rethinking the necessary murder, I moved the scene of the decapitation to the empty lobby of the funeral home. It would suck if I had to send Sasha to prison. She hadn't banged Damien yet, and everyone was eagerly awaiting the sexy buildup—including me. It was the fourth book in the series, and it was about time they got together. The sexual tension was palpable.

"What in the freaking hell?" I snapped my laptop shut and groaned. "Sasha doesn't have an ex-husband. I can't do this. I've got nothing." Where was my muse hiding? I needed the elusive imaginary idiot if I was going to get any writing done. "Chauncey, dammit, where are you?"

"My God, you're loud, Clementine," a busty, beautiful woman dressed in a deep purple Regency gown said with an eye roll.

She was seated on the couch next to Thick Stella, who barely acknowledged her. My cat attacked strangers and friends. Not today. My fat feline simply glanced over at the intruder and yawned. The cat was a traitor.

Forget the furry betrayer. How in the heck did the woman get into my house—not to mention my office—without me seeing her enter? For a brief moment, I wondered if she'd banged my husband too but pushed the sordid thought out of my head. She looked to be close to thirty—too old for the asshole.

"Who are you?" I demanded, holding my laptop over my head as a weapon.

If I threw it and it shattered, I would be screwed. I couldn't remember the last time I'd backed it up. If I lost the measly, somewhat disjointed fifty thousand words I'd written so far, I'd have to start over. That wouldn't fly with my agent or my publisher.

"Don't be daft," the woman replied. "It's rather unbecoming. May I ask a question?"

"No, you may not," I shot back, trying to place her.

She was clearly a nutjob. The woman was rolling up on thirty but had the vernacular of a seventy-year-old British society matron. She was dressed like she'd walked off the set of a film starring Emma Thompson. Her blonde hair shone to the point of absurdity and was twisted into an elaborate up-do. Wispy tendrils framed her perfectly heart-shaped face. Her sparkling eyes were lavender, enhanced by the over-the-top gown she wore.

Strangely, she was vaguely familiar. I just couldn't remember how I knew her.

"How long has it been since you attended to your hygiene?" she inquired.

Putting my laptop down and picking up a lamp, I eyed her. I didn't care much for the lamp or her question. I had been thinking about Marie Condo-ing my life, and the lamp didn't bring me all that much joy. If it met its demise by use of self-defense, so be it. "I don't see how that's any of your business, lady. What I'd suggest is that you leave. Now. Or else I'll call the police. Breaking and entering is a crime."

She laughed. It sounded like freaking bells. Even though she was either a criminal or certifiable, she was incredibly charming.

"Oh dear," she said, placing her hand delicately on her still heaving, milky-white bosom. "You are so silly. The constable knows quite well that I'm here. He advised me to come."

"The constable?" I asked, wondering how far off her rocker she was.

She nodded coyly. "Most certainly. We're all terribly concerned."

I squinted at her. "About my hygiene?"

"That, amongst other things," she confirmed. "Darling girl, you are not an ace of spades or, heaven forbid, an adventuress. Unless you want to be an ape leader, I'd recommend bathing."

"Are you right in the head?" I asked, wondering where I'd left my damn cell phone. It was probably in the laundry room. I was going to be murdered by a nutjob, and I'd lost my chance to save myself because I'd been playing Candy Jelly Crush. The headline would be horrifying—*Homeless-looking, Hygiene-free Paranormal Romance Author Beheaded by Victorian Psycho.*

If I lived through the next hour, I was deleting the game for good.

"I think it would do wonders for your spirit if you donned a nice tight corset and a clean chemise," she suggested, skillfully ignoring my question. "You must pull yourself together. Your behavior is dicked in the nob."

I sat down and studied her. My about-to-be-murdered radar relaxed a tiny bit, but I kept the lamp clutched tightly in my hand. My gut told me she wasn't going to strangle me. Of course, I could be mistaken, but Purple Gal didn't seem violent —just bizarre. Plus, the lamp was heavy. I could knock her ladylike ass out with one good swing.

How in the heck did I know her? College? Grad School? The grocery store? At forty-two, I'd met a lot of people in my life. Was she with the local community theater troop? I was eighty-six percent sure she wasn't here to off me. However, I'd been wrong about life-altering events before—like not knowing my husband was boffing someone young enough to have been our daughter.

"What language are you speaking?" I spotted a pair of scissors on my desk. If I needed them, it was a quick move to grab them. I'd never actually killed anyone except in fictitious situations, but there was a first time for everything.

Pulling an embroidered lavender hankey from her cleavage, she clutched it and twisted it in her slim fingers. "Clementine, *you* should know."

"I'm at a little disadvantage here," I said, fascinated by the batshit crazy woman who'd broken into my home. "You seem to know my name, but I don't know yours."

And that was when the tears started. Hers. Not mine.

"Such claptrap. How very unkind of you, Clementine," she burst out through her stupidly attractive sobs.

It was ridiculous how good the woman looked while crying. I got all blotchy and red, but not the mystery gal in purple. She grew even more lovely. It wasn't fair. I still had no clue what the hell she was talking about, but on the off chance she might throw a tantrum if I asked more questions, I kept my mouth shut.

And yes, she had a point, but my *hygiene* was none of her damn business. I couldn't quite put my finger on the last time I'd showered. If I had to guess, it was probably in the last five to twelve days. I was on a deadline for a book. To be more precise, I was late for my deadline on a book. I didn't exactly have time for personal sanitation right now.

And speaking of deadlines...

"How about this?" My tone was excessively polite. I almost laughed. The woman had illegally entered my house, and I was behaving like she was a guest. "I'll take a shower later today after I get through a few pivotal chapters. Right now, you should leave so I can work."

"Yes, of course," she replied, absently stroking Fat Stella, who purred. If I'd done that, I would be minus a finger. "It would be dreadfully sad if you were under the hatches."

I nodded. "Right. That would, umm... suck."

The woman in purple smiled. It was radiant, and I would have sworn I heard birds happily chirping. I was losing it.

"Excellent," she said, pulling a small periwinkle velvet bag from her cleavage. I wondered what else she had stored in there and hoped there wasn't a weapon. "I shall leave you with two gold coins. While the Grape Nuts were tasty, I would prefer that you purchase some Lucky Charms. I understand they are magically delicious."

"It was you?" I asked, wildly relieved that I hadn't been sleep eating. I had enough problems at the moment. Gaining weight from midnight dates with cereal wasn't on the to-do list.

"It was," she confirmed, getting to her feet and dropping the coins into my hand. "The consistency was quite different from porridge, but I found it tasty—very crunchy."

"Right... well... thank you for putting the bowl in the sink." Wait. Why the hell was I thanking her? She'd wandered in and eaten my Grape Nuts.

"You are most welcome, Clementine," she said with a disarming smile that lit up her unusual eyes. "It was lovely finally meeting you even if your disheveled outward show is entirely astonishing."

I was reasonably sure I had just been insulted by the cereal lover, but it was presented with excellent manners. However, she did answer a question. We hadn't met. I wasn't sure why she seemed familiar. The fact that she knew my name was alarming.

"Are you a stalker?" I asked before I could stop myself.

I'd had a few over the years. Being a *New York Times* best-selling author was something I was proud of, but it had come with a little baggage here and there. Some people seemed to have difficulty discerning fiction from reality. If I had to guess, I'd say Purple Gal might be one of those people.

I'd only written one Regency novel, and that had been at the beginning of my career, before I'd found my groove in paranormal romance. I was way more comfortable writing about demons and vampires than people dressed in top hats and hoopskirts. Maybe the crazy woman had read my first book. It hadn't done well, and for good reason. It was over-the-top bad. I'd blocked the entire novel out of my mind. Live and learn. It had been my homage to Elizabeth Hoyt well over a decade ago. It had been clear to all that I should leave Regency romance to the masters.

"Don't be a Merry Andrew," the woman chided me. "Your bone box is addled. We must see to it at once. I shall pay a visit again soon."

The only part of her gibberish I understood was that she thought she was coming back. Note to self—change all the locks on the doors. Since it wasn't clear if she was packing heat in her cleavage, I just smiled and nodded.

"Alrighty then..." I was unsure if I should walk her to the door or if she would let herself out. Deciding it would be better to make sure she actually left instead of letting her hide in my pantry to finish off my cereal, I gestured to the door. "Follow me."

Thick Stella growled at me. I was so tempted to flip her off but thought it might earn another lecture from Purple Gal. It was more than enough to be lambasted for my appearance. I didn't need my manners picked apart by someone with a tenuous grip on reality.

My own grip was dubious as it was.

"You might want to reconsider breaking into homes," I said, holding the front door open. "It could end badly—for you."

Part of me couldn't believe that I was trying to help the nutty woman out, but I couldn't seem to stop myself. I kind of liked her.

"I'll keep that in mind," she replied as she sauntered out of my house into the warm spring afternoon. "Remember, Clementine, there is always sunshine after the rain."

As she made her way down the long sunlit, tree-lined drive, she didn't look back. It was disturbingly like watching the end of a period movie where the heroine left her old life behind and walked proudly toward her new and promising future.

Glancing around for a car, I didn't spot one. Had she left it parked on the road so she could make a clean getaway after she'd bludgeoned me? Had I just politely escorted a murderer out of my house?

Had I lost it for real?

Probably.

As she disappeared from sight, I felt the weight of the gold coins still clutched in my hand. Today couldn't get any stranger.

At least, I hoped not.

Opening my fist to examine the coins, I gasped. "What in the heck?"

There was nothing in my hand.

Had I dropped them? Getting down on all fours, I searched. Thick Stella joined me, kind of—more like watched me as I crawled around and wondered if anything that had just happened had actually happened.

"Purple Gal gave me coins to buy Lucky Charms," I told my cat, my search now growing frantic. "You saw her do it. Right? She sat next to you. And you didn't attack her. *Right?*"

Thick Stella simply stared at me. What did I expect? If my cat answered me, I'd have to commit myself. That option might still be on the table. Had I just imagined the entire exchange with the strange woman? Should I call the cops?

"And tell them what?" I asked, standing back up and locking the front door securely. "That a woman in a purple gown broke in and ate my cereal while politely insulting my hygiene? Oh, and she left me two gold coins that disappeared in my hand as soon as she was out of sight? That's not going to work."

I'd call the police if she came back, since I wasn't sure she'd been here at all. She hadn't threatened to harm me. Purple Gal had been charming and well-mannered the entire time she'd badmouthed my cleanliness habits. And to be quite honest, real or not, she'd made a solid point. I could use a shower.

Maybe four months of wallowing in self-pity and only living inside the fictional worlds I created on paper had taken more of a toll than I was aware of. Getting lost in my stories was one of my favorite things to do. It had saved me more than once over the years. It was possible that I'd let it go too far. Hence, the Purple Gal hallucination.

Shit.

First things first. Delete Candy Jelly Crush. Getting rid of the white noise in my life was the first step to... well, the first step to something.

I'd figure it out later.

HIT HERE TO ORDER THE WRITE HOOK!!!!!

NOTE FROM THE AUTHOR

If you enjoyed reading *Run For Your Midlife,* please consider leaving a positive review or rating on the site where you purchased it. Reader reviews help my books continue to be valued by resellers and help new readers make decisions about reading them.

You are the reason I write these stories and I sincerely appreciate each of you!

Many thanks for your support,
~ Robyn Peterman

Want to hear about my new releases?
Visit https://robynpeterman.com/newsletter/ and join my mailing list!

ABOUT ROBYN PETERMAN

Robyn Peterman writes because the people inside her head won't leave her alone until she gives them life on paper. Her addictions include laughing really hard with friends, shoes (the expensive kind), Target, Coke (the drink not the drug LOL) with extra ice in a Yeti cup, bejeweled reading glasses, her kids, her super-hot hubby and collecting stray animals.

A former professional actress with Broadway, film and T.V. credits, she now lives in the South with her family and too many animals to count.

Writing gives her peace and makes her whole, plus having a job where she can work in sweatpants works really well for her.

Printed in Great Britain
by Amazon